THE PROBLEM WITH WHAT IF

On Friday morning, I say to Stu as we walk to Cap, "He's a nice guy, and I like him, but we aren't exactly having great conversations. It's just about school."

"Have you tried longer conversations?"

"Do you mean since homecoming?"

"Do you count homecoming as trying?"

"I count homecoming as an embarrassing disaster."

"Well, so does he, probably. He's the one who told you he only asked you out because you're tall."

"Yeah, and he apologized, and so did I for blathering all night. But now I think we're at the point of finding out just how much we like each other, so we need to show each other who we really are—beyond height and blathering—which creates a number of unpleasant possibilities." I tick these off on four fingers and ignore the exaggerated look of bemusement on Stu's face. "What if I like him more than he likes me? What if he likes me more than I like him? What if neither one of us likes each other all that much? What if we have a repeat of homecoming?"

"What if his head explodes while you're talking?"

I raise my thumb right in his face.

"Josie, you think too much," he says with a little laugh. "You also talk too much."

OTHER BOOKS YOU MAY ENJOY

LOVE

and Other

FOREIGN WORDS

ERIN McCAHAN

speak

SPEAK
An Imprint of Penguin Random House LLC
375 Hudson Street
New York, New York 10014

First published in the United States of America by Dial Books for Young Readers,
an imprint of Penguin Group (USA) LLC, 2014
Published by Speak, an imprint of Penguin Random House LLC, 2015

THE LIBRARY OF CONGRESS HAS CATALOGED THE DIAL BOOKS EDITION AS FOLLOWS:
McCahan, Erin.
Love and other foreign words / Erin McCahan.
pages cm
Summary: Brilliant fifteen-year-old Josie has a knack for languages, but her sister's engagement has
Josie grappling with the nature of true love, her feelings for her best friend Stu, and how anyone
can be truly herself, or truly in love, in a social language that is not her own.
ISBN 978-0-8037-4051-8 (hardcover)
[1. Interpersonal communication—Fiction. 2. Love—Fiction. 3. Sisters—Fiction.
4. Best friends—Fiction. 5. Friendship—Fiction.] I. Title.
PZ7.M47833747Lov 2014
[Fic]—dc23
2013027095

Speak ISBN 978-0-14-750959-8

1 3 5 7 9 10 8 6 4 2

Designed by Jennifer Kelly

Printed in the United States of America

FOR MY HUSBAND, TIM

CHAPTER ONE

There must be a way to figure this out.

I contemplate the possible formulae lying on Stu's bed, staring at the ceiling but seeing only x's and y's and parentheses and question marks. Across the room, Stu sits with his back to me at his keyboard, playing an occasional combination of chords and pausing to write or erase musical hieroglyphics in a notebook.

"It can't be done," I say. "There are too many variables."

"That's what I've been saying," he says.

"But I *have* to know."

"I think you can live without knowing this. I know I can."

I sit up, adjust my glasses, and notice a loose thread in the brick-red stripe of his serape-style blanket.

"You need to fix this before it comes undone," I say.

"Fix what?"

I tell him.

"Just yank it," he says.

"I'm not yanking it."

"Then ignore it."

"You realize I can never sleep under this blanket with this thread as it is. The thought of it would plague me all night."

"Were you going to?" he asks, looking over his shoulder at me.

"Well, I'm not going to *now*."

"Suggesting you *were* going to at some point?"

"Suggesting no matter where I sleep in the future, it will not be under *this* blanket."

"I was not aware our friendship included sleepovers," he says. "Will we be doing each other's hair as well?"

"Yes. I long to see you in an up-do."

"Okay, listen to this," he says, and proceeds to play, to perfection, the gorgeously trilling introduction of one of the greatest songs of all time, "Come Sail Away." (Words and music by Dennis DeYoung, former lead singer of Styx and now a composer, Broadway performer, and all-around superlative human being. I believe in his spare time he rescues stranded motorists across the country, chases purse-snatchers, and donates blood and plasma until the Red Cross temporarily bans him for his own good. Somewhere in his closet there must be a cape.)

Then Stu sings—and only Stu, as far as my listening experience extends, could do Dennis DeYoung justice, which is the highest compliment I can pay to any singing person. Stu sings in a couple of choirs and is so musically gifted that our high school choir director often consults him on arrangements for musicals and ensembles. I have a mere average singing voice myself, and the utter inability to play any instrument. I took piano lessons when I was nine for the longest six months of my life. The whole thing made no sense to me, and my teacher refused to answer my list of *why* questions. Why assign fingers to keys? Why include a tie? Why do you need a damper pedal; why not just *not* play that note? Why won't you teach me how to tune this thing? Why are there no blue pianos? No, really, why are there no blue pianos?

She and I were very happy the day my parents let me quit.

Just before the tempo of "Come Sail Away" increases, Stu stops singing and breaks into a classical version of the piece, somewhere between a minuet and a concerto, as if Johann Sebastian Himself had composed it. If I were not watching him with my own eyes, I would swear that more than one pianist was playing.

After only one and a half minutes or so, Stu stops and turns on the bench to face me.

"That's as far as I've gotten," he says.

"I like it."

"I aim to please," he says as Sophie shouts from across the hall, "That's not how it goes!"

"That's how I say it goes!" Stu shouts back.

"That's because *you* are just too freakishly weird!"

"And *you* are a fluffy poodle!"

"Freak!"

"Fifi!"

"Enough," their mom says as she leans into Stu's room. "Josie, are you staying for dinner?" she asks me.

"Thanks, Auntie Pat, but I can't. Kate's coming over tonight, and I finally get to grill her about Boyfriend of the Moment, who, by the way, none of us has met yet."

"Grill her? Josie," Auntie Pat says.

"I have to. It's for her own good."

"Her own good?" Stu and his mom ask simultaneously, which entertains Auntie Pat far more than it does Stu.

"Yes. I need to find out if there's anything wrong with him, which there probably is, which I say for three reasons."

Auntie Pat arches her eyebrows at me, skeptical but waiting, something Stu does at times too.

"One"—I hold up my index finger for emphasis—"there's something wrong with all her boyfriends. Two"—second finger up—"she's been going out with him for four months and hasn't brought him around, so she's probably hiding something. And three, which is related to one, Kate did not receive an ounce of the discernment Maggie got," I say of our older sister, "when it comes to picking guys who are right for her."

"And you did?" Stu asks.

I cringe, thinking back to homecoming, before I say, "Well, I'm better at picking for Kate than Kate is for herself. You know what it is? I'm not blinded by love the way she is. I take a much more logical approach."

"You have never liked any of her boyfriends," Stu says.

"My opinion is informed by the guy."

"Uh-huh. Tell us again what was wrong with the last one."

"Corn," I say.

"Corn?" Auntie Pat asks.

"Corn," Stu says.

"The guy ate only corn, meat, and chocolate," I tell Auntie Pat. "See, this is where Kate fails the discernment test. She likes to cook. She also eats loads of cruciferous vegetables. And it would be impossible to cook long-term for a grown man who doesn't eat any. Therefore, logically, he was not a good match for Kate. I knew they'd break up. All I did was suggest it a little earlier than she was prepared for."

"Cruciferous," Stu says. "Not tuberous?"

"Those too."

"How about legumes?"

"You get my point."

"What is her boyfriend's name?" Auntie Pat asks.

"Geoff with a *g*, three *f*'s, and a silent *p*." *Pgeofff.*

"Well, then I hope for Kate's sake that Geoff-with-a-*g* enjoys a variety of vegetables," she says.

"I plan on finding out tonight," I say. And when Auntie Pat turns to leave, I stop her with: "Did you know there's a thread coming loose here?"

"Show me," she says, coming close as I point. "Yes, I see. Just yank it."

Stu shrugs. "That's what I said."

"I can't. What if it doesn't come out in one try but gets longer? What if it puckers? What if it tears the whole—"

"Here." Auntie Pat reaches over me and snaps the thread off as I wince. "All fixed," she says, and shoots me a quick smile before leaving the room.

I look at my watch. Nearly five thirty. "I have to go." I hop off the bed, twist my ankle right under me, and crash to the floor.

Stu grins wickedly as he plays the first few chords of Beethoven's Fifth Symphony.

Buhm-buhm-buhm-buhmmmmm

"Dennis DeYoung would have helped me up," I say as I rise, pink but uninjured, and straighten my glasses.

"Stu Wagemaker thinks you're a klutz."

"Oh, hey." I stop in the door. "Jen Auerbach told me today she thinks she likes you."

"She doesn't know?"

I shrug. "She likes lots of guys at present. But, in your case, it doesn't matter since I told her to stay away from you."

"Oh, really. Why is that?"

"You mean in addition to your going out with Sarah Selman at the moment?"

"Yeah, in addition to that."

"I told her you're the love-'em-and-leave-'em type."

"No, I'm not."

"Yes, you are."

"No," he says clearly. "I'm not."

"Yes you are!" Sophie calls.

"See?"

"You're both wrong," he says, and plays a few light notes on the keyboard.

"Sarah is your third girlfriend this calendar year. And it's only March."

"It's the twenty-fifth," he protests. "And the last Tuesday of the month, no less."

"Still a Tuesday in only the third month of the year. That's a girlfriend a month, so far." I hold up three fingers for emphasis. "Need I say more?"

"No, because you're wrong, and I'd hate for you to keep embarrassing yourself."

"I'm not wrong," I say, which is confirmed by Sophie.

"She's not wrong!"

"Gotta go," I say.

I call out a good-bye to Sophie and pause in the kitchen to pet Moses, the Wagemakers' seventeen-pound cat, who is just allowing me to touch him again after I stepped on his tail last week. Twice.

Sophie is the love-'em-and-leave-'em type too. She and Stu have identical blond hair, long limbs, symmetrical

faces, and easy smiles. Stu writes music. Sophie paints—
bright collages when she's happy, bleak landscapes
when she's not. Having known both of them all my
life, though, I can say that Sophie, apart from her love life,
is much less complicated. Not a fluffy poodle, but also
breezily unconcerned with matters that neither interest
nor affect her.

No one will ever accuse Sophie of over-thinking,
which I, as an inveterate (my dad says incorrigible) over-
thinker, admire. I don't know how she does it. I find her
completely fascinating.

Auntie Pat says she and Stu bicker because they're
so close in age. Thirteen months. Stu's sixteen. Sophie's
fifteen, three months older than I am even though I'm
a year ahead of her in school. I skipped second grade,
making me a junior at the moment—like Stu.

Auntie Pat predicts by the time Stu and Sophie are
thirty and twenty-nine, well involved in their own families and careers and living in separate states, they'll get
along rather well.

My parents have owned our house across the street
from the Wagemakers for nearly twenty-two years,
which is at least how long Kate and our oldest sister,
Maggie, have been calling them Auntie Pat and Uncle
Ken.

For this reason, everyone at school thinks Stu and
Sophie are my cousins. We let them. It's easier to per-

petuate the rumor than to explain the intricacies of so close a relationship that isn't family but should be.

I leave the Wagemakers' house and cross the street. It's damp and cold, like the air, from typical late March rain. My thoughts return to the dilemma that had taken me out of Sophie's room, where I had listened, fascinated by her enthusiasm, to her latest break-up drama that included the description "cheese-sniffing rat bastard," and into Stu's room, where I tried to create a formula Stu called impossible. But he must be wrong. There should be—there *has* to be—some way for me to conclusively determine if I, in all my fifteen-point-four years of life, have eaten an entire rat.

CHAPTER TWO

I can determine the average size of a rat. That's easy. What I cannot determine is the consistency with which they fall into vats at meat-processing plants or the number of times I have eaten processed meats from the plants where rats have accidentally become part of the product, coupled with the frequency with which my mother has bought certain brands from certain stores. And this is all based on the assumption that rats do fall into these vats and find their way into hot dogs and hamburgers I've eaten. So it appears Stu was right. There are too many variables, and I'll just have to live without knowing. Or guess.

But I hate guessing, also estimations, and much prefer the precision of mathematical formulae and exact translations. Math is a language, and I like languages. Look at all the foreign words I've used just today:

hieroglyphics: Greek

serape: Spanish

ensemble: French

concerto: Italian

minuet: French

hamburger: German

Pgeofff: Josie

The single greatest word, of all languages in the world, is *teepee*. Comes from the Sioux. I could be born into a family of French-speaking goat herders in the Swiss Alps and still know immediately what a teepee is the moment I hear the word. No confusion. Perfect clarity. It is the epitome of lingual greatness.

Teepee.

If only every language were as clear as Sioux.

I enter the kitchen through the back door and am alone there long enough to deduce tonight's dinner. Mother has arranged an easy culinary formula for me with limited variables. Based on the juxtaposition of ground beef, an onion, and fresh tomatoes in the refrigerator, and red beans and spices on the counter, I conclude we're having chili. (Possibly with trace amounts of rat. I'll never know.) Neither of my parents gets home until six most nights. Chili needs to simmer, so I promptly get to work as sous chef, trained and frequently employed by my sisters and mother.

I have barely placed the appropriate pot on the stove when Kate breezes through the back door, holding her cell phone like a walkie-talkie.

"No," she says into it, setting her purse and briefcase

down, "I've got to be in Cincinnati on Tuesday and Dayton on Wednesday, and Thursday I'm in a training meeting most of the day, so I could only fit you in on Monday or Friday." She shoots me a smile, blows me a kiss, points at the phone, tosses both hands up, rolls her eyes at herself, makes me smile, and points, questioningly, at the pot.

"Chili," I say.

"No," she says into her phone. "I've been to his office three times, and he kept me waiting over an hour each time, and I won't apologize for finding my time as important as his," she says as she shoulder-presses the phone to her ear and pulls the meat and the onion—I grab the tomatoes—out of the fridge. "And he still won't switch from Squat-in-Lederhosen," or something like that. She names some drug I've never heard of and pours some olive oil into the pot, and then I follow her pantomimes to get dinner started. She hangs up after the onion is browned and all the tomatoes have been thoroughly diced.

"Well," she says, beaming another smile at me. "Hello."

Then I get a real kiss from her and ask her how many pounds of processed meat she thinks she's eaten in her life.

Kate's a drug rep—a sales representative for a pharmaceutical company—so she's forever visiting doctors in their offices and in hospitals to hawk the latest treatment for baldness or vaginal dryness.

She keeps me supplied with pads of paper and pens, all bearing the names and fancy logos of prescription drugs. My favorite was a four- by six-inch pad with large blue letters at the top—*CYLAXIPRO: One daily dose to reduce herpes outbreaks*. I asked Mother to write my school absence excuses on that, but she refused. I wrote last year's birthday thank-you note to Uncle Vic and Aunt Toot on it. They sent me ten dollars in a card with a monkey on it, and I felt genuinely grateful for both and said so. But then I had to use Mother-approved stationery to write them a note of apology for the references I made in my original note to genital herpes and the part Kate plays in preventing its spread.

Since then, most of my pens and pads of paper have borne the names of allergy and cholesterol-lowering meds.

Today, Mother arrives home before Dad. She teaches four days a week at The Ohio State University's College of Nursing, which is about thirty minutes from our house in the old suburb of Bexley. Yet it seems, somehow, closer than Kate's condo, a mere fifteen minutes away in downtown Columbus, which has felt like a world away ever since she moved out. Especially since she comes for dinner less and less frequently, depending on work and boyfriends who only eat corn or have maladies she refuses to disclose.

By seven thirty—a dinnertime my dad calls cosmopolitan but never with a straight face—we four Sheridans are seated at the kitchen table, where Kate appears too entirely happy over chili. It's good, but not blissful.

"I'm just thinking about Geoff," she says when Mother tells her she looks happy.

"I was thinking about him earlier," I say, "and I bet we were not thinking the same things."

"Josie," she says, adding a cheery little *tsk*, "you are going to love him."

"When do we get to meet him?"

"Well," she says, shooting eager looks in Mother and Dad's direction, "I was hoping to bring him over Friday. For dinner? Maybe a big family dinner?"

Special Family Dinner, in the Sheridan language, is Mother and Dad, Maggie and her husband, Ross, and Kate and me. We fill a room with height and words, making our number seem more than six.

For just a second, Mother and Dad share a look, a curious little nod too, which Kate misses entirely.

"That will be nice," Mother says. "Any special requests for dinner?"

"Spaghetti," Kate and I say in happy unison, since spaghetti has long been our family's preference for any and all special occasions that don't require a giant animal carcass on display. It doesn't signify exceptional dining to most people, but then most people haven't tried my mother's homemade sauce. Auntie Pat wants her to market it, and Mother accepts the compliment each time with only the slightest trace of satisfaction visible on her face. For such an exhibition, its roots must run deep.

By the end of dinner, where we were endlessly entertained by lists of Pgeofff's vague but extraordinary qualities—gorgeous, brilliant, interesting, brilliant, gorgeous—plans for this coming Friday's Special Family Dinner are set.

"Are you staying over tonight?" Dad asks Kate, checking his watch against the clock in the kitchen, which means—in our private Sheridan language—stay or leave, but now is the appropriate time to decide.

"She's staying," I answer for her, and I grab her hand and say, "Come on," and we run up to my room.

I hop on my bed, fold my legs underneath me, straighten my glasses, and say, "Now tell me everything you haven't told Mother and Dad about Pgeofff."

"I've already told you everything." Kate is rummaging through my pajama drawer. She pulls out two nightshirts—both of which she gave me—and I point to the blue one, leaving the burgundy one for her.

"Does he eat green vegetables?"

"Geoff has very sophisticated taste in food," she says as she starts to peel off the layers of her suit. "And, yes, I've cooked for him, and, yes, he likes it. We cook together frequently." She thinks a moment. "Yes, we do seem to cook together a lot."

"That's not a euphemism for sex, is it?"

"Josie! No."

"Because it could be, but I'd prefer it if it weren't."

"Stop. Geoff and I cook together. With pots and pans. And he likes and appreciates the meals we make."

"Well, I'm inclined to like him," I say, emphasis on *inclined*.

"I'm not worried at all," she says. "Did I tell you he's brilliant?"

"Couple times."

She pops into the bathroom and emerges minutes later in my nightshirt, looking like she just got home from cheering at a professional football game. Even at this hour, her hair is nearly perfect. I fool absentmindedly with my ponytail for a few seconds before she grabs the brush off my dresser and orders me to turn around. I promptly obey.

She slips the band off my hair and starts brushing as I take off my glasses and place them safely on the nightstand. Kate's brushing my hair is my first memory. I was three and a half. She was almost fourteen, and we talked about birds. I wanted to know why they didn't freeze to death in the winter and drop with loud clunks into the yard. Kate said angels flew down from heaven and used their wings to keep birds warm, but she had no answer when I asked why birds' wings don't keep their own bodies warm.

"I imagine you want to grill me now about Geoff," she says, and I bristle at my predictability.

"No," I say. "But I am going to grill *him*."

"Josie," she laughs.

"You should warn him before Friday that I have a list of thirty-seven questions I need to ask him."

"Only thirty-seven? Why not an even forty?"

"Because the number of questions has nothing to do with the questions themselves. I have as many as I need."

"Are you serious?"

"I am."

"Give me an example."

I twist around to face her. "For example, if he gives up his seat every day on the bus to a pregnant woman but then discovers she's not pregnant but faking it to trick her boyfriend into marrying her, would he still give up his seat to her? Also, would he tell the boyfriend?"

"Is that one question or two?" she asks.

"One," I say, "with two parts."

"Hmm," she says. "It's a good question." She twists my head around to continue brushing. "You should ask him that. I can't wait to hear his answer. It's going to be brilliant," she says as I simultaneously mouth the word.

I'm glad I'm facing away, since I feel my lip starting to curl.

"What are his faults?" I ask.

"He doesn't have any."

"That's impossible, and you know it."

"Well, then, I haven't noticed any because everything else about him is so wonderful."

"So you could say you're blind to his faults?" I ask.

"Happily. That's what happens when you're in love. You overlook the unimportant things. Satisfied?" she asks as she sets the hairbrush down and climbs into bed.

"No, because I need to know how you're defining *unimportant*."

"What do you mean how I'm defining it?"

I turn out the lights.

"Unimportant like staying up too late reading," I say, slipping into my side of the bed, "or unimportant like large hairy facial moles and compulsive nose-picking?"

"Compulsive— Josie." She giggles some. "No."

"Hunchback? Troll hair?"

"Neither."

"Tertiary syphilis?"

"Good night, Josie," Kate says, kissing me quickly before turning over.

"Unnatural interest in ventriloquism?"

"No."

"Uncontrollable watery stool? Diapers? Does he wear adult diapers? Or does he wear adult diapers but doesn't really need them? See, that would be something important you shouldn't overlook, don't you think?"

Kate pulls her pillow over her head, and I grin and snuggle a little closer. How can Stu accuse me of not liking any of Kate's boyfriends when each one provides me with moments like these? I hope she's never single again.

CHAPTER THREE

Jen Auerbach bounces herself against my locker after school today and launches into a conversation well past its starting point. Her wide, dark brown eyes seem to smile even when she does not, making her look as if she's about to hear not good but great news. I'm always a little sorry when I don't have it to give to her.

"That far from my face," Jen says. "I'm telling you he was that far from my face." She holds her thumb and index finger two inches apart. "Oh, he smelled soooooo good. Why is it that great-looking guys just smell good, no matter how they smell, you know? I mean, it's like, if he smelled like day-old pizza grease, I would be think-ing oh, I want pizza with him. Now. Right now."

I mentally shift into Jen's natural language and re-alize she's talking about Josh Brandstetter, best-looking guy in our class and Jen's current chemistry lab partner, chosen by random name-draw back in January. She said she tried to look like she didn't care when he pulled her name out of a large beaker, but it's next to impossible for Jen Auerbach to look indifferent about anything.

I've been friends with Jen since seventh grade. We're the tall girls in school. Jen, Emmy Newall, and a couple others who play volleyball. I, thanks to my maternal DNA, am the tallest on the team but not the best. Jen and Emmy are. They already have my vote as next year's cocaptains.

"What were you doing?" I ask. "In lab?"

"I don't know. Some stupid whatever, but it was great because we had to be *this* close"—she shows me her thumb and index finger again—"to read the results."

"You don't even know what they were, do you?"

"I have no idea. I just copied what he wrote down. I was too busy smelling how good he smelled."

"Who smells good?" Emmy Newall asks, inserting herself into our space and conversation.

"Josh Brandstetter," Jen says.

"What does he smell like?"

"Day-old pizza grease," I say, making Jen smile as Emmy, wrinkling her nose at the thought, asks, "You think that smells good?"

"No. It was a joke," I say.

"I don't get it," she says, and Jen explains in a rapid, abbreviated manner, which Emmy unenthusiastically calls cool at the end.

I grab my stuff for track practice. Emmy runs track too, so she's waiting to walk down to the locker room with me.

"Oh, hey, Jen," I say, shutting my locker. "I can't meet you at Easton on Friday."

Easton Town Center is the fancy indoor/outdoor mall-hangout for half the city under thirty. Usually, I find it a kaleidoscopic maze of fluorescent light and pounding music and endless strangers, interspersed with moments of happy refuge when my friends and I reenergize with sodas and soft pretzels in the food court. And I like the recap in Jen's car on the way home when everyone assesses the outing so I know exactly how much fun I had.

"You're going to Easton Friday, and you didn't ask me?" Emmy, trying to liberate a strand of hair from her lip gloss, asks Jen. "Thanks a lot."

"Check your phone," Jen says. "I asked you like a week ago. We're all going."

All to Jen is all, most of, part of, or one friend from the volleyball team.

"Why aren't *you*?" Emmy asks me.

"My sister's bringing her boyfriend over for dinner, and I haven't met him yet, so I have to be there."

"So can't you just meet him and then come?" Emmy asks. "Just tell your parents you have plans. I'll even pick you up if you want," she offers, sounding irritated.

"No. I want to be there. She says she's in love with him, so I need to spend some time there to check him out," I say, and Jen further defends me to Emmy with: "You know how Josie is about her sisters."

"I know how she is about her whole family. It's completely bizarre," Emmy says in a tone I dislike. But she has only a small repertoire of tones and none of them is particularly pleasant, so it's easy to ignore—or at least re-interpret—some of the things she says.

There's a lot more to meaning than just words. And sometimes, as in Emmy's case, there's a lot less.

CHAPTER FOUR

On Friday, it's nearly five thirty by the time I get home. I walk into the kitchen pungent with the smell of fresh, chopped basil, collected into a tidy pile on the cutting board by the stove. Mother, who has Fridays off, emerges from the pantry carrying a large bottle of olive oil, and we greet each other with kisses on cheeks.

"Did you have an interesting day?" she asks. She never asks if I had a good day. If it was interesting, it was necessarily good, and my mother is never redundant.

"I did," I say, and tell her briefly about a conversation I had in French class today—one of those spontaneous scenarios between two students in front of the class— that involved bread, cheese, the mayor, a cello, and death.

"C'est une longue histoire," I say.

It's a long story.

I run upstairs to shower and change for dinner, texting Stu on the way to remind him of tonight's momentous occasion.

Text to Stu, 5:31 p.m.
Pgeofff's coming to dinner tonight.

Text from Stu, 5:31 p.m.
Pwho?

He knows who Pgeofff is, and he'll be curious about the details later.

It's a little after six when I return to the kitchen, where Ross and Maggie greet me with hugs and quick pecks. Ross is wearing my favorite cologne.

"You smell better than day-old pizza grease," I tell him.

"Well, we were out of pizza grease," he says, "so I went with aftershave."

He bends his neck toward me, and I enjoy another sniff.

"Josie, I do hope we have a daughter like you someday," Maggie says.

"One with my impressive sense of smell?" I ask.

"One who says hello in the most unpredictable ways."

"I wouldn't mind one with an impressive sense of smell," Ross tells Maggie.

"When *are* you going to have kids?" I ask. They've been married five years now and are finally out of residency. Maggie's a pediatrician. Ross is a pediatric endocrinologist. They've joined viable practices. They bought a house a few blocks away. They really have no excuses for not starting a family, and I'm desperate to stop being the youngest Sheridan.

"We'll let you know," Ross says.

"Just don't expect me to babysit until the kid is old enough to clean up her own mess. I don't do sticky or gross," I say.

"We know," Ross and Maggie say in cheery unison.

"Hey," Ross says, pulling out his phone. "Did you see this?" We stand shoulder to shoulder looking at the latest list of *Dennis DeYoung and The Music of Styx* concert dates.

"Nothing in Columbus yet, but at least he's getting closer," Ross says.

It was Ross who introduced me to Dennis DeYoung's music, for which I am eternally grateful.

I love my sisters and never longed for a brother, but since Maggie forced one, in law, upon me, I'm very glad she chose Ross. He plays guitar and piano and does sticky and gross in his job—all things I cannot do—all of which increased his standing in my estimation and made it easier for me to grant Maggie permission to marry him. Which I did in writing. I was eleven at the time. Maggie framed the letter, and it hangs now in their home office—a permanent reminder of the blessing I gave their union.

Dad arrives home shortly, and we settle into the kitchen, remodeled and enlarged three years ago to include a small sitting area around a fireplace we never use. The remodeling lasted months longer than predicted and was the source of the one and only meltdown my mother has ever had. Before she became an instructor, she was a surgical nurse. Normally, nothing rattles the woman. Not even me.

Kate is late, of course. It's her mildly passive-aggressive response to Maggie, who inadvertently steals all the attention in any room simply by entering it. She is, without exaggeration, *that* stunning, made all the more gorgeous by her utter obliviousness to her own beauty. Strangers have stopped her in public—I've seen it—just to tell her how pretty she is, and she receives the compliment every time with a blush and an embarrassed *thank you*.

Friends—myself among them—constantly tell Sophie Wagemaker how beautiful she is too, which she receives with a casual *shut up,* which is the high school translation of *thank you*.

Sophie and Maggie, to varying degrees of formality, speak the language of beautiful women. I can translate it because I grew up hearing it, but it is not my mother tongue.

It is nearly six thirty when Kate finally arrives, thirty minutes late and happily unconcerned. Behind her comes a tall, hazy, male-like creature, an artist's sketch of a man becoming a stork, erased and redrawn several times and never fully defined. Since he bears no resemblance to Kate's description, I can only deduce that this is not Pgeofff.

We stand. Kate hooks her arm through the human rough draft and says with some alarm, "Hey, you're engaged!"

Okay, that was me.

"Josie. *Erm*. Mom."

That's Kate.

"That's an engagement ring," I say, pointing. "So who's the guy?"

"Josie. This is Geoff," she says.

"No, it isn't," I say, and get shushed by Mother, who then asks, "Kate?"

"Well, eh—" She deflates.

"Do you have something to tell us?" Mother says, trying to re-inflate her.

"Josie already did."

"If you wanted it to be a surprise, you shouldn't have worn the ring," I say. "Though I'm definitely surprised by Pgeofff. You're sure that's him?"

"That's Josie," she says as an aside to Pgeofff, and then announces, "Yes, we're engaged."

The room swells then with congratulations and happy chatter, and I hug Kate but reserve my enthusiasm until I have thoroughly vetted Pgeofff, who waits until the merriment subsides before introducing himself.

"Geoffrey Stephen Brill. Nice to meet you," he says to my dad.

To my mother:

"Geoffrey Stephen Brill. Nice to meet you."

To Ross and Maggie:

"Geoffrey Stephen Brill. Nice to meet you."

To me:

"Geoffrey Stephen Brill. Nice to meet you."

"What was that again?" I ask.

Kate giggles. Mother shoots me The Look, and Geoffrey Stephen Brill says with grim sincerity, "Geoffrey Stephen Brill. Nice to meet you."

"I'm done," I announce, and try to leave the kitchen but am scruffed by Mother, practically picked up by the back of my neck and set right back down next to her. This nearly jars my glasses loose, and I promptly straighten them.

All thirty-seven of my carefully prepared questions evaporate the moment Pgeofff presses his cold, damp hand against mine and grips it for a queasy one . . . two . . . three . . . four . . . *ew* . . . seconds and says through a crooked smile, "Josie. I've heard a lot about you."

"Really?" I ask, wiping my hand dry on my jeans.

"I think we're going to get along very well," he says, and then smiles at my parents when he adds, "I have a pretty good rapport with adolescents."

"I'm eating at the Wagemakers' tonight," I say to Mother.

"No, you're not," she says.

"Well, then I'm eating alone in the kitchen."

"No, you're not."

I am about to protest when Dad intervenes. He shanghais Geoffrey Stephen Brill, nice to meet you, into a tour of the house with Kate in tow. First stop, the study to view and admire Dad's collection of odd and slightly gruesome medical antiques. He presses every new visitor into this temporary service. He's a psychiatrist, which means he's insane.

"'Good rapport with adolescents'?" I practically shout at my mother. Then I turn to Ross and demand, "You would never use the word *adolescent,* would you?"

"Not to you I wouldn't."

"See!" I say, pointing at Ross for emphasis, which fails to impress my mother.

"I expect you to give him a chance, my dear," she says. "You've just met him. At the very least, I expect you to be pleasant and not ruin this evening for your sister."

Those words always pinch my heart. *For your sister*. I love my sisters, and, unlike Stu and Sophie of the future, I hope we never live in separate states.

"I'll try for Kate's sake," I say. "But if he uses the word *adolescent* again while I am one, I'm going to have to insist they break up. At least until I'm twenty-one."

A few minutes later, with our little crowd reassembled in the kitchen, Maggie asks Geoff—who is clearly not the type of guy whose name translates into Josie, so I shall miss that silent *p*; maybe I'll give it to Pstu—"Did you enjoy Dad's tour of the house?"

"For the most part. It's nice," he says. "It's a little large and excessive to suit my sense of intimacy, but it's exactly what I expected when Kate told me she grew up in Bexley."

"Excuse me?" I ask.

"Oh, forgive me if I just made a faux pas," he says. "I assumed everyone was familiar with Bexley's reputation."

"We are. We are," my dad says as he pours glasses of wine and as my mother—*ow*—pinches my arm. It never really hurts. She means to warn me to consider my next response.

True, Bexley does have a reputation throughout Central Ohio as home to families with generational wealth where inheriting is considered a talent, and the schools are filled with kids who would much rather sue than fight. But that's the reputation, not the whole population. We have lovely friends here and a lovely house my parents worked hard for, and I'm bristling at Geoff's remark.

Ow.

Okay. I won't say anything. Yet.

"What do you do, Geoff?" Ross asks.

"I'm the director of the medical library at Mount Carmel West," Geoff says, citing a downtown hospital, as he sets down his glass, settles himself against one of the counters, crosses his ankles, folds his arms, and gets comfortable.

My dad copies his pose—a favorite psych trick he employs without thinking sometimes—and tries not to smile when he asks, "And what exactly does the director of Mount Carmel West's medical library do all day? I imagine it has something to with books."

"Uh. Well, it's a little more involved than that. My job entails eight particular elements, each with its own subset of duties and responsibilities, beginning, naturally, with administration."

"Not books?" my father teases.

"Administration," Geoff says, and for the next fifty-eight hours he lists every single detail of his excruciatingly boring work-life and its subsets of toe-curling monotony. And all the while, Kate stares dreamily at him. The whole scene is nauseating.

"Excellent," my dad finally says. "As fine a job description as I have ever heard."

"I suppose I do go on about it. It's really a great job," Geoff says. "And I owe it a debt of gratitude since it's where I met Kate, which really was ironic."

"Ironic?" I ask.

"Yes."

"It would only be ironic if neither one of you could read," I say.

"Josie," Mother says. I have moved across the kitchen, away from the reach of her very long arm and lobster-like pincher claw.

"Well, it was ironic because I never expected to meet

someone so amazing in a place so dusty and serious," Geoff says.

"That's not irony," I say. "That's not even a coincidence."

"Enough," Mother says, and I concede with, "Okay, but it's still not irony."

"Well, I'm glad to hear you enjoy your job," Dad says.

"Plus I get to read all day," Geoff says.

"Do you like to read, then, in your spare time?" Maggie asks.

"Geoff reads everything, I mean everything, you could ask him about anything and he's probably read about it," Kate gushes as Geoff smiles paternally at her.

"Who are your favorite authors?" Ross asks.

"Well, I'm an intellectual, so I go for the highbrow stuff. I don't know how familiar you'd be with some of the authors I like. They're pretty obscure."

"Yeah, our family just likes books with pretty pictures in them," I say, and he produces a sound like a laugh, more an airy snort, accompanied by that half smile.

"Oh, that's right," he says as he snaps his fingers—*excuse me?!*—and points at me. "I forgot I was talking with the gifted sister." He pantomimes quote marks around the word *gifted*.

"The what?" I ask, equally irritated and offended.

"Josie," Kate says, dismissing me with a combination smile/eyelid-flutter. "You're so cute. You know you are."

"Well, then, what sisters are you and Maggie?"

"Maybe I've met my match," Geoff says.

"Geoff's gifted too, you know," Kate adds.

"Gifted?" I ask. "Or"—I sham his incorrectly applied quote-marks move—"gifted?"

"Josephine," Mother and Dad say in quiet, serious unison.

"Well." Geoff pretends to demure before telling a story about himself in first grade having a fourth-grade reading level and being the favorite of his school's librarian. They probably had matching shoes.

"Didn't I tell you he was smart?" Kate says to us all while tipping her head against Geoff's shoulder. "I still say you should let Dad test your IQ. He tested Josie."

"I was merely out of lab rats that day," Dad says. "Didn't know what to do with all my cheese."

"You know, I've never had it tested," Geoff says. "Labels merely pigeonhole people. And, anyway, I don't feel the need for a number to confirm what my academic record has already shown."

"If you get it tested and find out you're actually retarded, *that* would be irony," I say, and receive the most reproachful version of The Look so far tonight. If I push it, I'll lose my iPod for a week.

"So what is yours?" Geoff asks me.

"Didn't you just say it doesn't matter?"

"Well, for me, but since you know yours, I thought I'd ask."

"And yet my parents don't like me to say," I reply.

"Really?" Geoff asks.

"Really. House Rule. Large and Excessive House Rule," I say as Mother clears her throat, but I catch her suppressing a smile. "Broken upon pain of death."

"Not pain of death but torturous grounding," my father says. "No, all I'll say is that it's up there. Makes up for the surprise that you were, eh, Josie?"

We share elbow nudges and smiles while Kate quietly explains to her fiancé that I was a menopause baby. Mother thought she had the flu.

"Ah," Geoff says to my father. "That must have been quite a challenge."

"Yes," Dad says with contrived solemnity. "But I do believe I handled every contraction admirably. Wouldn't you say so, dear?"

"You were very brave," Mother says, and I volunteer to set the dining room table then, just to escape the kitchen.

I should have volunteered to set the Wagemakers' table too. And Mrs. Easterday's. She lives next door.

Isn't this how people stage their disappearances? They claim they're going to run an errand. *I'm going out for a pack of cigarettes. I'll be right back.*

I'm going to have to learn how to smoke.

Later, as we begin to make our way into the dining room for dinner, my dad hooks his arm through mine and steps with me away from the others.

"Josephine, I would like you to observe much and say little at the table," he says before producing his most imperative expression, letting me know he is wholly serious.

"Do I get to share my observations with you later?"

"You do."

"Unabridged?"

"I expect nothing less."

"Okay then."

"You're a good girl, Josie," he says. "Most of the time."

Geoff addresses me only once at dinner, with a predictable question about music, which is the language of adults who don't know how to talk with *adolescents*. This language consists of questions mostly and always about music, school, and pastimes. It is a language that does not create real conversations but merely the impression of them.

In response to Geoff's question, I grin at Ross when I speak about the perfection of Styx and Dennis DeYoung.

"Styx," Geoff repeats. "Kind of an edgy rock group turned prog-rock turned synth-pop turned concept-album group. Not quite soft or mainstream pop but nowhere near jangle or power pop either, don't you agree?"

Seconds pass in silence.

"I have no idea what you're talking about," I say.

"You really have met your match," Kate teases, and I

shove an enormous bite of salad in my mouth and chew in protest of Dad's rules.

"No, it's not that," Geoff says. "It's just the genres and sub-genres they experimented with. I don't think they ever fully identified with one, which is one of the reasons why I've never been able to embrace their music."

"Uh-huh," I say.

"But I think it's great that you like music from previous generations. I do," he says. "I think it shows a real maturity in taste. So very good for you."

He winks at me and ignores me for the rest of supper, during which he instructs Ross about current diabetic treatments, corrects Maggie's perfectly pronounced *Renoir* as *Ren-wah,* and keeps fondling Kate's breasts. Okay, not exactly, but he touches her arm or hand whenever he talks or she does, and it's so frequent it's bordering on molestation. I can't believe no one's putting a stop to this.

After dinner, we womenfolk clear the table, leaving Geoff lecturing my father and a glassy-eyed Ross about the number of tick-borne diseases other than "the over-diagnosed Lyme disease." All the while, my father interjects with too much enthusiasm, "You don't say?" And, "Well, imagine that."

When I retrieve the last plate, Dad says, "Did you get

a load of that, Josie? Tularemia can be spread by deer-flies as well as ticks."

"You don't say?" I ask with dad-like enthusiasm on my way back to the kitchen.

Ross and Maggie cannot leave fast enough. I think they leave skid marks in the driveway. Taking the hint lost on Geoff, Kate finally announces that they must leave too. I open our front door before either one of them dons a coat.

Just across the threshold, Geoff says, "Oh, and my compliments to the chef tonight."

"Thank you," Mother says.

"If you don't mind my saying, there was a bit too much basil in the sauce, but it's a common mistake American cooks make."

"Is it?" Mother asks.

"Next time, if you put in about one-third less, you'll notice the difference. You'll be able to enjoy the other flavors and not feel assaulted by basil."

Mother thanks him plausibly, and the moment she closes the door, I say, "I feel the need to inform you both that I dislike him . . . very, very much."

My parents bristle at the word *hate,* except in reference to injustice, vulgarity, and thugs who mug old ladies. But I come close to using it tonight.

"Did you see how he kept touching her?" I demand, wriggling at my mental image.

"I thought it was endearing," Mother says to my horrified, "What?!"

"Now, Josie," Dad says, hooking his arm through mine and leading the three of us slowly to the study. "In this family, we like the ones each other likes and love them if we must."

"No, we don't. We don't like Uncle Vic. You called him organically unpleasant after last Thanksgiving."

"That's true. I did. You think he heard me?" he asks hopefully.

"Your father means our immediate family."

"Geoffrey Stephen Brill is never becoming immediate family," I say. "I, for one, won't stand for it, and I don't think you two should either. You need to call Kate tonight and tell her to give the ring back. He is all wrong for her, and we should not make room for him in this family."

"Now, now," Dad says. "You need to give Geoff more of a chance than this one evening. He may improve in your current estimation."

"It will never happen."

"Not with that attitude, it won't. But you may be glad of knowing someone like Geoff one of these days," Dad says.

"That will never happen either."

"Oh, I think it may. Imagine if Sophie Wagemaker goes for a walk in the woods with one of her many admirers and contracts Tick-Borne Relapsing Fever.

Whom would we call? Why, Geoffrey Stephen Brill."
Dad pats my hand. "Yes, we may find that he is very use-
ful, indeed. I believe you could learn a great deal from
Geoff if you will allow him to teach you."

"About ticks?"

"Ticks and other things, my dear." He cups his hand
against my cheek and smiles maniacally. "You never
know what you're going to learn from another person—
about him or about yourself."

"So you're not going to say anything to Kate?"

"I am not," he says.

Well, then I'm going to have to, I think as I pick up a
gray stoneware jar with *Leeches* printed across it, drop
into one of the big wingchairs, and plot my strategy
while nibbling on the M&M'S Dad keeps in the jar
for me.

CHAPTER FIVE

I call Kate first thing this morning. Well, second thing. Minutes ago, I learned via a thorough Internet search that Geoffrey Stephen Brill is not a deadbeat dad, wanted fugitive, or registered sex offender. Not in *this* state.

At the moment and for the foreseeable future, I cannot dislodge his triptych name from my head, nor can I forget the repulsiveness of his handshake. Shivering at the memory, I wipe my hand on my sweatpants, and I dial Kate's number.

While her phone rings, I glance at the framed, autographed photo of Dennis DeYoung on my desk and tell him, since he's looking keenly at me, "I'm taking care of this right now."

He'd do the same.

"Josie," Kate answers in a sleep-gravel voice. "It's Saturday. What time is it?"

Kate is not the morning person my dad and I are. He rises even earlier than I do so that he can be at his office by 7:30 at the latest. Even on Saturdays I naturally rise early and fall asleep around ten at night, which makes dances and parties arduous. I actually need a nap before most of them. Or I leave early. Or both.

"It's seven thirteen," I say. "And I know it's early for you, but I couldn't wait. I have to talk to you about Geoffrey Stephen Brill."

"He's great, isn't he?" Kate says.

"No. He isn't. He's horrible."

"He is not."

"He is obnoxious, unpleasant, and overbearing, and if I keep going with this list, eventually I'm going to come to *asshole*. But I'm stopping now so I don't upset you too much."

"Josie! You don't even know him."

"Kate, he's the single most uninteresting person in the world. You're not really going to marry him, are you? Is this a delayed rebellion? Is this the boyfriend—"

"Josie, stop it!"

"—you should have had when you were sixteen just to piss off Mother and Dad?"

"Josie, I'm hanging up."

"Tick-borne diseases? Need I say more?"

"Oh," she says. "Well." I hear her sitting up. "He was just nervous about meeting everyone. I mean, think about it. You know, you guys are kind of an intimidating family to join."

"Who?"

"You. All of you."

"You're part of us," I say, irked.

"Especially Dad and you."

"We are not."

"Right. Not to anyone with IQs higher than Einstein's."

"You're the one who brought up gifted. Didn't Dad teach you not to?"

"I'm hardly the one he'd say that to."

"What?"

"Anyway, Geoff would have figured it out, and he just wanted everyone to know that he's smart too."

"So he chose to display his stunning knowledge of ticks? Kate."

"Josie, stop. Well, yeah," she concedes. "That was an odd topic, but it was an article he'd just read, so that's what came to mind."

"Well, lucky us that he hadn't just read about rectal lesions."

"Josie, enough. He's a great guy. Really. Just give him a chance. You'll get to know him better. He'll be less nervous, and you'll see."

"No, you're the one who needs to see."

"See what?"

"That he's all wrong for you. As usual. Gorgeous, brilliant, interesting." I tick them off on my fingers, and Kate can tell. She can feel the sting of my finger-ticking over the phone. "You said he was all these things."

"He is."

"He's none of them. There is something wrong with

your ability to accurately assess the men you date. You should not trust your own judgment here, which means you need to listen to me and break up with him right now."

"Josie, I love him. He loves me. We're getting married, and you're going to love him."

"He's—"

"And if you don't right now, then you'll learn to," she nearly snaps at me.

"Apparently I'll have to learn about ticks too."

"Josie, stop it."

"No, Kate. I'm telling you the guy is wrong for you."

"You may be fifteen going on thirty, but you're still fifteen," she says, wielding *fifteen* as if it were a knife, "and you have no idea what you're talking about in these matters."

"What matters?"

"Love."

"I know what love is."

"Right, with all your vast experience?"

And, *ouch,* she twists the knife in.

"It's more than a dictionary definition," she says. "So fall in love, and then we'll talk. Until then, you have no ground to stand on. So I'm done talking with you about this."

"Well, I'm—"

Click.

"—not."

I hang up the phone completely irritated and fuming under my own little black cloud. I hate this cloud. It smells like toes. Every time Mother finds me in a black, cloud mood she says I look as if I'm smelling someone else's toes. Therefore, black clouds smell like toes. Who knew?

"I'm not giving up," I tell my photo of Dennis, pointing at him so he knows just how serious I am.

Text from Stu, 9:05 a.m.
How was the dinner?

Text to Stu, 9:06 a.m.
We were assaulted by basil.

Text from Stu, 9:06 a.m.
Sorry to hear it. Food poisoning?

Text to Stu, 9:07 a.m.
Close.

Text from Stu, 9:07 a.m.
Feel better.

Text to Stu, 9:07 a.m.
Working on it.

Text from Stu, 9:08 a.m.
So what's wrong with this Pgeofff guy?

Text to Stu, 9:08 a.m.
He spells his name wrong.

Text from Stu, 9:09 a.m.
A tragedy.

Text to Stu, 9:09 a.m.
I knew you'd understand.

I set my phone down and wrinkle my face at the smell of toes. Kate's right. I am woefully inexperienced about the actual application of love and am reduced to learning from secondary sources such as Stu, Sophie, and Jane Austen.

Here, I think Sophie, of my living experts, has more experience—or a better track record, anyway—than Stu. Her relationships, while many, last longer than Stu's, and the break-ups are dramatic and always her choice. They are rarely Stu's. Yet they never truly unsettle him either.

Text to Stu, 9:11 a.m.
U R the love 'em & leave 'em type.

Text from Stu, 9:12 a.m.
I realize this is not a non sequitur 2 U, but . . .
WHAT?

* * * * *

I have gone out with exactly three people in my life—count them, which I do, grimly raising fingers: one dance freshman year, one dance last year, and dinner and the homecoming dance with Stefan Kott just five loveless months ago in October.

I'm hoping my date-a-year history is not becoming a pattern. I also hoped Stefan and I might go out a little longer than just one night, but that didn't happen. He's nice and cute in a gangly way, with a mop of curly sand-colored hair that gets thicker, not longer, as it grows. And he plays bass guitar in a band with three friends, calling themselves Blue Lint Monkey, who haven't had any paying gigs yet, but someday they might.

I admit I have a thing for musicians.

Text to Kate, 9:15 a.m.
Can Geoff sing or play guitar?

Text from Kate, 9:17 a.m.
No. Y?

I knew it, I quietly grumble and set my phone on my desk.

Stefan had told me at dinner, before the homecoming dance, as we furiously searched for conversational commonalities—well, I did—that he only asked me out because of my height. He's one of the tallest guys in our class, and I am all legs—flamingo legs at that, long, skinny, knobby-kneed, and nearly as pink. Sometimes I think I have more than just two. Then he added in the nicest possible way, "But it turns out I kinda like being with you too."

And I thanked him but felt so thoroughly undermined, first by the height remark and then by the word *kinda*, that I became quietly fixated on these things and could think nothing other than *I'm tall and he only "kinda" likes me?* To compensate for the few minutes of awkward silence that followed, I spoke for most of the remainder of the evening in what can only be described as Stream-of-Consciousness Josie.

During our first slow dance, he said to me, "Do you think you could stop talking for the rest of this song?"

Sure. Of course. Got it. No talking during slow dances, which were few and left a lot of other time for yammering—all the way into my driveway, where I hopped out of the car before he even turned it off, and I darted inside the house. Exhausted.

Oh, and I tripped, stepped on my dress and tore it somewhere between the recipe for my mother's spaghetti sauce and a brief history of how English became a global language in the modern era.

Then, just to prove I could be quiet at will, I consciously said very little on the phone the next day when he called, and again the following Monday when I saw him at school. Tuesday too. By Friday, we just said hi to each other in the halls when we passed. And, yes, I felt disappointed because I liked him, but height? Height was it for him? I keep a growing list of qualities important to me in the guy I fall in love with. I'm up to twenty, and I admit that height is on the list, but it's not the *only* thing on the list.

Text to Sophie, 10:02 a.m.
Know of anyone who wants to ask me to the prom?

Text from Sophie, 10:04 a.m.
Really? OK, I'll ask around. Who do U like? BTW no 1 says know OF.

Text to Sophie, 10:04 a.m.
Thx. He should have as much in common with Dennis DeYoung as possible. BTW, I say know OF.

Text from Sophie, 10:04 a.m.
I know. I love it. I'd sound so stupid.

Text to Sophie, 10:05 a.m.
U never sound stupid.

Text from Sophie, 10:05 a.m.

Text to Sophie, 10:06 a.m.

Having Sophie find me a prom date is not exactly the modern equivalent of *their eyes met across a crowded room,* but it's a start. Like Kate said, I need some love experience here. If I don't gain any soon, I won't be able to prevent Kate from making the worst mistake of my life. And hers.

CHAPTER SIX

"I'm definitely ready to be in love," I say.

"Do I want to hear this?" Stu asks.

"Ohmigosh, be quiet. I do," Sophie says.

It's Monday. We are in Stu's car on our way to school on yet another cold, drizzling morning this last day of March. He drives a bright yellow Subaru station wagon that he bought last summer from a woman who covered the bumper with stickers about quilting. He, Sophie, and I spent a Saturday scraping off such slogans as *I ♥ Quilting*; *Love to Bee a Quilter*; *A Quilter is happiest when her life is in pieces.*

He kept the only one that had nothing to do with quilting: *Hot Granny on Board.*

This morning, Sophie twists all the way around in the front passenger seat to face me, her eyes vivid with an excitement I don't share and can't match.

"I've worked this out," I say.

"You can't work love out," she says, wistfully pulling her long blond hair over one shoulder.

"I can work anything out," I say.

"How much rat have you eaten in your life?" Stu asks via the rearview mirror.

"Fine. I can work *most* things out," I say.

"You two stop," Sophie says, unbuckling her seat belt and climbing over the center console to join me in the back. "Tell me everything," she says. "What kind of guy are you looking for?"

Stu turns the radio up—some unidentifiable jazz piece.

"You really want to hear this? Because I have a list," I say.

"I know you do," she says, rolling her eyes and smiling at the same time, which is a look only Sophie, in all her beautiful blitheness, could master so inoffensively. "Yes. Let's hear it."

"Okay. He has to be older than I am. And taller. Preferably handsome but not so gorgeous that he knows it. And smart in a way that makes me just want to sit and listen to him talk."

"About what?" she asks.

"Just—everything interesting. We have to be able to have marathon conversations. But we also need to be comfortable being quiet together." *He will appreciate the value of self-possessed silence and practice it judiciously,* I want to add, but don't.

"He should play some instrument too," I say. "Preferably guitar or piano, but I wouldn't mind a woodwind. Bagpipes would be my first choice, but percussion is out of the question."

"Bag——? Josie," Sophie says.

"Well, he has to be able to do things I can't do that don't drive me crazy so that I stay interested."

"Like walking a straight line without falling over?" Stu asks.

"Yeah. Like that," I agree, pointing at Stu and shamming a smile.

"Stop listening to us," Sophie orders him. "Just go back to driving."

"You realize I haven't stopped driving," he says.

"Be quiet," she says. To me, she asks, "What else?"

There's more. There's lots more.

He will never ask me to eat gray, slimy, gelatinous food nor will he tousle my hair. Not that he could tousle it since I wear it daily in a neat and tidy ponytail, but there are times—showering, blow-drying—when my hair is, in fact, tousle-able. I'd prefer it if he just never touches my head or touches it only with my permission, which I will grant on special occasions such as Arbor Day, poor, neglected holiday that it is, but never on my birthday.

He will not collect white crud in the corners of his eyes or mouth. He will be athletic, but his interest in sporting events will stop well before obsession. He will understand the difference between:

- coincidence and irony
- smart and gifted
- ticks and things that are interesting

He will agree that the single greatest musical talent of our times is Dennis DeYoung, whose picture we will enshrine in the foyer of our first home together. He will never criticize my mother's cooking or my parents' house but will, instead, fit seamlessly into the Sheridan family dynamic. And his name will easily lend itself to a silent *p*.

He will be Pperfect.

But I don't say any of this to Sophie. Instead, I ask, "What else do you want to know?"

"Well, is there anyone at school you like?"

"I don't think so," I say.

"Not even Stefan?"

"Homecoming?" I say by way of reminder.

"Yeah," she says, producing an entirely too cheerful cringe.

Stu pulls up to the high school, and Sophie grabs her backpack.

"Okay, so this afternoon, come find me, and I'll let you know what I find out," she says of her new mission. Stu watches me in the rearview mirror, his lips parted and frozen halfway between a smile and a laugh. I slouch in my seat a little and ride the rest of the way to Cap like this, impatient and pessimistic about the future of love in my life.

Cap is the nickname for Capital University, a small liberal arts university of old brick buildings on lush green grass, about a mile from Bexley High School and two miles from my house. This semester at Cap, Stu and I are finishing up our freshman year.

We're in our high school's Early College Program, slightly tweaked. Usually, it's only for seniors, but Stu and I were accepted into the program last year as sophomores.

We should have graduated high school last year, but my dad refused on our behalf. His specialty is creating educational programs for highly gifted teens that also meet social and psychological needs. He insisted on this division between high school and college for what he calls age-appropriate socialization.

To him, we're like a couple of kittens in training before we leave the birthing box and explore the real world. If improperly socialized, he fears we could become skittish and strange our whole lives, peeing in potted plants and hissing at people who just want to pet us.

So in the spirit of socialized cats, I am not allowed to go away to college until I am eighteen, by which time I'll be a senior at Cap, so I figure I'll graduate from there and go away to graduate school. Unless, of course, my dad catches me urinating in one of Mom's Boston ferns. I should do it someday, with a camera handy just to capture his expression.

"So what about this Geoff guy?" Stu asks when we exit his car.

I pop up my umbrella even before I get out since rain

and eyeglasses do not mix. "Kate is not going to marry him," I say.

"Oh, really?"

"Really. It's a phase. It's an engagement phase."

We've parked a couple blocks from the campus because Stu won't spring for a student parking pass. On nice days, we park near the high school and walk.

"But she'll come to her senses soon and call it off," I add. "Also, I'm not exactly sure what he looks like, but I'm pretty sure he's not gorgeous."

"You don't know what he looks like?"

"Well, I can't trust my memory of him at the moment. I remember his words, and I really disliked every single one of them, so now when I try to remember him, I'm remembering that I don't like him, and that's corrupting my mental image of him. So I need to try to remember him separate from my feelings, which is no easy task."

"So he could be an okay-looking guy?"

"No. I just have to remember the degree of his hideousness distinct from his degree of boringness."

"Let me know when you do."

"And he did this," I say, making air quotes. "In reference to me."

Stu smiles some.

"And he snapped his fingers at me too," I say. "Then he disparaged IQ testing right before he asked me what mine is. He was completely rude."

"Not necessarily," Stu says. We are nearing the corner of Drexel and Main just opposite the campus, which also marks the beginning of Bexley's little downtown of boutiques, cool restaurants, coffee shops, and condos. "Given your dad's work and you, I can see how the topic would come up."

"Kate brought it up."

"She's proud of you."

We stop at the corner to wait for the light.

"No, she brought it up in reference to Geoff, who then referred to himself as an intellectual."

"Well," Stu says, raising his shoulders and stretching his mouth to the sides in a kind of hesitant smile, as he does when deciding whether or not to speak his mind.

"Say it," I demand.

"Yeah, I think if you are one, you don't have to announce it. As for IQ, I don't know. I appreciate the research, but—" He shrugs again. "I know people like this Geoff guy who don't."

Stu's IQ is one hundred fifty-one—eleven points above genius on some scales. Mine is three points higher than his. Now, I mean these as statements of fact, not bragging, because we came this way with these IQs, this blond hair—mine's a little darker than Stu's—these eyes, these fingers, this height, these flat chests, and so on. We had nothing to do with it.

I like to think of human beings as coming from a divine vending machine, like the ones in hotel game rooms and old gas stations where you press a letter and a number and watch your item drop to the bottom.

B-3 you get Sigmund Freud.

D-12 is Beyoncé.

C-7 is me.

A-8 you get Twix.

Stu and I part ways in the center of campus. He heads off for a history class. I head off to algebra. I'll see him again later this morning for a lit class called Modern Drama. Then we'll walk to Fair Grounds, our favorite coffee shop a couple blocks east of campus, for what I consider lunch and what Stu considers a brief reprieve from starvation. He eats like a furnace and never gains weight. Actually, I think he's growing. Lately I've noticed his shoulders are just a little higher than mine.

We split every day between the two schools—mornings at Cap, afternoons back at Bexley High. Showing my high school ID at the door feels a little like going through customs at an airport. Every school day is like this, consisting of two different cultures, requiring two languages different from my own mother tongue.

The language of high school could be called Ohmig*d since just about everyone says it a hundred times a day. But I can't say it, even as a name, because I think it's so unfair to G-d. It's not like He's sitting around Heaven spitting out ohmijosie every time He loses his keys or His computer crashes.

It's only in Ohmig*d where *shut up* means *thank you*, *hot* is either *wildly popular* or *sexy*, *chill* means *relaxed*, and *cool* and *sweet* are synonymous. In college, it's Ohmig*d 2.0—with some shared vocabulary and some different. I'm a high school *girl* but a college *woman*. I mature and regress all on the same day depending only on my location.

I like studying languages. At Cap, I've already declared Romance Languages as my major, but I don't know yet what I want to do with the degree. I don't know that I'm wildly ambitious beyond the things I like to study, and pretty stubborn about the courses I dislike, doing the bare-bones minimum for the grade and not for the knowledge itself. I only know I want to do something that keeps me engaged, and the puzzle of foreign languages and the tangle that is sometimes English do that. Like Ohmig*d and Ohmig*d 2.0, there are a lot more foreign languages in the world than the ones identified by national or international boundaries.

I find Sophie at her locker a little after three this afternoon. She's engrossed in conversation with a couple of her friends from Art Club, and I'm headed to track practice, so I say, "I'll just call you later." But she grips my wrist, and tells her friends, "Hang on a minute. This is important.

"I put some feelers out," she says when she turns to me. "I'm doing this slowly. Trying to be really subtle, you know."

"Well, I prefer subtlety to a sign on my locker that says, 'Help, I'm desperate for a prom date.'"

"I'd make a gorgeous sign for you, though."

"I'm sure you would."

Emmy Newall appears next to me and demands, "You coming?" She doesn't like going anywhere alone. Ever.

Sophie turns back to her friends with a promise to catch up with me later.

"Okay, so get this," Jen says, running to join Emmy and me as far as the gym. "Today in chemistry—did you hear?"

"Stefan Kott?" Emmy asks as Jen says, "Yes," and I ask, "What?"

"Stefan Kott," Jen says, and stops walking and pauses for excited emphasis as we stop too. ". . . lit his hair on fire."

"What?" I ask. "Is he okay?"

"He's absolutely fine," Jen says. "He just got his front, but—"

"He's got thick hair," I say, worried.

"Exactly. And it went—" She snaps her fingers. "Like that. Ohmig-d, it stank too."

"But you're sure he's okay?" I ask.

"Yeah. I mean, he slapped it right out. Didn't get burned at all. But, you know, his hair," she says, and pulls a sad face. "He's gotta get that fixed. Like, today."

"Ohmig-d, he's so stupid," Emmy says, and I turn deliberately to stare at her. "What?" she says.

"He's not stupid. He may have been clumsy, but that's not the same as stupid."

"Whatever. Sorry," she puffs at me. "Come on. Let's just go."

We part from Jen and head toward the locker room, and I say, "He's actually pretty smart."

Emmy uses a pinky to hook a captive hair stuck in her lip gloss, frowns, and says, "Whatever," again. A couple seconds later she adds, "I'm glad he didn't get hurt."

"Yeah," I say, happy that she said it, so I concede, "He doesn't always focus."

He also doesn't appreciate the value of self-possessed silence and practice it judiciously, I want to add but don't. Our silence beyond *hi* in the halls isn't self-possessed. It's just plain awkward.

CHAPTER SEVEN

Stu says nothing for several seconds, just looks sideways at me, waiting for me to admit to exaggeration, which I do when I do, but today I speak the unadulterated truth.

"A bird on a pogo stick?" he finally asks.

"Yes. It came to me this morning. That's what Geoff looks like."

It's Tuesday morning, and we're walking across Cap's campus. It's chilly today, and windy, which isn't bad for early April in Columbus. Last year at this time we had snow. Stu and I have had to stop twice so I could align and then realign the seam on my left sock, which drives me mad when it slips. None of Stu's socks have seams—he can't stand seams, so he understands.

"I'm not entirely sure I'm getting an unbiased report here," he says.

"First of all, nobody presents a one hundred percent unbiased report of anything. It's impossible. But I was able, for the most part, to mentally separate Geoff from my *experience* of Geoff, and the result was that I remember him looking like a bird on a pogo stick."

"Let me ask you this. Do you think it's possible for a person to find someone she dislikes attractive?"

"*She* dislikes?"

"Or he."

"I'd have to say no," I say.

"That's what I thought."

"But then answer me this," I say. "Is it possible for a person to find someone she loves more attractive than he actually is?"

"Yes," he says without hesitation.

"Well, that explains Kate and *her* particular bias."

"So this Geoff guy's appearance is somewhere between gorgeous and bird-on-a-pogo-stick," Stu says.

"Probably. So he's a parrot in khakis walking down the street."

Stu raises his eyebrows at me, just like Auntie Pat does when she's skeptical. "How is a parrot in khakis halfway between gorgeous and bird-on-a-pogo-stick?"

"Parrots can talk," I say, making my hands into scales, "and so can Geoff."

"I don't think you're embracing the spirit of halves here."

"That's because you haven't met Geoff yet."

"Call me the next time he's over," Stu says. "Especially if he's molting."

That makes me smile more than I mean to, which always amuses Stu. He grins crookedly with quiet satisfaction.

We part ways here—Intermediate Spanish II for me, Music Theory for Stu.

French for pogo stick is *baton de pogo*. I have no idea how I know this, but since I do, I think I should also know it in Spanish and will ask my professor at the end of class today. If I don't, it will plague me for life.

It's an advantage that I'm good with languages, since knowing the local language is always the first step to blending in. And at Cap or the high school, Stu and I do—no more or less than anyone else, really. It helps that we are not social misfits who are beaten up or stuffed in lockers. We have friends. We play sports. We do not carry briefcases, wear suits to class, or have hobbies involving formaldehyde or kites. Our mothers don't cut our hair along the outline of a bowl. We aren't rude to the C students. And no one—at least no one in this high school—hates us because we're smart. A bunch of people I know hate Emmy Newall but not because she got into AP Chemistry this year.

No, Stu and I learn the languages and copy the customs and get along. Though, sometimes it's hard. Living in foreign cultures and constantly translating Ohmig*d into Josie and back again gets fatiguing. It does for me more than it does for Stu, I've noticed. He's like my mother—nothing much rattles him, not even me.

I like school. I like college. I especially like having two different IDs that show I belong to both places. But usually it's a relief to be home or at my sisters' or at the Wagemakers', where I can just speak Josie without having to translate a thing.

Emmy Newall is waiting for me to gather up my track gear. She taps her heel repeatedly against Danny Shiever's locker, next to mine, and sighs when he stops in front of her and says, somewhat aggressively, "What?" Which is Omig*d for *Move*.

Unfazed, Emmy takes up post on the other side of me. I grab my backpack, shut my locker, and pause at the sight of Sophie, strolling toward me and trying not to smile overly.

"Can we talk?" she asks, darting her eyes discreetly at Emmy.

"Yeah," I say. Emmy sighs again and moves over several locker-lengths.

"I have some good news. I think you'll think it's good. I do."

"Is there a particular person in this news?" I ask.

"Oh yeah," Sophie says as Emmy sighs once more and checks her watch.

"Did you tell her?" Jen Auerbach asks, rushing into

us and grabbing our arms in a way that practically turns us into a Trinity knot. Sophie untangles all our hands and casually cautions Jen, "Subtle. Let's be subtle."

"Tell me," I practically plead—so much for subtlety—as Emmy moves closer and asks, "Wait, is this about Josie and a guy?" She confronts Jen: "And how come you know and I don't?"

Jen inhales as if she's about to dive for the answer, but before she can speak, I turn to give a friendly nod to Stefan Kott, walking past me with a couple of his buddies who are happily ribbing him about his spiky new haircut.

"Hey, Josie," he says.

"Hey, Stefan."

When I return my attention to my friends, their entirely too amused faces—the kind that are about to burst into laughter over how long it takes me, their idiot friend, to deduce the obvious—tell me everything I need to know. And I try to copy their enthusiasm, but all I can manage to think is . . . *oh*.

CHAPTER EIGHT

Text to Kate, 3:22 p.m.
Stefan Kott still likes me.

Text from Kate, 3:23 p.m.
Thought U liked him 2

Text to Kate, 3:23 p.m.
He likes me because I'm tall. How can I
comfortably date someone who only likes me
because I'm tall?

Text from Kate, 3:24 p.m.
I DOUBT thats the only reason—y dont u go out
with him & find out

Text to Kate, 3:24 p.m.
Maybe.

Text from Kate, 3:25 p.m.
Call me later. Want 2 talk more. 2 busy now

Thoughts of Stefan Kott—more specifically thoughts of me projected into the future with Stefan Kott at the prom and dinner beforehand—preoccupy me throughout all of track practice. For a moment, my thoughts turn to Stefan's haircut, which I like. It seems to brighten up his whole face, especially his eyes, which now look more gold than brown. It completely suits the kind of guy who would—and did—write *playing baseball, making funny faces, and helping old ladies across the street, but never at the same time*—under *About* on his Facebook page.

Quiet contemplation is one of the things I love about running.

I don't know how couples run together and chat. Or why.

I must be more absorbed than usual because after practice Emmy grabs my arm and fairly hangs from it—a sensation I thoroughly dislike—as she asks, "Josie, what's going on? Are you ignoring me? I called your name like nine times just now."

"Sorry. I didn't even hear you."

"So?"

"I'm just thinking."

"About Stefan?"

"Yeah," I say.

"Shut up," she says, opening her mouth in a manner that alarms me. So I explain—in keeping with the day's idiocy theme—that we're just friends, and by Wednesday afternoon it is all over school that Stefan and I are a couple, and by Friday we confirm it when he asks and I agree to go to the prom with him.

He asks me at my locker.

"And it's not just because you're tall," he says. "I'm such a jerk for saying that. And so stupid."

"You're not a jerk. And you're not stupid."

"Yeah," he says, puffing out a laugh. "I heard you told Emmy that."

"Well, it's true."

"Still, I'm sorry about that whole homecoming thing. I know it bothered you."

"Yeah, I guess you could tell I was a little upset."

"A little," he says, smiling at me. "So the prom?"

"Yeah. That'd be nice," I say.

"Yeah? Cool," he says. "So—maybe I'll call you this weekend. Maybe we can hang out, do something."

"Sure," I say, and lose myself in happy contemplation at track practice once again, and if Emmy Newall calls my name nine times, I do not hear her once.

Sophie hangs out in the art room after school this afternoon, working on an abstract oil painting for the school's art exhibit next month. After track practice, she walks several blocks with me to Thane's Discount Drug Store, where she searches for a particular shade of lipstick for me.

"I'm so glad prom's not until May tenth this year," she

says. "I want it to be warm so I don't have to wear a coat, which will look completely hideous with my dress."

"Sophie, I doubt you could ever look hideous, even if you tried."

"Aw, Josie, shut up," she says, briefly smiling up at me. Then she spies her target and hands me a tube of pale pink lipstick called Candy Bliss. "This will be perfect on you no matter what color your dress is. Trust me. Stefan will appreciate it."

I don't have my dress yet and only have about a month and counting to find one. Sophie's had hers since before she had a date, who is Adam Gibson, by the way. He's a senior. I know him the way I know everyone in school, the way everyone knows everyone in school. There are only about two hundred in each class, so we all have a kind of familiarity outside of real relationships.

Sophie has their entire night—including a warm, moonlit evening—scripted, which she describes to me on our long walk home. When I script my own prom night with Stefan, I don't see weather or moonlight. I only see myself falling off my shoes, crashing to the floor, breaking both an ankle and a wrist as I nearly take Stefan down with me. But he falls into a table, where the votive candles ignite what's left of his hair. We end up in the emergency room, I in two casts, he with his bald head bandaged. When the nurse checks on him in the next gurney over, I quickly reapply my Candy Bliss lipstick, and later, when we're alone in Bay 8 of the ER, he

notices and says, "I really appreciate that color on you."
And I say, "I thought you might."

This would be romance in what has been my dating life. I'm definitely looking forward to the prom.

The Wagemakers come for dinner tonight to meet Geoff and congratulate the happy—*shudder*—couple.

Right before they arrive, Mother cautions me, "Do consider your remarks before speaking tonight, my dear. And then reconsider your initial consideration."

I love the warning for its succinctness and privately fume about it for the same reason.

With the Wagemakers and the Sheridans under one roof, the evening flies by in a delirium of festive and frequently loud conversation, leaving Geoffery Stephen Brill few opportunities to hold forth beyond the early getting-to-know-you questions. He is neither loud enough nor verbally flexible enough to jump into brief conversational spaces, nor is he bold enough—and this surprises me—to charge headlong into the middle of conversations as all of us except my parents do.

Instead, he remains close to Kate tonight, looking at times like a cardboard cutout of himself and smiling passively at the buzz around him.

It's self-serve tonight—Chinese takeout with enough options to suit our varied tastes and nearly enough to satisfy Stu's bottomless pit of a stomach. A third of the

way through the evening, he, Sophie, and I find ourselves alone at the kitchen table buffet, where I demand
of them, "Well?"

Stu shrugs and starts to load his plate with everything
but the centerpiece.

"He's kind of cute," Sophie says. "And Kate is so
much in love. You can see it on her face."

"What?" I turn to Stu. "Did you hear that?"

"You realize I'm two feet away from you and not
deaf," he answers.

"Do you agree?" I ask.

"I have no opinion on the appearance of another guy,
because it's another guy," he says, shrugging. "But, over-
all, he's not as bad as I thought he'd be."

"Well, he's barely talking tonight," I say, and Sophie
lets me know with a cheerful "Hello" that someone has
just entered the kitchen behind me. And it turns out to
be Kate and the self-adhesive fiancé.

"So, Geoff," Stu says in a falsely cheery tone I recognize and dread. "Josie tells me you know a lot about a
lot."

Oh, no.

"That's nice of her," he says with a kind of bob in my
direction.

"Know anything about birds?" Stu asks.

"Birds?"

"Yeah. Specifically parrots," Stu says. "Josie was just
telling me this week how interesting she finds the parrot."

"Well, parrots are very interesting," Geoff confirms. He looks at me when he says, "I don't know as much about them as I do about the myna, which you may know as the myna bird, but there are actually over two dozen species of mynas, and myna bird isn't, officially, among them."

As Geoff continues, Stu pops a whole pork dumpling into his mouth and shoots me a wickedly happy grin before returning to the fun in the family room. Meanwhile, Sophie and Kate coo over Kate's ring while I listen to something about the crested myna and wonder, through my boredom, if I am remembering to blink.

"Don't make plans next Saturday," Kate tells me at the back door, with a more vividly grinning Geoff still pressed up close behind her. The Wagemakers went home twenty minutes ago, and Mother caught me by my arm trying to leave with them.

"I'm taking you shopping," Kate says. "We're getting your prom dress. Then plan on spending the night."

"Just the two of us?" I ask her.

"Just the two of us," she says, looking over her shoulder at Geoff and adding, "You don't mind, do you?"

"Not at all. If I had a sister, I'd do the same."

"Aww. You will have a sister. You'll have two in just—"

"Okay. Next Saturday. Just the two of us," I say, and

we kiss cheeks, and I close the door and find myself thinking, *Unlike most other mynas, the crested myna's beak is off-white instead of orange.* Startled, I shake my head to dislodge the language of Geoff. I'm afraid it might spontaneously paralyze my eyelids.

Stefan doesn't call over the weekend but sends me dozens of text messages. I respond as promptly as possible. He tells me in one, "U even punctuate texts—cool."

I receive three texts from him at Mrs. Easterday's house Sunday afternoon, but I politely ignore them, preferring Mrs. Easterday's conversation to just about anybody's text messages. I admit it: I like speaking the language of old ladies. It is surprisingly similar to Josie and, therefore, easy to speak.

The Easterdays owned their house for sixteen years before my parents moved in next door. I'm over here at least twice a week. I pop in to say hello, hang out, play cards, talk. And if Mrs. Easterday doesn't have anything sweet in the house, we'll bake it while she tells me perfectly constructed stories of growing up in the 1940s, and I tell her about classes at Cap or the high school and about the variations in Ohmig*d and Ohmig*d 2.0.

She taught fourth grade for more than twenty years and refused to allow her students to say *yeah* instead of *yes*.

Mr. Easterday died three years before I was born.

Whenever Mrs. Easterday finishes a story about him, her heavy-lidded eyes become abstracted and a bit of a smile spreads across her lips. If I remain quiet, she'll hold the look for up to a minute. And I always manage to remain very quiet then.

Mrs. Easterday met Geoff Friday night, joining us for cocktail hour before dinner—she had cranberry juice— and promising Kate she would not miss the wedding, which, by the way, has been set for Saturday, November eighth. I'm working against a deadline here.

When I ask her today what she thinks of Geoff, she tells me, "I think I am very happy for Kate because she is so very happy, herself."

"Yeah," I concede, which causes Mrs. Easterday to lower her eyebrows disapprovingly at me. "Yes," I correct myself through a warm-cheeked grin. *Yeah* is Ohmig*d and Ohmig*d 2.0, into which I sometimes slip. *Yes* is from a number of languages—Teacher, Grandparent, Job Interview, Marriage Proposal. I'm sure Kate didn't say *yeah* when Master Myna Bird proposed.

I do not feel like belaboring the topic of Kate's relationship with Geoff, especially since very lately the thought of *the two of them* produces an odd sensation in me. I feel as if I'm riding in a car on a newly paved country road and suddenly traverse an unforeseen bump that lifts my stomach slightly higher than it should.

Reason Number Nine Why Geoff Should Not Marry Kate, behind crested mynas, pogo stick, adolescent, intellectual, *Ren-wah,* breast-fondling, ticks, and basil: The mere thought of him induces nausea.

"I think I have a new boyfriend," I say to Mrs. Easterday as she pulls a tray of chocolate peanut butter cookies from the oven. "Well, I'm going to the prom with him."

"How very nice. You like this boy?"

"I do."

"And he makes you happy?"

"He does."

"Imagine that," she says, and I feel that bump in the road again, and she grins ever so slightly at me, and I turn the topic to the cookies, which really are decadent and perfect. I love these. Mrs. Easterday can probably see it on my face.

CHAPTER NINE

"So," Stu says, pausing for dramatic effect, into which pause he inserts a playful smile I see from the corner of my eye. "You and Stefan Kott."

"So, you and Sarah Selman."

He shrugs. It's Sunday night. I had dinner here at the Wagemakers', and now Stu and I are lying on his bed, staring at his ceiling.

"You're breaking up with her," I say.

"No," he says a little too unconvincingly.

"You're doing it after the prom, aren't you?"

He shrugs again.

"It's just not working," he says.

"Imagine that. I do *love* being right."

"You're not right," he says as Sophie pops into the room, quickly examines the ceiling, and asks, "What are you guys doing?"

"Talking about why I'm right that Stu's the love-'em-and-leave-'em type," I say.

"Not right," he says as Sophie crowds onto the double bed on the other side of her brother.

"You so are," she tells him.

"He's breaking up with Sarah," I say.

"I knew it," Sophie says. "Does she know?"

"Not yet," I say.

"Before or after the prom?" Sophie asks.

"It'll be after," I say.

"How did I literally get in the middle of this?" He turns his head toward Sophie. "And who invited you in?"

"Be quiet," she says. "We're not done discussing this."

"Okay, well, come find me when you are," Stu says as he climbs off the bed and leaves.

Sophie and I are quiet for a few seconds before she says, "This is fun. We should talk like this more often."

"We've driven Stu out of his own room."

"Yeah, I know," she says. "That's the fun part."

Every day this week after school, Stefan waits at my locker, grinning nearly to the point of laughter. It's completely contagious. Then we walk together to my track practice, his baseball practice.

On Monday, we talk about the weekend and Mrs. Easterday.

On Tuesday, we talk about Cap and Early College, which he'll join next year.

On Wednesday, we talk about Emmy Newall's screaming break-up that afternoon with shell-shocked

Nick Adriani in the crowded senior lobby, and on Thursday we keep talking about it because four of us were unable to calm or quiet her, and her truck-driver adjectives earned her two days' detention.

On Friday morning, I say to Stu as we walk to Cap, "He's a nice guy, and I like him, but we aren't exactly having great conversations. It's just about school."

"Have you tried longer conversations?"

"Do you mean since homecoming?"

"Do you count homecoming as trying?"

"I count homecoming as an embarrassing disaster."

"Well, so does he, probably. He's the one who told you he only asked you out because you're tall."

"Yeah, and he apologized, and so did I for blathering all night. But now I think we're at the point of finding out just how much we like each other, so we need to show each other who we really are—beyond height and blathering—which creates a number of unpleasant possibilities." I tick these off on four fingers and ignore the exaggerated look of bemusement on Stu's face. "What if I like him more than he likes me? What if he likes me more than I like him? What if neither one of us likes each other all that much? What if we have a repeat of homecoming?"

"What if his head explodes while you're talking?"

I raise my thumb right in his face.

"Josie, you think too much," he says with a little laugh. "You also talk too much."

"Okay, this is not helping."

"No," he says, now sounding a little serious. "I know." Then he shrugs. "Relationships are tricky. You need to speak the same language. Or learn each other's, but that doesn't always work."

"Is that why you're the love-'em-and-leave-'em type?" I ask, earnestly wanting to know.

"I'm really not."

"You are."

"Am not," he says, shaking his head and confidently staring forward.

"You need to come see my dad about your denial," I say, and we debate the issue for several more blocks.

At 3:05 this afternoon, there's Stefan, making me smile, casually leaning one shoulder against my locker, waiting for me.

"How was class this morning?" he asks. "Intermediate Spanish II and Sociology of Aging and Society, right?"

"Right," I say. "And interesting. They were interesting. Let me ask you something."

"Shoot."

I've been thinking about this since Stu mentioned language this morning, so I inhale and forge ahead. "If you give up your seat every day on a bus to a pregnant woman but then discover she's not pregnant but faking it to trick her boyfriend into marrying her, would you still give up your seat to her? Also, would you tell the boyfriend?"

Stefan blinks at me for a second or two, his lips frozen halfway between his easy grin and a round-mouthed gape. I find myself frozen with nervous anticipation, immediately wondering if I should have just asked about baseball. But then his grin predominates his face, and I quietly exhale, and he says, "Cool question. Okay, ask it again."

I do. He repeats it. Emmy steps between us with a curt hello to us both and hurries me off to track practice, and Stefan and I say *see ya* to each other.

"You're so cute, you're sickening," Emmy says.

"So are you with your hair like this," I say as I remove several strands from her gooey pink lips.

Tonight, Stefan calls me at home with his well-reasoned answer. He would keep giving up his seat, but if he ever met the boyfriend, he'd tell what he knew.

"You can't stay quiet in the face of a lie," he says.

"Even if it causes a more disturbing scene than Emmy and Nick?"

"Oh, yeah. I mean, you know what they say. I'm just the messenger. What would you do?"

"I'd say something immediately and let her stand for all eternity."

"Cool."

"And even though I'd just be the messenger, I'd be prepared to get shot."

"Yeah, that's it! Don't shoot the messenger," he says.

"No one likes to be told bad news," I say.

"Yeah, but sometimes you have to, right? And I think most people understand eventually, so that's cool. And the ones who don't, hell with them, you know."

"I guess," I say, giving it some thought.

"Hey, you want to go to breakfast tomorrow?" He names a popular diner just outside Bexley.

"I can't," I say.

"Sunday?"

"I can't Sunday, either," I say, and before I have a chance to explain, he says, "Well, that's cool. We'll do it some other time maybe."

Cool, I'm discovering, has many different meanings in Stefan, a language I think I like learning. But like all languages, fluency takes a very long time.

On Saturday mornings, I volunteer at Sutton Court Assisted Living Center, a formal redbrick manor sitting on three acres of land in New Albany, an entire community of formal, redbrick homes about twelve miles outside of Bexley. Schools, churches, synagogues, even shopping centers create a sea of Georgian and slightly corrupted Georgian architecture that is surprisingly beautiful in its redbrick uniformity, not at all monotonous.

My dad drives. He volunteers his therapeutic skills there, while I volunteer my literacy, conversation, and knowledge of roughly three dozen card games, courtesy of Mrs. Easterday. My dad sings, in his perfect baritone voice, with the radio during the drive out. If he has had a troubling session, he stays quiet on the drive home. Lately, he tells me it will be a relief when I finally get my temporary driver's license this summer so that I can drive us home and he can lose himself in thought.

He drives the way I run.

I've been volunteering at Sutton Court every Saturday morning for over a year now, having first come out with Mrs. Easterday to visit her sister, who lived there only temporarily following a hip replacement. The Schmader sisters—their maiden name—are sturdy women who, Mrs. Easterday often says, come from good, hardworking, long-lived German stock.

"Our husbands knew before they married us that we'd have healthy babies," she said to me once. "No one thinks of that anymore, but they should."

Breakfast out on weekends is impossible. Sutton Court Saturday, church and youth group Sunday. Between that, track meets, homework, baking cookies with Mrs. Easterday, and keeping a piece of my schedule open for Kate or Maggie, I don't have much free time on weekends.

Stefan calls Saturday afternoon, asks me over to his house tonight for pizza and a DVD, which I think should be called a movie since DVD is the vehicle by which we watch the movie and not the movie itself. But I am in the minority, so I translate movie to DVD, but it still privately bugs me.

I explain I have plans with Kate, which he pronounces *cool*.

He's going to see his grandparents in Indiana the following weekend. I have an away track meet the Saturday after that. We compare schedules and find they don't coordinate until prom night, four weeks from today.

"That's cool," he says, sounding resigned. "At least I get to see you at school."

After I hang up, I think about *at least I get to see you at school*. I think about these words as I pack my bag for Kate's. I think about these words as Kate drives me to Nordstrom, out at the ever popular Easton Town Center, and I think about these words as I try on the first three of seven dresses Kate has picked out in Shopping Commando Style.

I love her Shopping Commando Style. She dons her imaginary shopping-vision goggles, declines all help from salespeople, moves with intention, speed, and determination, and obtains the target or targets within minutes. Minutes. Unlike Sophie and Jen Auerbach and other friends I go shopping with, who take forever, leave with nothing, and consider the excursion a success, which makes absolutely no sense to me, even though I go along with it.

The only person I enjoy shopping with is Kate.

And the only reason I stop thinking about *at least I get to see you at school* and the pleasant feeling it induces is because a tag on the inside of dress number four is trying to lacerate my flesh over my bottom rib.

"This one's no good," I call to Kate through the dressing room door.

"I need to see it."

"No you don't."

"Josie, let me see," she says, opening the door and peeking in. "Okay, that one's perfect. Stop fussing."

"I'm not fussing," I say, holding a pinch of dangerous fabric out from my side. "I can't wear this."

"No. That's the dress. I'm telling you, that's the one."

"Then I have to wear it like this all night," I say.

"What? A tag?" She knows me so well. "A seamstress can remove it."

"No."

"Yes. She can."

"No. She can't because what if she misses one little piece? What if she creates a big or bigger knot or bump where there isn't any? What if she—"

"Okay, stop," Kate says, and sighs. "I get it. Let me see the others."

Eventually, she chooses a long dress of navy blue satin with spaghetti straps and a fitted, ruched bodice gathered at the waist with a large teardrop-shaped crystal brooch.

"It gives you the illusion of having hips," she says.

"Well, then I ought to have brooches here and here," I say, grabbing my non-existent bust.

"Josie, it fits you perfectly. You don't need a thing, but that reminds me," she says before grabbing her phone out of her purse and typing notes.

"Reminds you of what?"

"Reminds me," she says, dropping her phone back in her purse and shooting me a quick smile, "that I need to get you a strapless bra before the wedding."

"I have a strapless bra. It doesn't stay up."

"I need to get you a padded one, and we'll find one that stays up. You're going to need it for the bridesmaids dresses I chose." And her description of them and how she found them carries us through Nordstrom, to the parking lot, back to her place. At least I think it does. I have stopped listening and am thinking only *at least I get to see you in school*.

CHAPTER TEN

I am sitting with my backpack on my lap, underneath the glowing light on the front steps of Kate's condo in German Village, a historic but trendy part of the city consisting mostly of red bricks and young lawyers. German Village abuts downtown Columbus, sharing nothing but proximity with the city. The sweet scent of crabapple blossoms fills the air tonight, courtesy of a warm start to April. It's quiet too, but for the clicks the moths make overhead against the light.

Positive phototaxis, I say to myself, looking up. So succinct. Two words to describe the attraction of bugs to light. Some bugs. Roaches run from light, which is negative phototaxis, and I realize I sound like Geoff and his Traveling Tick Show, but it is not my fault that I remember the entomology section of eighth-grade biology. And I'm not at a dinner party. Not anymore.

Mother arrives about fifteen minutes after Kate has called her. I climb in, drop my bag on the floor, shut the door, and try to avoid Mother's unavoidable look. The car does not move. I know my mother will out-wait me, but I have to challenge her a little.

So one second after just long enough, I say, "It was an accident."

"I'd like your version of it."

"My version is the truth. Kate's the one who gave you a *version*, completely biased because of her association with Geoffrey Stephen Brill. I think he's corrupting her sense of reality. You and Dad should be worried."

"I'm waiting."

"Here's what happened."

"I want to do your hair and makeup for prom," Kate said the minute we entered her condo, which is decorated in warm shades of burgundy and white and predominated by candles on tables, counters, and the mantel.

I had not yet set my backpack down nor hung up my dress.

"Okay," I agreed.

"Let's practice now. Oh, and I have the perfect necklace you can borrow, and . . ." She leaned in close to examine my ears and sighed with mock disappointment. "Well, I was going to say the perfect earrings too, but . . ." She shrugged. "Just get them pierced before the wedding."

She picked up a stool from in front of her breakfast

bar, and I followed her to the bathroom. We do this all the time—relocate a stool so I can sit comfortably while Kate plays with my hair.

"You want me to get my ears pierced?" I asked along the way.

"Everyone has them but you. I want everything to be uniform for the wedding pictures, and I know exactly what earrings I want you to wear."

"I'm not getting my ears pierced," I said as I sat down.

"Why not?"

"Do you have any idea how common infections are from ear piercings? Bacterial infections, abscesses, allergic reactions," I said, raising fingers. "Some of these are disfiguring. With yellow discharge. *Yellow discharge*. How's that going to look in your photos?"

"Josie, you're not going to get a disfiguring, weeping ear infection. Have Mom do it. Your ears will be sterile for a month."

She slipped my hair out of the black band holding my ponytail in place.

"Maybe."

"Come on. Please. For me?" she asked via the mirror, and I found the reflected plea difficult to resist, so I responded with a considered nod. "You're the best," she said as she kissed the top of my head.

Kate is the only person in the world I allow to touch my hair because she is the only person in the world who manages to do so without driving me crazy—touching me too much, tickling my head, roughly scratching my head, or, worst of all, moving my hair against its natural bend, which makes me want to crawl out of my skin screaming.

Plus she knows I only ever wear it in a ponytail and knows how to create at least seven different ponytail looks I endorse.

She set to work and talked mostly of her wedding and how all of us bridesmaids would be getting our hair and makeup done professionally, and she ignored my suggestion for Candy Bliss lipstick and how guys will appreciate the color. Kate's talented enough to do our hair and makeup herself but plans on being a Psychotic Freak on her Big Day. She said *stressed*. I've seen Kate stressed. It's the same thing.

I changed the subject three times—or attempted to. Nothing took. I felt like asking her, "If you give up your seat on the bus every day to a pregnant woman," but didn't.

As she applied what little eye shadow I can tolerate— it's the feel of the spongy applicator dragged across my eyelids that I cannot stand—she said I ought to consider getting contacts, that I'd be much prettier without glasses and then tried to cover what could have been a horrendous insult with, "Oh, but everyone is."

"It's okay," I said. I know I don't look like Maggie. Or Kate. But I didn't agree to the contacts. I like my glasses and tend to feel incomplete without them.

Then she finished, and I pronounced it nice, and I washed my face, and Kate returned my hair to its normal, tight, neat ponytail.

I had just set the stool down in its rightful place when Kate announced that she had a surprise for me—a surprise that caused her own shoulders to rise as she smiled in private anticipation.

"What is it?" I asked.

"Well, we're going to cook. Spaghetti."

"Okay."

"Not Mom's but a new, different, authentic sauce."

"So—surprise?!" I said with mock cheer.

"No, that's not the surprise," she said just as her doorbell rang. "That's the surprise."

She fairly ran to the door on her tiptoes, and just as I began to apprehend the source of the adoring look on her face, Geoffrey Stephen Brill stepped inside, and they kissed. Kate shortened and sanitized what Geoff's hands on her back told me he hoped to prolong. Still, I felt my lip curl but managed to merely grimace when Geoff chirped hello at me and winked.

"You're not staying, are you?" I asked.

"Josie," Kate laughed nervously.

"Now, what kind of greeting is that for your future brother-in-law?" he asked.

"When I meet him, I'll let you know."

"Josie," Kate laughed again.

"You're quick. I like that about you, but you say things like that often enough and I just might believe you," Geoff said.

"Well, you know how we adolescents can be," I said as he made his way past me into the kitchen, allowing me an unobstructed and explicit glare at Kate.

"I've been invited to give you both a cooking lesson," he said.

"Well, I'm sure the issuer of the invitation"—glare, glare, glare—"was mistaken about the date. This was supposed to be just the two of us tonight."

"Now, Josie," Kate said, drawing close and grasping my hands. "I know. But I thought you might like this."

I allowed my eyebrows, raised contemptuously, to answer for me.

"Okay, I'm hoping you like it," she said.

"You've gone insane, which is actually good. You're not legally well enough to consent to marriage."

"Josie, please. Please. I knew if I said anything in advance, you wouldn't stay."

"So you opted for an ambush? Good thinking, Kate."

"I know how you feel about Geoff," she whispered.

"I *might* have given him a chance. I was just starting to think about it."

"Really?"

"Something Mrs. Easterday said."

"What did she say?"

"I'm not telling you, particularly now that I'm mad at you."

She ignored my remark and hugged me quickly.

"I didn't know you were coming around, but I love that you are," she said. "I thought I *had* to ambush you." I sigh in defeat. "And he's here now, so please? Please? You love studying foreign cultures. So does Geoff. You have that in common. And he knows how to make an authentic Italian spaghetti sauce that he's made for me before, and it's really good." She leaned in close. "Josie, you and he are two of the most important people in my life, and I want you to love him, and him to love you, so, please, will you try to have a good time, for me?"

The words *for me* landed right on my heart where Mrs. Easterday's remark about Kate being happy lodged itself. So for the second time tonight, I tacitly conceded and watched Kate glow with happy appreciation. Then I took my seat on the stool I had just set down and watched the cooking show that, after two minutes, neither interested nor included me. It was the *Master Chef and His Giggling Apprentice Spectacular*. Between prep work and stirring, they stole quick kisses and fed each other bits of bread with sauce. They looked almost as if they were dancing, which bothered me terribly because kitchens are no place for such foolishness.

Finally, Kate remembered I existed. By then, I was flipping through her mail, piled in a sloppy stack on the counter in front of me. I had no idea she spent so much money at Ann Taylor, but I wasn't surprised since she always looks perfect in her outfits. And everything she wears constitutes an outfit, complete with just the right shoes and one funky element—a huge ring, usually, or cool pendant—that prevents her seeming stiff or too studied in her appearance.

"Josie, you've got to try this," she said.

"No, thanks. I'm waiting for the big moment at dinner."

"Food should be a big moment," Geoff said, and then proceeded to pontificate on what he considered The Only Way to Truly Experience Food.

"First with the eyes," he said, gesturing to his own in case I forgot where eyes are generally located. "Then through the nose." He demonstrated sniffing. "Then in motion," he said as he began pouring ladles of sauce over the pasta. "And then, at last," he said, producing a fork from a drawer. "The Big Moment." He twirled a bit of pasta onto his fork. "When taste and texture combine on the tongue for the ultimate experience of pleasure. Food," he said, and popped the bite in his mouth, "is meant to be a multisensory experience."

We sat in the infrequently used dining room. It wasn't until Kate finished saying grace that I looked at my plate and saw noodles fairly swimming in sauce that looked and smelled perfectly edible and which I thought I would probably like. But the sauce-to-noodle ratio precluded me from even sticking my utensils in the stuff for a taste. At this rate, my bowl was more soup than sauce, likelier to spill, splatter, or drip, and I shuddered at the thought of a glob of it clinging to my shirt like a baby spider monkey hanging on to its mother's underbelly, or worse—much, much worse—dribbling down my chin.

Shudder

Shudder

Shudder

I picked up my plate and started toward the kitchen, saying, "There's too much sauce on this."

"No, there isn't," Geoff said, and put his hand on my arm.

"There is," I said. "And actually, you need to stop touching me."

"Oh, uh, Geoff, Josie doesn't eat a lot of sauce. I forgot to say."

"No, this is how you eat it," he said.

"This is how *you* eat it. This is not how *I* eat it," I said.

"Josie," Kate said worriedly.

"I think you should sit down and be taught," Geoff said. "You're being very rude."

"Because *you* put too much sauce on my plate?"

"Because you won't let me teach you the proper way—"

"I just need to fix this. Let go of my arm."

"Geoff."

"Josie, sit."

"Let go. Let go."

I blink at my mother, who blinks back at me.

"That's it," I say. "That's how Geoff ended up with *my* plate of spaghetti in *his* lap. It was an accident. Oh, and by the way, he used oregano, which is not Italian. It's Greek, and you should be very proud of me for not correcting him."

"Yes, you exercised remarkable restraint. Kate says you laughed."

"I didn't laugh." I reconsider. "I might have . . . tittered. But it was nervous anxiety, a totally spontaneous response over which I had no control."

"And then?"

"Well, then, you already know this part."

Kate and Geoff sprang to their feet in the confusion of sauce and pants and anger and distress and some, little, tittering. I offered Geoff my napkin, which he petulantly declined in favor of the massive amounts of paper towels and a big wet sponge Kate retrieved from the kitchen. They cleaned him up the best they could. He declared his pants ruined, and we resumed our seats, and Geoff fussed over his pants, and Kate fussed over Geoff's fussing, and I asked them to pass me the breadbasket that sat between the two of them, but they didn't hear me. So I reached for it myself in haste and annoyance, and I swear, I swear, I swear I did not mean to, but I knocked Geoff's glass of red wine over and, yes, right into his lap.

Kate erupted into a shrieking fit—especially when I said something about the crotch being part of the ultimate dining experience; who knew?—and she called my mother, who came to fetch me, alone on the steps of the condo and tittering ever so slightly.

CHAPTER ELEVEN

My parents refrain from involving themselves in this mess. When necessary, they mediate volatile arguments, which rarely occur in our family. They prefer that the people involved in a conflict resolve said conflict on their own before it escalates into a fight.

I hardly view an accident as a conflict, and there wouldn't have been one had Kate not shoehorned Geoff into our evening. So, in terms of a causal relationship, this is entirely Kate's fault.

I scroll quickly through my list of text messages and click the thing off without reading any of them.

"Nothing from Kate?" Stu asks.

I shake my head. "She's still not speaking to me," I say.

We are walking this rare gorgeous spring afternoon back to the high school from lunch at Fair Grounds.

Stu bumps his elbow against mine and says, "She'll call."

"When? On my thirtieth wedding anniversary?"

"Yes," he deadpans.

"If she waits until then, I will not pick up the phone."

"Yes you will."

"Yes," I quietly agree. "I will."

He bumps my elbow a second time and says, "Josie, she'll call. Much sooner than you think."

I thank Stu with a nod but hope rather than know he's right. Kate's never done this before, and I don't know the rules of this contest, but I know I miss her terribly. I try to ignore the ache, but it's there, waiting for my attention, continuously lurking behind my Spanish homework, and walks with Stu, and Stefan's contagious smile.

I feel it at home on the nights Kate normally comes for dinner but now declines, leaving Mother to tell me, "She's busy tonight." I feel it at school when Stefan says something funny or sweet that I want to share via text with Kate but can't, knowing she won't write back. I feel it most at track practice when I try to run in quiet contemplation, but all my thoughts are drawn like a compass needle to the magnetic pull of that thing I am trying to ignore, which is this: Kate is not speaking to me, and that hurts.

At least at track practice I eventually find a good distraction. I run with Emmy Newall and listen to her colorful disparagement of Nick Adriani and what a "piece of shit" he is to break up with her so close to the prom, and she's thinking of suing him for the cost of her dress and hair and makeup. Days later I listen to how they've reconciled even though she's still angry with him but loves him or hates him. She can't decide and concludes with a laugh that it doesn't really matter "because, you know, they're so close to the same thing."

"I really think they're not," I say.

"You've never been in love before."

Does the whole world know this?!

"I love my sisters, and I know that I could never easily hate either one of them," I say.

"I'm talking about romantic love," she says. "It's not the same thing."

"So when I fall in love with a guy, I could, at any minute, start hating him?"

"Yes, especially if he's like Nick and nearly f-cks up your prom."

Later that night, Stefan calls and I tell him what Emmy said about love and ask him if he believes she's right.

"Don't know," he says. "Never been in love before."

"Yeah, me neither," I say, happy to admit it, at last, to a kindred soul.

"Cool."

"So tell me what you mean when you say *cool*," I say.

"What do you mean what do I mean?"

"Well, it could mean a lot of things."

"Yeah, cool's cool, you know. Easy. Cool. Got it. Whatever you want it to mean."

"Okay," I say, and hope Stefan can hear my smile when I say, "Cool."

I'm speaking Stefan, and it's a nice, sweet, easy language—just what I need right now as an antidote to the torturous silence that is the language of Kate.

Maggie tries to soothe me with an invitation to dinner at her house a couple weeks before the prom. I go, and we eat Greek takeout, and Ross wears my favorite cologne. Maggie tells me I don't need my ears pierced. Ross says my glasses suit me, and no one spills anything. Everything they do to take my mind off Kate makes me miss her all the more.

Her silent treatment continues right up to the prom. Maggie arrives around two thirty to help me with my hair and makeup.

"This shade of lipstick is perfect for you," she says as she dabs it on me. "But you don't really need it."

I pull my hair into a ponytail, of course, and let Maggie style the thing into one big curl with the aid of a round brush Kate gave me when she moved out.

Sigh.

"There," Maggie says to my reflection, which I can see only when I put my glasses back on.

"Very pretty," she says in a way that almost makes me believe her. In any case, I thank her for saying so.

Maggie's one of three beautiful women I know who doesn't make me feel bad about myself. Sophie's the second. Kate used to be the third.

"I like this," Sophie says, bouncing my big-curl ponytail on the palm of her hand.

We're in her bedroom, overdressed for mere hanging out, but it is the prom, after all. Sophie looks like she stepped from the pages of a bridesmaids' catalog, with her one-shoulder, knee-length, chocolate-colored dress. I look like someone's prom date, but since I *am* one, I really don't mind.

"Stefan'll like it too," she says, "but don't expect him to say anything. Guys are like that. They know you look different. They just don't know how exactly or how to say it, so they just say you look great. So when he tells you that, just say thanks. Don't ask him if he's noticed anything."

"Including my perfect lipstick?" I ask.

"It *is* perfect. He just won't say so specifically. *Great* is the best you can hope for. Watch, I'll show you. Stu!" she calls as he passes her room, dressed in a tux but for the tie hanging loose around his neck.

"What do you think?" she asks, pulling me next to

her and gesturing between the two of us as if we are prizes on *The Price Is Right.*

He shrugs and says, "You look great," and leaves the room confused by our shameless snickers.

"You know Kate's still not speaking to me," I say.

I pop a huge piece of a chocolate chip cookie into my mouth, careful not to drop a crumb on or down my dress as Mrs. Easterday slides another tray into her oven.

"That's not like Kate," she says, directing me out of the backlight of her kitchen window with a wave of her hand. "Stop just there," she says, and snaps a picture.

"Perhaps your apology wasn't sincere enough," she says, examining the photo for a second.

"I didn't"—I cringe at the realization—"apologize."

"Didn't you? Hmm," she says, still finding great interest in her camera.

"Well, the whole thing was an accident."

"Yes, of course it was," she says, and smiles up at me through pale blue eyes, slightly magnified by her glasses.

"I'll . . . apologize. But don't you think Kate should apologize to me too, for refusing to speak to me?"

"I think you and Kate will work this out in your own special way," she says, and offers me another cookie, which I eat while she describes formal dances she attended when she was my age. They were all held in the school gymnasium. They drank punch and ate cookies, and everyone went home by eleven thirty. I think I'm nostalgic for a time I never experienced.

> *Text to Kate, 4:47 p.m.*
> I'm sorry about the spaghetti.

> *Text to Kate, 4:48 p.m.*
> And the wine.

> *Text to Kate, 4:49 p.m.*
> The whole thing WAS an accident.

She doesn't text back.

Stefan arrives at five o'clock just ahead of Adam Gibson. Jen Auerbach and the eloquent Danny Shiever—who are just going as friends—and Emmy and Nick arrive within minutes. We're triple dating, but having group pictures taken at my house and the Wagemakers'. Ross is here with Maggie, just to watch, and when Nick Adriani stares too long at Maggie, Emmy slaps him, hard, on his chest.

Stu and Sarah are dining alone tonight at her request, something romantic and private that Stu has already described to me as uninteresting. Adam is taking Sophie out with a group of his friends tonight to flaunt the most beautiful girl in the school as *his* date.

He glances a little too long at Maggie too, and Sophie doesn't even notice.

He tells her at hello that she looks great.

"And I mean great," he says.

"Shut up." She beams.

Emmy tells her, "You are so beautiful, I hate you," and Sophie receives the compliment with her standard "Shut up, I am not."

Stefan says "Nice dress" to me in lieu of hello, so, in speaking Stefan, I say "Nice tux" back.

Later, I produce sufficient if forced smiles for Dad's and Uncle Ken's cameras. Behind the poses, I think of Kate, still not speaking to me and not even here. And the ache is hard to mask. Not impossible, but hard.

It is a gorgeous blue Saturday, made even sunnier, I think, by Mrs. Easterday's blooming forsythia bushes. At seventy-three degrees this May tenth, it's just a bit warmer than normal. Sophie got her wish. No hideous coats required.

After many minutes of posing in the Wagemakers' front yard and many more minutes of mingling with Mrs. Easterday and some of the other neighbors who turned out to watch, we in gowns retrieve our purses from those we assigned to hold them and start toward our dates' cars. Stefan opens the door for me, and I step one foot in when I hear, "Josie! Josie!" and look up to see Kate dashing across the street. She greets me with a quick hug and kiss, ending, if not our conflict, then this minor and awful campaign of hers.

I will never tell her how she has wounded me.

"I'm so glad I didn't miss you," she says.

"Thirty seconds and you would have," I say. I am not letting her off the hook so easily, especially since she hasn't apologized for her part.

"I'm Kate," she says cheerily to Stefan and shakes his hand, repeating my earlier line, "Nice tux," but in a language entirely different from the one I used, a language I wish I had spoken instead. She actually looked at the clothes before offering her assessment, making her compliment sound like a compliment instead of a jokey greeting.

"Let's get a picture," she says to me. "Dad!"

Dad directs us to a spot in the Wagemakers' yard. On the way, Kate gently places the palm of her hand against the curl of my ponytail and says, "Nice. I like it. We'll have to think of something like this for the wedding."

Dad snaps a couple of shots and pronounces each one excellent after scrutinizing it a good four seconds—the man can't see the screen without his glasses, which he isn't wearing—and Kate beams when she whispers, "Can you imagine how funny he'll be at the wedding?"

And all the while I feel strangely sick, worse than an unexpected bump on a smooth country road. More as if a great weight repeatedly drops from my throat to my stomach.

"Okay, have fun," Kate says, and sends me back to Stefan with a hug.

As I wave good-bye to my family, I allow the barely suppressed thoughts I've had about Kate into the forefront of my mind and ride to the restaurant in quiet if irked contemplation, interrupted a time or two by Stefan asking me, "What's on your mind?"

"Kate," I say each time and return to contemplation.

I am not soothed by this so-called détente. I like it, but I'm not soothed. In fact, I feel more concerned—or *as* concerned—certainly not *less* concerned—than before, since the entire episode was so utterly uncharacteristic of Kate. Well, of Kate before she met Geoffrey Stephen Brill.

"How can Person A claim to love Person B if Person B is completely wrong for Person A, *and* how can Person A fail to see it?" I ask.

"Sorry?" Stefan says. "Who?"

"Kate and Geoff," I say. "He's all wrong for her. She doesn't see it. He's wrecking my relationship with her. He's going to wreck my entire family, so I need to get rid of him. But not in a felonious kind of way. I just need Kate and him to break up."

"Felonious?"

"Yeah. Related to a felony."

"Did you ace every single vocabulary test you ever took?"

"Actually, yes."

"I'm not surprised."

"Do I sound weird?"

"No, you sound cool. And I'm glad you're talking about your sister. I thought you were talking about us."

"Us? We're not completely wrong for each other, are we?"

"*I* didn't think so."

"We do have height in common," I tease, which makes Stefan smile. "But, no, don't worry. I wasn't talking about us. Anyway, that would imply that I believed one of us was in love with the other, and, as far as I know, we're not."

"Oh. Cool," he says, and after *cool*, he withdraws for most of the evening into what I can only describe as quiet contemplation.

I like this side of him since I speak this language and know not to ask *What's on your mind? What's on your mind*—or, worse, *Penny for your thoughts*—breaks the flow of ideas that percolate in quiet contemplation until they either produce a plan of attack, a resolution, or the need to scream *how* and *why?!*

At dinner Jen whispers to me, "Is Stefan okay?"

"He's fine."

She widens her eyes at me and waits—hopes—for more, but all I can tell her is, "He's really fine."

Later in the ladies' room, Emmy asks a little too enthusiastically to suit me, "So, did you and Stefan get in a fight on the way here?"

"No. He's just thinking."

"About what?"

"I don't know yet. He'll tell me when he's ready."

She looks at me the way Jen earlier looked at me—as if she knows something I do not.

At the prom, Stefan and I chitchat comfortably, and he even laughs a little when I tell him how I grilled my mother about the sanitary standards of the Breathalyzer test required for entry here. Several years ago, the chaperones *finally* noticed that couples were showing up to the prom bombed, so the administration implemented the test at the doorway. I needed to know from my mother that I'd have my own plastic tube to blow into, or I'd have to refuse the test—I who have never had a drop of alcohol in my life outside of church. And part of me actually worried a little about taking the test. What if I didn't blow hard enough? What if I blew too hard? Or for too long a time? Or not long enough? It's a test, after all, and I wanted to get it right on the first try.

"Only you would want to get an A on a Breathalyzer," Stefan says with a goofy smile, and it embarrasses me into the admission that, yes, I would.

We dance, and he asks me, "What do you call people who have something weighing really heavy on their minds?"

"Do you?" I ask, tilting my head to the left to look at him.

"Maybe not weighing on it. But what's a good word for just thinking?"

"Contemplative," I say. "Or meditative. Pensive. Reflective."

"Geez, where were you last semester? You could have tutored me all through College Comp." Then some seconds pass and we're nearing the end of this song when he says, "You know I really like you, Josie."

"I really like you too."

"Yeah?" he asks. "Good."

But this seems an unusual admission to me. I took it as a given in our relationship. If Person A agrees to go to the prom with Person B, who asked Person A in the first place, Persons A and B can be reasonably understood to like each other.

I am about to say this to Stefan, but in his language, not mine, when I am distracted to the point of giggling—well, suppressed snickering, anyway—at the sight of Stu's face, pained with boredom as he dances with a clinging Sarah Selman. She's like an enormous pink dryer sheet stuck via static electricity to the front of Stu's tux.

I bury my face in Stefan's neck to keep from laughing, and he startles me by tipping his head against mine. We finish the song this way and smile at each other when the music ends. I can't interpret his smile, and I know he can't interpret mine. It's the one I reserve for Emmy when I have to speed-translate one of her snarkier remarks. It's the one I use when I'm trying to figure out what she means.

I do not want to attend the after-prom party but agree since it's included in the price of the tickets. But I can only reasonably handle thirty minutes of the thing before I begin to fray at my mental health edges.

Long before now I have had my fill of:
loud music
flashing lights
constant motion
constant noise
shouting to talk
straining to hear
speaking Ohmig*d
translating Ohmig*d

I have overloaded my nervous system to its breaking point and now must go find peace, solitude, stillness, darkness, and quiet. And I need the entire world to stop touching me—friends grabbing my arm to talk, all of us squeezing past one another in crowds, even Stefan and I dancing. It is all too jarring.

Stefan knew this about me beforehand. I even offered, when I explained my sensory limitations, to have my parents come pick me up so he could stay at the party, and I make the offer again tonight.

"No, it's cool. I'm ready to go too," he says, and for several long, luxurious moments, we soak in silence in his car. I could ride the whole way home like this. In fact, I do ride the whole way home like this, feeling some disappointment when Stefan pulls into my driveway that the soothing car trip is over.

"So," he says as if it is a complete sentence.

"I'd invite you in, but I'm so tired, I'm just going to fall asleep."

"Well, don't before I tell you something. Or ask you something." He thinks a second, moving his big, gold eyes up and to the right. "Or both."

"Okay," I say, and wait.

He inhales. Lets it out. Squirms a little. Inhales again.

"It's—you said neither of us—it's just that—well, what would you say if I told you I like you a lot?"

"You said that," I say, smiling because he actually grows cuter when he's nervous.

"No, I mean a lot," he says very seriously. "A lot."

I quickly think, trying to decipher—to translate—*a lot* into a language I can understand because, at the moment, I don't know what it means in Stefan. A lot is a lot, a great deal, very much. But why the gravity? And just when I think I begin to comprehend, he says, "Josie, I think I could fall in love with you."

"Really?" I ask, stunned. Genuinely stunned. "Why?"

"Why?" he nearly laughs.

"Yeah. I don't mean why me. I mean why do you think you could? Fall in love, that is. And that would, necessarily, imply with me, so maybe I do mean why me, but more *why* than *me*."

"Well," he says, and puffs out a laugh. "That's part of the reason right there. I mean, the way you talk. It's like I never know what to expect, and it's all good. Though sometimes, you know, I have to take a minute to figure it out."

"Translating," I say. "I do it all the time."

"Exactly. I hardly have to talk sometimes, you know. It's like you know what to say when I don't. You're great. You're fun. You're interesting. You're smart. And ..." He leans in, reaches for my glasses, which makes me flinch. "... Sorry," he says as he slips them off.

"You realize I can't ..."

He kisses me.

" ... see without them," I say.

"Then close your eyes," he says, and kisses me again, and this time I think about the kiss, his kiss, his lips, his tongue, his teeth when ours bump, and all of it is sweet. Soft and smoother than I imagined. So soft and so smooth that it has the very opposite effect on my nervous system than it should. It doesn't overload me. It soothes.

Eventually, he leans just a few inches back and says,

"Now would be a good time for you to tell me how you feel about me."

Now would *be a good time for that,* I nearly say. It's an excellent idea with perfect timing. He waits, eyes bright with anticipation, as I ponder this whole moment.

"Do you, um, do you think you could, maybe, fall in love with me?" he asks.

"Can I think about it?" I ask. "Because I actually want to get it just right."

I could not be more serious, and Stefan smiles his contagious smile at me and says, "Yes. I mean, if anyone else had said that, I might be upset, but you . . . See, this is why I really think I could fall in love with you."

And he kisses me again, which initially I like, but I admit that now I'm paying more attention to the question and its potential answer than to his lips. Which is too bad since I'm probably missing a really nice kiss.

CHAPTER TWELVE

I wake at 7:10 a.m. to a handful of texts resembling this one from Jen Auerbach:

Text from Jen, 12:53 a.m.
U R missing such a fun after-party call me when you get this unless its b4 2 pm which it will B so call me after 2

As I scroll through the rest of them, I find this one from Stefan sent just after he got home last night from dropping me off:
gnite Josie. I had a really great time. Thx

I smile as I continue scrolling.

Text from Stu, 7:03 a.m.
Sarah broke up with me last night.

Text to Stu, 7:13 a.m.
Stefan told me he thinks he could fall in love with me.

Text from Stu, 7:14 a.m.
What did U say?

Text to Stu, 7:14 a.m.
I need time to consider this.

Text from Stu, 7:15 a.m.
Sarah cried.

Text to Stu, 7:15 a.m.
Stefan didn't.

Text from Stu, 7:16 a.m.
Neither did I.

Text to Stu, 7:16 a.m.
I need to hear this story. Tell Auntie Pat I'm coming over for breakfast and meet me in your kitchen in 15 min.

I'm sitting at the granite-topped breakfast bar in the Wagemakers' kitchen, nibbling on buttered toast, when Moses the cat jumps up on the stool next to me—Stu's stool if he were down here. Stu's a pseudo morning person—awake and cogent early but not ready to move for hours, if he has the choice. I dip the tip of my finger in a bit of unmelted butter and allow Moses to lick it off before Auntie Pat notices.

When I hear Stu thudding down the back stairs, I quickly scratch Moses' head and pick him up with the intention of safely depositing him on the floor. But he squirms, and I slide. He jumps. I topple right off the stool and end up as Swiss Army Josie on the floor—legs and arms folded at all sorts of odd angles at Stu's feet.

"Good morning," I manage, looking up and untwisting myself.

"Impressive," he says, taking his seat. "Even for you."

"Stu—Josie," Auntie Pat says, hurrying to help me up.

"That cat is never going to come near me again," I say, straightening my ponytail once I'm vertical.

"*I* barely want to," Stu says, exaggerating a look of wild-eyed bewilderment.

Within a couple of minutes, we are settled again at the breakfast bar. Stu's eating cereal out of a mixing bowl and answering me between and during bites, which doesn't really bother me. I speak Stu Chewing.

"So dinner was boring," I say, recapping his story so far. "Prom was okay. What happened at after-prom?"

"She gah ma a mih," he says.

She got mad at me.

"Why?"

He swallows that mouthful, and I put my hand on his wrist to prevent another bite. I speak Stu Chewing, but I want to hear this loud and clear.

He pushes the bowl aside and looks directly at me to say, "She told me she loves me."

116 ⌒⌐

"And you didn't say it back!" I nearly shout, happily and quickly, before he can finish the story.

"Yeah. Okay. I didn't."

"I knew it," I say under my breath.

"So she goes running out of the place, and I follow her, and we can't get back in once we leave, so I drive her home, which gives her the opportunity to vent her vitriol against me about eleven inches from my ear, listing, among my other faults, that I don't listen, don't care about her feelings, don't love her—ignoring me every time I told her how much I *like* her"—he sighs—"and ruined what was supposed to be the best night of her life."

"And you said?"

He raises his shoulders high as he grudgingly admits, "I told her I was sorry and hoped senior prom would be better for her."

"Oh, geez."

"Yeah, she wasn't happy with that response either. She started crying."

Stu hates it when girls cry. He says no guy knows how to react to that, and he's always afraid, in that moment, he's going to offer her his car or one of his kidneys just to make her stop, and calls that a verbal contract he wouldn't want to keep.

So I ask him about cars and kidneys, and he says, "My name remains on the titles to all three."

"All *three*?" I ask as he slides his bowl closer. "You're assuming you don't have a rare third kidney."

"Yah, I shu geh tha che ow."

Yeah, I should get that checked out.

"I like him," I tell Kate the following Saturday. We are lying on her bed, heads tipped together, looking at the long, curvy shadows the streetlights and her curtains create on her walls and ceiling.

"This is great, Josie," she says. "But do you think it could turn into love?"

"I don't know." I have just told her about Stefan. "How can you predict something like that? Did you start off liking Geoff and then discover, some moment, that it had turned into love?"

"I don't know how to explain it, other than . . . no, I just knew I did. I mean, of course I liked him first, but then, yeah, pretty quickly, I guess, I felt something more."

"Why? How? How did you know? And while we're on this topic, you actually liked Geoff when you first met him?"

"Josie, we agreed. No Geoff tonight."

"No Geoff live and in person tonight," I clarify.

"You said 'no Geoff' when I invited you over, and I promised you no Geoff tonight. So I'm extending that even to our conversation."

"I'm just trying to understand why you're going to marry him."

"No, you're not. You're trying to pick a fight with me about him. I know you don't like him."

I prop myself up on my elbows.

"I just don't think that he's right for you," I say.

"Oh?" She sits up. "And who do you think is right for me?"

"Someone other than Geoff."

"Such as?"

"Well, go pick someone. I'll vet him, and then I'll let you know. Better yet, let *me* pick someone this time."

"Josie," she says, raising one hand toward me as if I'm traffic she's stopping. "I'm not going to argue with you, and I'm not going to defend Geoff."

"Because you'll lose the argument since there is no defense."

She pushes her traffic cop hand at me a second time, which is new, and I dislike it. Then she repeats herself —*I'm not going to argue with you*—which I dislike even more.

"Now. Tell me about Stefan," she says, and after a tense couple of seconds spent in standoff, I flop back down on her bed. She does the same, copying my sigh but trying to cajole me with a shoulder nudge.

"I know you're trying to redirect me," I say.

"It is impossible to redirect you. But I still love you."

"I know," I say, and nudge her shoulder back. "I love you too."

We talk about Stefan and all the things I like about him until somewhere between his smile and the way he kisses, we both fall asleep.

In the morning I overhear Kate on the phone to Geoff.

"We had a great time," she says, "and it worked perfectly. I said exactly what you suggested and even did the hand gesture exactly like you showed me."

What?!

"It was fabulous." She giggles as she adds, "I think for the first time in Josie's life, she really has met her match."

My parents pick me up from Kate's at nine forty for church, and in lieu of hello, I say to them, "I want you to know that I am not putting up with Geoffrey Stephen Brill much longer. I have no intention of attending their wedding, nor will I ever speak to Geoff again if Kate goes through with it. Please pause to imagine how much fun holidays will be. And if you dread the thought as much as I do, then you should side with me in opposing this wedding. His very presence will disrupt the perfect harmony that is our family. Now, shall I redirect us with an uplifting account of last night's events?"

"If you wouldn't mind, my dear," my mother says, and I oblige, omitting the part about Kate's new job as traffic cop.

CHAPTER THIRTEEN

Studying for finals, writing papers, and state finals for track and baseball keep Stefan and me busy through May. Neither of our teams places, but any team "going to State" is a good distraction from the general lethargy that affects everyone—even teachers—near the end of the school year.

We're all tired by the third week of May, walking with heavy-lidded eyes through slightly quieter halls.

The quiet is nice.

Stefan and I talk on the phone most nights. I've gone to his house a few times for dinner and to play video games, at which I'm horrible, which makes him smile uncontrollably as he trounces me in whatever we're playing. He hasn't been back to my house since prom, just for lack of time. Neither one of us has revisited the topic of potential love since other topics predominate our conversations.

I've run through almost all thirty-seven questions with him I wanted to ask Geoff.

Last one before I ask him his thoughts on the word

teepee: "You come into possession of a magic potion that will cure all cancer in all people for all time *if* it is ingested by one person you love, but it will claim the life of that one person. Would you give it to someone you love or would you leave it untouched?"

"Cool question," he says to me at my locker. "I have to think about it."

He thinks about it overnight and meets me at my locker this morning. Classes at Cap ended two weeks ago, so, being an early riser, I come into the high school in the mornings to help my former Spanish teacher grade papers. Stu just sleeps in.

It's the last Friday of May, last Friday of the year, and the halls are quieter, even grimmer, than normal thanks to a steady rain that lacks the guts to produce thunder or lightning or anything more interesting than rain.

Emmy Newall tromps in, pulling a hundred wet pieces of hair off every part of her face.

"No umbrella?" Stefan asks her.

"Duh," she says as she passes, which only makes Stefan laugh.

I wrap up my own umbrella and hang it in my locker.

"So, the magic potion that will cure cancer if I ask someone I love to drink it," Stefan says. Then he smiles at me, more meaningfully—it's in his eyes—than I've ever seen him smile. I think I feel myself turn pink—or warm anyway—but I try to ignore it.

"I just couldn't do that to someone I love," he says.

"You know what would be even more interesting?" I ask. "What if you gave it to someone you love, but that person doesn't die, because it turns out, you don't really love her?"

"Well, I'm pretty sure how I feel about one person, which is why you'll find no magic potions in your locker today."

Then we steal a quick kiss before heading off to homeroom, and I wonder what it would feel like if I were sure of my feelings for him. I can't be certain I'd risk the potion on him. And I'd hate to be responsible for not curing cancer when I had the chance.

Stefan is utterly patient and thoroughly easy with me as I continue pondering my side of our relationship. He comes to my house for dinner this rainy night but first has to view my dad's collection of medical antiques, pronouncing the Civil War–era bullet forceps cool as he repeatedly opens and closes them.

The blue and brown glass bottles with brittle yellow labels catch his attention. *Schaffner's Celebrated Influenza Mixture, Dr. Bicknell's Blood Purifier, Duda's Fig Syrup for the cure of constipation, safe for infants and adults in all cases.*

"Quackery," my father says, smiling maniacally.

"That's a Josie word," Stefan says.

"Stefan, can you guess what all these medicines had

in common?" He shakes his head, and my dad says, "Heroin."

"No way," Stefan says, and my dad tells us briefly of the poisonous history of medicine, and afterward Stefan tells me that someday he's going to have a dog named Quackery.

"And a cat named Felonious," he adds.

Later, when the house is quiet and dimly lit, and Stefan and I are alone in the family room, we kiss some and then some more, which feels soft and good at my lips but strange in my stomach and stranger in my head when I begin to consider the precise sensation in my stomach. It's neither pain nor nausea but some kind of discomfort.

I slide across the sofa finally, joking—a little—that I need some air.

I cite my early morning and long drive as reasons to end the evening and send him home. I took finals early and am leaving tomorrow for a month in Michigan, skipping next week's last four days of school. I really won't miss the chaos that the halls become—full of guys shouting *yes!* and *all right!* to each other, group hugs, and everyone's junk from their lockers spilling onto the floors.

Every summer since before I was born, my parents have rented one of several cottages for five weeks on Lake Michigan in a town called Holland, settled by the Dutch, including the terribly blond forebears of Uncle Ken and Auntie Pat. It was they who introduced my landlocked parents to the place.

Holland is home to Hope College, the terribly blond counterpart to Cap, where last summer I took Intro to Global Politics, and this summer I'm signed up to take Ecology of Our Changing Planet during a four-week session called June Term. It starts Monday, and I'm looking forward to it even though the class sounds dull as rain. I love the consistency of the whole trip—the reliability of it—and that a college course that fulfills a science credit fits seamlessly into our well-ordered lives, even far from home.

"I can't believe you're going to be gone over a month," Stefan says at our open front door, and I tell him about Stu's eight-week course on an archaeological dig in Crow Canyon, Colorado.

"I'm glad you're not going with him," Stefan says. "Five weeks away from you is going to be hard enough. I don't know if I could handle eight weeks. I'm really going to miss you."

"I'm going to miss you too," I say, and then add this before I fully consider the gravity of it: "I promise I'll think about us when I'm up there and tell you how I feel when I get back."

"Good," he says. "I think you already know how I feel."

"Hmm," I say through a smile, knowing very well that he will mistranslate it as *yes* when, in Josie, it means *I really do not want to say what I'm thinking just yet. I need more time to figure this out.*

* * * * *

I don't have my temporary driver's license yet. I've just been lazy about getting it when I can walk almost everywhere I need to go or ride with Stu or other friends. Without the distraction of driving, I am left with my own thoughts, which even Dennis DeYoung's perfect voice flowing through my earbuds cannot completely impede. I promised Stefan I'd think about him. On the six-hour ride to Holland, alone in the backseat of the car, I find I can do almost nothing but think of him, yet I come to no conclusions—except that my dad's bald spot is increasing in diameter.

I continue thinking about Stefan and sweet kisses and sick stomachs all the way inside the cottage, where, I'm relieved to say, nothing has changed since last summer. It's a four-bedroom white house with highly polished poplar walls and floors, overstuffed blue-and-white furniture, and a large porch from which thirty-two steps descend to the beach below. I have never been able to navigate them without getting splinters. And flip-flops make me trip.

I contemplate my feelings for Stefan for two days, interrupted only by Ecology of Our Changing Planet, which I drop at the break on the first day. I have to. The professor's upper lip sweats droplets, and he says *buh-cuz* instead of *because,* and by break, it is the only word I hear, which is soon to drive me insane.

At the registrar's office, I switch to Exercise Physiology, which fulfills a health sciences credit at Cap and which entertains my father when I tell him about it tonight at supper.

"Perhaps you can ask your professor about the dynamics of coordination," he says. "You could submit yourself as the subject for a class project."

"I'm not *that* klutzy," I protest, and fume under a toe-scented cloud two nights later when I miss the last step before the beach and end up sprawled on my stomach in the sand.

"Nicely done, my dear," Dad says, stepping over me.

"It's my flip-flops' fault."

Dennis DeYoung would have helped me up. Stefan probably would have too.

Text from Stefan, 9:45 a.m.
just heard come sail away in the car—thought of U

Text from Stefan, 9:53 a.m.
putting come sail away on my playlist—kinda a long song tho

Text from Stefan, 10:17 a.m.
Miss U—R my texts getting thru up there

I am in Exercise Physiology. It is Wednesday, day three of class. I wait until break to text Stefan back, to explain that professors are no different from high school teachers. Phones must stay off during class.

Tonight I establish a signature nightly closing:

Text to Stefan, 10:32 p.m.
Thinking of you. Good night.

Text from Stefan, 10:33 p.m.
U2 g-nite

Next night:

Text to Stefan, 10:32 p.m.
Thinking of you. Good night.

Text from Stefan, 10:33 p.m.
U2 g-nite

Next night:

Text to Stefan, 10:32 p.m.
Thinking of you. Good night.

Text from Stefan, 10:33 p.m.
U2 g-nite

Next night:

Text to Stefan, 10:32 p.m.
Thinking of you. Good night.

Text from Stu, 10:33 p.m.
U R? Y?

"Oh, geez," I say, squinting at my phone.

Text to Stu, 10:34 p.m.
I hit the wrong button. Meant 2 send 2 Stefan.

Text from Stu, 10:35 p.m.
Josie & Stefan sittin' in a tree . . .

Text to Stu, 10:36 p.m.
Josie sittin' alone on the beach, trying 2 figure things out.

Text from Stu, 10:36 p.m.
UR alone on the beach? It's past 10:30.

Text to Stu, 10:37 p.m.
No, I'm in bed.

Text from Stu, 10:37
Then Y did U say U were on the beach?

Text to Stu, 10:38 p.m.
Well Y did U say I was in a tree????

Text from Stu, 10:38 p.m.
UR the 1 who went up there with Stefan.

Text to Stu, 10:39 p.m.
Good night, Stu.

Text from Stu, 10:39 p.m.
Good night, Josie.

Tree or beach. There must be a way to figure this out.

CHAPTER FOURTEEN

I went to the beach to love deliberately.

This is only partially true, of course. But according to a high percentage of novels I've read, it appears that falling in love at the beach is both easier and more satisfying than falling in love in a grocery store or mall. So far, I am not finding it to be easy. In fact, each time I think about saying the words *I love you* to Stefan, every feeling in me reacts as if I'm lying. I *want* to say it, but I can't. I just can't.

I watch Ross and Maggie here for a long weekend, quiet and easy in each other's presence. He glances up from a book now and then. She tries not to smile but cannot help herself. I watch my parents walk on the beach, laughing, bumping elbows, tipping their heads now and then toward the sky. I do not have with Stefan what Ross and Maggie or what my parents have with each other—a deep and private connection that is a language all its own. I can speak Stefan, and I like speaking Stefan, but it does not come naturally to me. Any more than Josie does to him. Without that, I don't think I can say I love him.

Kate and Geoff do *not* speak the same language. Not that I can perceive. She and he are here this week, allowing me five whole afternoons and evenings of observation, which I conduct from a distance. He reads endlessly and is forever saying to her things such as, "You might find this interesting," or "I think you'll like how the author puts this." Then he reads out loud to her, as if she's five, and if she's lucky, she can help turn the pages.

When she isn't discussing work or wedding plans with him, she's running wildly into the water, shrieking and laughing along the way, more amusing than including Geoff, who accompanies her but does not match her enthusiasm.

Out of the water, they look like two people in a towel-drying contest. Kate wins, and I giggle from the porch when Geoff cringes and contorts his body as Kate applies sunscreen. When it is his turn to apply the stuff to her, he takes his time, by which I mean he takes forever, touches Kate as if she's made of glass, which she nearly is, so that much I understand, and then inspects and pronounces his work well done. And he starts reading to her again while she stares over the water.

"Is it possible," I ask my dad, who is sitting next to me on the porch, reading yesterday's edition of the *Holland Sentinel,* "that Geoff is like Rasputin and has hypnotized Kate into believing she's in love with him?"

"No," he says without looking up.

"I'm going to find an explanation for her attraction to him, you know."

"I expect nothing less."

Five weeks pass much too quickly, and soon we are home again in pretty if lake-less Bexley. I am lying this July Fourth afternoon on Stu's bed, staring at the ceiling and seeing nothing but its vast blankness.

"There has to be a better way—or a gentler way— of saying I don't see myself falling in love with you," I say, and Sophie sighs for about the eighth time. I've lost count.

"You can't say that. Just say, 'I'm not in love with you.' It's better. Trust me."

"But that's not what Stefan asked me. He asked if I thought I *could* someday, and I don't think that's going to happen." I prop myself up on my elbows. "No offense, but I need Stu's advice on this."

"Mine is better," Sophie says. "I'm always the dumper. He is often the dumpee."

"I just want his perspective too."

"Well," she says, sitting up and putting her shoes back on, "you can call him—"

"Weak signal."

"—or text him—"

"He won't get it until tonight."

"—or wait a month until he's home."

"I don't have a month. I don't have two hours."

Sophie turns to me. She's smiling, but it's a little sad. "Just tell Stefan that even though you're not in love with him, you really like him and you still want to be friends."

"You aren't friends with a single one of your exes."

"I know," she laughs. "It never works, but it's a good line." She stands up. "Josie, just do it, get it over with, and then come over because I'll be here waiting for you."

She leaves. I flop back down on Stu's bed and pull my phone from my pocket.

Text to Stu, 3:47 p.m.
U R no help to me at all at the moment, and there's a crack in ur ceiling. I'll tell Uncle Ken to get it fixed. Ur welcome.

There was a parade this morning. I skipped it. Mother, Dad, and I returned home two days ago, too tired and with too much settling in to attend downtown's fireworks yesterday or Bexley's tonight. This is the excuse I initially use when Stefan invites me to both, but since I know I cannot delay a necessary conversation, I walk to his house after my brief and fruitless consultation with Sophie.

After an awkward hug hello—I am so glad his little sister was in the room—we sit on the steps of his front porch, and he teases me some about having no tan. I lecture him about skin cancer, and I describe and mime my twice-daily application of broad-spectrum sunscreen.

"I really missed you," he says. "Did you think of me and what we talked about?" he asks.

"Day and night," I said.

"And?" he asks, coming close for a real kiss, which I thwart by leaning back and placing my hand against his chest, a move that needs no translation in any language.

"I like you a lot, Stefan."

"Like?" he asks. "Not love."

"No," I admit, and follow that with a long, sad sigh. "I'm sorry. I don't think what I feel for you is love or will ever turn into it. But that doesn't change how much I like you. It doesn't diminish that."

"It's not the same."

"It *is* the same," I say. "I don't like you any less. I'm not saying I don't want to be with you."

"I don't really see how I can keep being with you. And before you explain how I can," he says, flashing me a quick, sad grin, "let me ask you. Would you want to be with someone who just told you they could never love you?"

"But that's not *all* I'm saying. I'm saying I like you. A lot." And as the expression on Stefan's face turns from sadness to pain, I launch right into a list of all his wonderful qualities in a slightly more directed version of the Homecoming File Dump.

"... and the stuff you write on Facebook is really fun and funny, and you've got this great smile that I wish I were seeing right now and hate that I'm the cause of its sudden disappearance, and—" The list continues and contains dancing, kindness, and athletic ability. "—and you're a good friend. A really good friend. And to me, closer than a friend. And I think that's valuable, and I don't want to lose that. I don't want to lose someone closer than a friend. I don't want to lose you."

"But I think," he says, tearing up a little, and I do the same, "you already did." He clears his throat. Stands. "I gotta go."

He walks in his house and shuts the door behind him. And I walk home in hot, humid misery, sniffling over the phone to Sophie on the way. She pulls me into her arms at the back door, and I sob on her shoulder. By the time I step back, she is crying too, and before I can ask why, she says, "I just hurt that you hurt so much."

I sit in one of the chaises on our patio, holding my legs folded up against my chest, my head on my knees. Only the lamps from the family room cast any kind of light onto me. In a few minutes, over the tops of trees to the southeast, I should be able to see some of Bexley's fireworks and hear the muffled thuds of the loudest mortars.

Kate slides the door open, steps outside, and sits on the end of my chaise.

"You okay?"

"I'm fine," I say, wiping my eyes with the back of one hand. "I'm sad but fine."

"I'm sorry you're sad."

She waits for the details, which are not long in coming.

"And he deleted me from Facebook," I say at the end of my rendition, dropping my face into the crook of my arm for a big sob.

"Josie," Kate says, squeezing my knee gently. "It'll be okay."

"I know," I say into my arm. "Everything just hurts at the moment."

"What hurts worst?" Kate asks.

"I don't know."

"I do," Geoff says, startling me into looking up and discovering his silent materialization next to Kate. And it's his hand on my knee, not hers! Slowly, I slide back in the chaise.

"It's hard to lose a friend," he says, and—*erm*—I have to concede, which I do with a nod. "Especially when you don't have that many."

"Excuse me?" I nearly shout.

"Geoff," Kate laughs nervously.

"No, I just meant—"

"I have friends," I say, wiping my face with both hands.

"No, I know. I just meant—"

"Nice," I say as I stand. "Really nice."

On my way to my room, I broadcast Geoff's remark via text, and my phone chirps in supportive response almost immediately. Then I post it on Facebook and find, in the morning, that over three-fourths of my class, teammates, church, Cap associations, and distant relatives who comprise my Friends List think he is an idiot. My page has become a Love List with hearts, *X*'s and *O*'s, and reassurances that Geoff is, once again, wrong.

"See? I have friends," I say to my photo of Dennis DeYoung.

But even in my quiet triumph, there at my desk, my heart aches and my stomach sinks over the one response I wish were here—the one from Stefan, who I still like as much as I ever did, even if I can't say I love him.

CHAPTER FIFTEEN

Text from Stu, 10:44 a.m.
Sophie told me you broke up with Stefan. U OK?

Text to Stu, 10:45 a.m.
Sad but fine. Thx.

Text from Stu, 10:45 a.m.
Sorry. Break-ups are hard.

Text to Stu, 10:46 a.m.
Unless U R U.

Text from Stu, 10:46 a.m.
No. Even then. Not my favorite thing.

Text to Stu, 10:47 a.m.
What is?

Text from Stu, 10:48 a.m.
Watching monkeys groom each other. U?

Text to Stu, 10:49 a.m.
Same.

Text from Stu, 10:50 a.m.
Cheer up, Josie. It'll get better. I promise.

I do have one thing to look forward to that cheers me considerably. Kate is moving home at the beginning of August, when the lease on her condo is up. Her old room connects to mine via a bathroom, and already I'm filled with the happy anticipation of late-night chats or just calling good night through the open doors.

I spend July helping her pack. I spend the weekend before she moves home cleaning the bathroom where she brushed, to perfection, my hair nearly every morning for years. Until college took her away but summers, and now an alleged wedding, brought her back. I'm considering feelings of gratitude toward Geoff for that. But I'd be significantly more grateful if he called off the wedding and she stayed forever. Then I can go away to grad school and return in the summer, and she can have her turn waiting eagerly for me.

But first comes August fifth, the day Kate moves home. She fails to notice the sparkling comfort and memories of her old room and instead moves her things into Maggie's at the far end of the house. "For space and privacy," she says. Between work and her evenings out with friends or the fiancé she seems determined to marry, I rarely see her.

She's too far away to call good night to. Stupid large and excessive house.

Ironically, my favorite nights are Sundays now when Geoff comes for dinner. At least I can count on seeing Kate with weekly regularity. Lately, I've been requesting spaghetti on Sundays and always help Mother set the table and always manage to jiggle the plates past Geoff. I know just how much of a tremor it takes to make him nervous.

Kate and I set the table on the patio for dinner on this muggy mid-August night. Across the way, Geoff and my dad man the grill. Geoff is pantomiming how to place and flip burgers, and my dad is copying the gestures with theatrical enthusiasm.

"Oh, Josie, I'm sorry," Kate says, producing such a pained expression that I forget about Geoff and Dad for a second. "I forgot. I completely forgot. I have a meeting with the florist tomorrow." She had promised to take me clothes shopping for school, which starts Wednesday, the 27th, which I entered into my phone's calendar with far less enthusiasm than I entered *shopping w/Kate* for tomorrow.

"It's not going to take all day, is it?" I ask.

"Who knows? There's so much to plan. So"—she

stretches an embarrassed smile across her lips—"can we do it next Saturday? I promise you are the only thing on my schedule."

"Sure," I say, and she hugs me and calls me *the best* and remembers to tell me the following Friday night that she and Geoff have to meet with the church organist tomorrow to pick out music.

She pledges to be back by two but isn't and doesn't even remember to call or text.

Mother takes me shopping instead. We zip through a few stores at Easton, examine colors, rub T-shirts and denim between our fingers, underwear too, and tell every salesperson who approaches us, "No, thank you. We're just looking." We keep lists, and later at home we sit in front of her computer in the kitchen and order my size and color choices online.

At home, my dad asks, "How was your shopping excursion today?"

"Interesting," my mother says.

"Successful," I say.

"Excellent," he says.

But I still prefer going with Kate.

I wake this morning as a senior in high school and greet the muggy day with a shrug. Kate has been telling me all summer—on those rare occasions anymore when she isn't talking about her fast-approaching wedding—that her senior year was the best, and she predicts mine will be the same. I predict it will be tragic if she insists on going through with this farce come November, which, by the look of things, she does. I'm going to spend part of this year dreading the thing and the rest of this year mourning it. Thanks a lot, Kate.

Most of Kate's bridesmaids think *a lot* is one word.

Text from Jen Auerbach, 7:04 a.m.
OMG!! WE R SENIORS!!!!

In the kitchen, I say a quick hello-good-bye to my dad, who dashes out for work, and find Kate sitting at the table cultivating a ridiculous smile she somehow manages to maintain through two sips of coffee.

"Yyeeess?" I ask, by which I mean *Why are you up, and why are you staring at me like that?*

"It's your senior year, Josie," she says as she rises and hugs me. "I had to see you before you left. Let me get a picture," she says.

"No."

"Oh, come on. Just one."

"No," I say as I begin my morning routine.

Kate takes her seat across from me as I flip through the paper, scanning grim headlines that betoken the end of the world.

KATE SHERIDAN DETERMINED TO RUIN SISTER'S LIFE BY GOING THROUGH WITH NOVEMBER WEDDING

Less ominous headlines report hurricanes and bank failures.

The minute Mother enters the kitchen, I say, without looking up, "Mother, please tell Kate it's rude to stare."

"Tell her yourself," she says before she kisses my cheek, then Kate's.

"I just want a picture, Josie. You are so cute. Doesn't Mom take a first-day-of-school photo every year?"

"Ask her yourself," I say, and glance sideways in time to see my mother grin a bit.

"I do," Mother says.

"Well, I want to be in it this year. Come on." Kate hops up and super-induces me to pose with her by saying, "This will be one worth framing."

We choose a spot near the kitchen fireplace and get comfortable with our arms around each other while Mother retrieves her camera. She clicks off two shots and sighs contentedly as she examines the images. I'd have quietly giggled a little longer if Kate hadn't said: "A couple more. Only this time, Josie, take your glasses off."

"Why?"

"We're practicing for the wedding," Kate says, resuming her pose with her arm around me.

"What?" I ask

"We really have to do something about your glasses soon," she says as I break the pose and end the photo shoot, leaving Kate to call after me, "I mean, they're fine for every day, but not for special events." Then she sighs at me as if she's eighty and says, "I remember the first day of my senior year. Oh, it was so much fun."

I wash my cereal bowl and glass and place them in the drying rack before texting Stu and Sophie. As I gather my things and drop my phone in my backpack, Kate turns to Mother and asks, "Don't you think it's about time Josie got contacts?"

"Ask her yourself," Mother says, but I am out the door before she can.

Across the street, Auntie Pat greets me with, "Seafood Delite or Chopped Chicken and Kidneys?"

She shows me a can of cat food in each hand.

"It feels like a Seafood Delite kind of morning," I say, and add, "I'll do it."

"Thanks, hon. You're a doll."

I spoon the stinky stuff onto a plate and place it before Moses, who waits for a good head-scratching before tucking into his breakfast. He's finally letting me pet him again.

"Okay if I run up to Sophie's room?" I ask.

"Of course. Tell her if she doesn't beat her brother downstairs, she's getting the chicken and kidneys for breakfast."

On the stairs, I see Stu before he sees me. He's yawning, scratching his left shoulder, and wearing the T-shirt and shorts he likely slept in.

After his time in Colorado, he came home much too

tan and got the melanoma lecture from me. Over the summer, he filled out some and let his hair grow into a short, wavy ponytail, and now he has a soft patchy beard a couple shades darker blond than his hair. On his first day home, he said he just got out of the habit of shaving. When I asked if he got out of the habit of peeing indoors, he just smiled at me as he ate a huge powdered donut in two bites.

"Seafood Delite for breakfast," I say.

"That's why I'm up early."

I'm at the top of the stairs. He's at the bottom when he says, "Oh, I got your text and no."

I smile.

It was: Kate wants me 2 B excited about 1st day of school. I'm not. U?

I knock on Sophie's door and hear, "Anyone other than Stu, come in."

When I enter, I find her sitting at her desk, holding her phone, which she promptly clicks off.

"I was just texting you back," she says. "And, yes. I'm excited to see everyone. But I'd be more excited if I were you."

"Why me?"

"Senior year? Oh, I can't *wait* until next year. Senior year is always the best."

"Why?"

"Everyone says so," she says. "But this year is starting off with pretty good potential."

"Any developments?"

"Not yet." She grins.

She broke up with Adam Gibson at the end of July and promptly produced a stunningly dreary painting of a deserted beach. Very lately she's been determined to fall in love with Josh Brandstetter—the cute guy in my class who smells good—once *he* falls in love with *her*. She's never the first to say it.

"He's—" she begins but stops herself, squints critically at me, and asks with some urgency, "What's wrong?"

I drop myself onto the corner of her bed as I ask, "Don't you think Kate's making a huge mistake marrying Geoff?"

"No, I don't, and I can't believe you're starting off your senior year still worrying about *this*."

"I worry about this daily."

"Well, stop it. I can't wait for her wedding. Oh, hey, tell her to put *and guest* on my invitation, okay?" She tries not to smile as she says, "Maybe I'll bring Josh. Wouldn't that be great? Falling in love at someone else's wedding."

"I'm not going."

"It's Kate. Of course you're going."

"It's number five on my list of things I refuse to do in my life—right after having the calluses on my feet exfoliated by flesh-eating doctor-fish in Turkey."

"What are one through three?"

"They all involve crime and body fluids."

"Josie," Sophie says, sighing at me with a kind of patient smile on her lips.

"And what is so wrong with my glasses?"

"Nothing. I love your glasses." She should. She picked them out.

"Kate says I can't wear them at the wedding."

"She just doesn't want a glare in her photos," Sophie says. "She wants everything to be perfect."

"Then she definitely shouldn't marry Geoff."

"Josie, stop. I keep telling you. Kate's in love. And that's the greatest thing in the world. And she's going to have a gorgeous wedding, and it's going to be so romantic, and you're going to go, and you need to be happy for her."

"Well, I'm not. I don't like Geoff, and I'm not happy she's marrying him."

"Josie."

"Hopefully, I can find some way to prevent the whole thing."

"You can't. They're in love, and love conquers everything," she says, flopping back on her bed so that her hair pools around her and slowly exhaling at something only she can see. "That's one of the things I love about love."

Her phone beeps.

"It's Josh," she says, beaming a smile at her phone. "I have to get this."

I walk back downstairs and try to ignore the burgeoning concern I have that this may, in fact, be my worst year yet. It doesn't help to be reminded at almost every turn that I am not in love, never have been in love, and would be significantly more excited about senior year if I were. Especially since I'm told senior year is the best.

CHAPTER SIXTEEN

Classes started yesterday at Cap, where I am now a sophomore. My Exercise Physiology class this summer tipped me over by one credit, which my parents celebrated with a card with a pony on it. Inside my dad wrote, "Graduate with honors and we'll buy you one for real."

He knows I'd rather have a goat.

Stu broke up with Amanda Meyers, whom he started dating two weeks after Sarah Selman broke up with him. Amanda asked him not to go away for eight weeks. They fought. She accused him of not caring enough about her, and he said, "If proof of my caring is that I stay here instead of take this great class in Colorado, then I don't care. But I disagree with your definition of *caring*." And, oh, the Facebook fireworks after that.

Now he's contemplating someone else from our class. He won't tell me who, but I think it's Jen Auerbach. He's a bit too adamant that it is not.

"You have to tell me who it is," I say. "I promise I won't interfere."

He stares sideways at me a full five seconds, letting his incredulous expression answer for him.

"I won't," I say. "Unless it becomes necessary."

"Which it will, I'm sure you think."

"Of course it will. I like Jen, and if you start going out with her now, you won't be together by Halloween, and she should know this up front. But actually she already does. I told her last year." He says nothing, so I add, "So I have no reason to interfere. So now you can tell me."

But he doesn't.

It's a nice morning, so we park at the high school and walk to Cap for our first Wednesday classes. This year, like last, we're taking two classes apart from each other and one together, a sociology class called Sociolinguistics, which I've been dying to take since I read about it but had to slog through some lower level soc classes first.

From the course description: *Soc. 310 is an introduction to sociolinguistics, specifically the social use of language. In this course students will examine the origins and evolution of language by modern speakers, paying particular attention to how language identifies social groups and changes in both emphasis and meaning from group to group.*

This class was designed for me. And it is the only thing I am happily anticipating at the moment.

"So, what about Stefan?" Stu asks. "Seen him? Heard from him?"

I shake my head and say, "Neither."

"You'll probably see him today. You ready for that?"

"I'm dreading that," I say. "But I've rehearsed several possible exchanges."

"Which aren't going to happen," Stu says, followed by a big shrug.

"I know. So I figured I would just present him with a big, warm smile and an equally friendly hello."

"Show me."

"I can't show you. I'm not in the moment. It'll look stupid."

"Come on, Josie," he says, nudging my elbow.

"Okay," I say, and we stop walking. I draw a breath, smile slowly and say, "Hello."

"Yeah," Stu says, nodding. "You're really not in the moment. That was definitely stupid."

I slap his shoulder. "I told you. I'll do it right when I see him."

"Just say hi."

"I will," I say. "I just want to do it in a way that lets him know I still like him as a friend even if he doesn't like me all that much anymore."

"Good luck with that one," Stu says in a tone that actually means *not going to happen*.

I just refuse to give up a friendship so easily or to believe that love and hate are remotely close on any emotional spectrum. I like Stefan and have every reason to believe I always will.

And then I walk into my sociology class and everything changes.

Their eyes met across a crowded room . . .

I've read this dozens of different ways, and never thought it could happen outside fictionalized Victorian England. But it's happening. To me. Right now.

I see him—Him Whom I've Never Met—the one in glasses, beautiful brown frames that match his beautiful brown hair. Suddenly, in a split second, a palpable force, like a seismic wave, hits me, but instead of knocking me over, it wraps itself around me before rushing into my body, where it twists my stomach, squeezes my lungs, and thumps on my heart. Sounds diminish to indistinct murmurs. The whole peripheral world fades. I cannot move, and, at the same time, I think I might be able to fly. And now—feet anchored to Earth, wings starting to sprout—he looks at me, directly at me, with those eyes the color of sky, and he smiles. And he nods, just once— an elegant, sophisticated, and entirely personal acknowledgment, between him and me alone.

I couldn't say hello to Stefan Kott like this if I practiced for a year.

What is this?

Heart pounding. Breath quickening. None of it within my control. I manage to free one foot enough to take a step toward him when I am stopped by less cosmic energy.

"Pick a seat," Stu says to me, spreading his arms wide.

I stand for a few seconds in front of three chairs slightly to the right of center and make my sensory assessment. No draft, no glare, no foul odor, and no strange sound coming from anywhere. If the person sitting next to me whistles through his nose or smells of pickles or something equally edible, I have to move. Immediately.

"These are good," I say, and we encamp.

Since class doesn't start for another few minutes, I decide I should probably meet the guy who caused such a peculiar—almost supernatural—reaction in me, get the introductions over, find out who he is and what this is all about. Mr. Brown Hair and Glasses must be eager for it too, because he's glanced at me twice more since the moment our eyes first met. Glanced and smiled.

He's standing with four people I know from previous classes, so I wander over to say hi to them.

A girl named Samantha, a friendly if reserved junior who always stands with her arms folded across her chest, greets me with a nod and, "Hey, Josie. How was your summer?"

"Nice, thanks. How was yours?"

"Good, thanks. I was just talking about this internship I did, and it turns out he's from Chicago," she says, nodding toward—*heart pounds*—Him.

"I'm Ethan," he says in a warm, confident voice as he extends a hand to me.

Very sophisticated.

"I'm Josie."

"Very nice to meet you, Josie."

"You too." *Ethan,* I say to myself and manage to refrain from sighing heavily. "I haven't seen you on campus before. Are you new here?" I ask.

"I am. New to Cap and to Columbus."

"You'll like them both. The people are really nice."

"So I'm finding out," he says, gesturing toward Samantha and me, and Samantha, still wrapped up tight in her arms, says, "The people here are great."

"Okay, then," Ethan says, looking at his watch. His watch? "I think we should get started."

Get started?

"Excuse me, Josie," he says, gently touching my shoulder before he steps to the front of the room and says authoritatively, "Okay, everyone take your seats, and we'll get started. Welcome to Sociology 310: Introduction to Sociolinguistics. I'm Ethan Glaser, and I will be your instructor for the next fifteen weeks."

CHAPTER SEVENTEEN

This is one of those moments when my loud, racing thoughts temporarily turn my ears deaf, and I miss the next few things Ethan—or Dr. Glaser or Professor Glaser or what do I call the guy?!—says, but suddenly I see the class arranging desks in a circle, so I robotically copy.

When I tune back in, I hear him say, ". . . a few minutes just to introduce ourselves. I'll start." Most of my professors at Cap do this, especially when, like Sociolinguistics, the classes are small, and there will be loads of discussion in the course.

"As I said, my name's Ethan Glaser, and you can call me Ethan. I'm an instructor, not a professor, and"—he smiles some—"I don't think I'm all that much older than some of you, so Ethan's fine. Or Mr. Glaser. Whatever makes you comfortable. I'm twenty-six. I have a master's in sociology from the University of Chicago, where I've been doing educational research for a couple of years, but decided I'd leave the lab and teach, so here I am.

"I'm new to this area, been here about three weeks, and so far I like it." He looks at me—AT ME—and he smiles when he says, "The people are really nice.

"Let's see," he continues. "I run. Need to find some local 5Ks. I like playing hockey and soccer. I play guitar, write a little music, and—what else? Oh." He laughs. "I like lots of different kinds of music, but mostly I am a closet Styx fan."

Stu nudges me with his elbow, nudges what I'm sure was an absurd smile off my face, and almost nudges me right off my seat. I pretend to search for something in my backpack so that I don't look as if I suffer from some strange seizure disorder that sporadically sends me toppling out of my chair.

When it is my turn to introduce myself, I say, "Hi, I'm Josie Sheridan. I'm a sophomore here, but also a senior at Bexley High School, where I'm on the volleyball team and the track team. I run 5Ks, so"—I look at Ethan—"I can give you a list. There are lots of them throughout the year."

He nods and—*ah*—smiles again.

I say something about my major, which I can barely remember at the moment, and then, "And I'm a huge Styx fan too. But only the Dennis DeYoung years. And I'm not closeted about it. I'll tell anyone."

"She will," Stu confirms.

"High school?" Ethan asks, surprised.

He's new. I forgot. And out of the whole Look How Much We Have in Common List, the wrong thing catches his attention.

"She and Stu are our resident geniuses," a guy I know from last semester—a football player—says. "They're both like twelve."

"Yeah," I say dryly. "We're tall for our ages."

This gets a chuckle from much of the class, including Ethan, who then asks the single most embarrassing question in the world:

Exactly how many butt zits do you have at this moment?

But it comes out:

"How old are you, if you don't mind my asking?"

"I'll be sixteen in October," I say, pretending I had just said *I'm practically thirty with my own home, office, and ex-husband.*

"Fifteen? And a sophomore here?" he asks. "Huh."

"Spooky, aren't they?" Mr. Football teases.

"So they're the ones who are going to set the curve?" Ethan asks as some in the class playfully groan their yeses, which amuses Stu, but I feel heat—and heat means pink—rising in my cheeks. It actually does not abate but worsens when Mr. Football adds, "But they're pretty cool, so it's okay."

We are?

It is?

And what version of *cool* is this? And what language—Ohmig*d, Ohmig*d 2.0? Football? Stefan? No, not Stefan. Or is it? I can't think.

"Well, in the spirit of full disclosure," Ethan says, "I was the same way in my classes. I graduated high school at sixteen, so"—he looks at Stu and me—"I know where you guys are coming from."

"So what you're telling us," Mr. Football continues, "is that you were the class brain."

"Yeah," Ethan says. "But." He holds up a cautionary finger. "I never carried a briefcase."

"Cool," Mr. Football says.

Then Ethan nods at Stu to begin his bio, and after his, the next until we're done, and I hear none of it. I am too busy quietly contemplating everything I have just learned about Ethan and chiefly my initial reaction to him. And how I could say to him, already, what I could never say to Stefan, which is that, yes, I think I could fall in love with you one day, in the future, quite possibly. Not impossibly at all.

I want to linger after class, talk some more with Ethan, maybe time my exit from the room with his, but that is not to be today. Samantha has rushed him in order to finish her conversation about Chicago, so Stu and I gather our things and walk to Fair Grounds.

On the way I text Kate.

Text to Kate, 9:54 a.m.
What would you say if I told you I just had an extraordinary experience with a guy I just met, don't know what it is, think it's serious, but that—

"What are you writing? A novel?" Stu asks. I ignore him and keep typing.

Text to Kate, continued, 9:55 a.m.
—there are some immediate obstacles?

Text from Kate, 9:56 a.m.
Josie! what happened?!?!

Text to Kate, 9:56 a.m.
I have no idea, but I think it was profound.

Text from Kate, 9:57 a.m.
want to hear everything!!!!

Text to Kate, 9:58 a.m.
Tell me honestly. Do you believe in love at first sight? Or at least its potential to become love?

Text from Kate, 9:59 a.m.
Josie!! I do, I do, I do, I do! Can't wait to talk!
XOXO

I click off my phone and grin my way to Fair Grounds, thinking Kate may be right. This may be my best year yet.

There's just one problem. I don't believe in love at first sight. But maybe I am wrong.

CHAPTER EIGHTEEN

Text to Mother from Bexley High School, 12:57 p.m.
Got Mrs. Beckwith for AP French. She is an idiot.

Text from Mother, 12:58 p.m.
Cope

This year, I am back at the high school for only two late afternoon classes. AP French and Government and Econ.

I spend all of sixth period French ignoring Mrs. Beckwith, intensely involved in this one thought: There must be a way to figure this out, *this* being whatever happened to me this morning at Cap. With Ethan.

I am distracted from my contemplation in Government and Econ because Cassie Ryerson, in the seat ahead of me, smells like pancakes, a smell akin to pickles insofar as both are food. And unless the food is in your possession or you are in a kitchen, you should not smell of it. Brush, floss, gargle, air out. Food smells belong in food spaces, not classrooms. And anyway, who smells of pancakes at two in the afternoon? Pancakes are breakfast food.

So this is why I cannot concentrate on my feelings for Ethan until I am at my locker at the three o'clock bell. But my contemplation is interrupted there too, when I am assailed by the shrieks of Jen, an unusually cheery Emmy, and the enthusiasm of four other friends from the volleyball team who are, we are told annually by our coach, each other's BFFs.

They have been waiting all day, all summer, all of high school to celebrate senior year. And I celebrate with them, in their language, copying their customs, which, at the moment, are hugs and huge smiles and breathless excitement. I don't shriek, though. There are certain foreign words and phrases I just can't reproduce, and shrieking is one of them. *Woo-hooing* is another. These things have never and will never sound authentic coming out of my mouth, so I don't even attempt them.

"Can you believe it? We're seniors. How cool is that?" Jen says, hugging me for the second time, and I tell her, "I know. This is going to be our best year yet."

"Okay, wait," Jen says, pulling her new camera from her backpack, saying, "I love this camera. I just got it. Wait. Here." She grabs the arm of the nearest person. "Take our picture, will you," she says, and I smile up at the photographer but can't manage to produce that greeting I've rehearsed. Just a weak, "Hi, Stefan."

He takes the picture, nods at me, and walks away, leaving Jen and the other girls saying such things as "Aw, Josie," and "Oh, it'll be okay, Josie." Emmy leans in close to gloat, "See? Love and hate, practically the same thing."

Tonight, I set the table for five, which means Geoff is coming. He arrives a few minutes after Kate, who arrives talking to him on her phone. Minutes later, he slips through a crack in the door, slides up to her, attempts to suck her blood, but there are witnesses, so he merely gives her a quick kiss hello.

He has taken to kissing my mother's cheek and sporadically makes overtures to do the same to me, but these overtures end each time in awkward hesitation. So usually he pecks a hello at me. Occasionally he winks.

"Geoff," I say in response, emphasis on the *eh* of his name.

Just before dinner is served, Kate squeezes my arm and whispers, "Tonight. After Geoff leaves. I want to hear everything."

And I beam my approval of the plan at her, but the beam, the approval, and the plan disintegrate at the dinner table with Geoff's first remark in that pause right after grace.

"So, Josie," he says. "Kate tells me you've had quite the day. Love at first sight, I believe she said. You know, there is some science behind that."

Kate bumps her elbow against Geoff's and frowns ever so slightly but not subtly enough to go unnoticed.

"What?" he whispers.

My parents seamlessly continue dining, waiting for further information.

"It's true," I say. "I've fallen."

"Whom for?" my mother asks.

"The Cap football team," I say. "I saw them practicing, and that was it."

"Planning an active social life this year, are you, Josie?" my father asks. "Excellent. Of course, we'll have to meet them first."

"Well, this is the year I get to date college boys. You and mom said."

"Should we meet them as a team or individually?" my father asks my mother.

"I suppose that depends on how Josie decides to date them," she says.

"Date them as a group," Kate says a little nervously.

"No, I've decided to date one a week for the next—what?—ninety weeks. That's Round One. For Round Two, I'll just date the guys I like. Again, one a week. And I'll just keep narrowing it down over the next several years until I'm down to a handful."

"Dating play-offs. An excellent plan," my father says. "Of course, you realize that you and most of them will graduate before you've chosen your final winner. It's unlikely you'll all be living in Ohio then."

"So I'll have to commute on some dates. Or they will."

And as my dad dissects this plan even further, Geoff catches my eye and mouths the word *sorry* to me and adds a little bit of a chagrinned look, which catches me by surprise, but I manage a little absolving nod in his direction. Curiously, I am not angry with him but Kate. But he still should have thought before he spoke. Of course, I don't always, but—whatever—I return to listening to Dad.

Later, Mother and I find ourselves alone in the kitchen, washing the dinner dishes. Geoff and my dad are in his study talking about antiques, and I don't care where Kate is.

"Thank you," Mother says when I take a glass baking dish from her dripping hands and begin to dry it. And the quick look she gives me—the smallest hint of a grin and eyebrows raised expectantly—persuades me to say, "Yes, I met someone today at Cap that I think I like. I think I could like him very much. Eventually."

"I figured you would eventually."

"Yes. Eventually," I say quietly, ignoring a twinge of sadness at such a remote word. Eventually. Really, really eventually. I clear my throat, clear away the blight on such a lovely experience. "He does seem perfect. Nice, smart. He even likes Styx."

"But he's older."

"He's older," I say, and *eventually* I will be too.

How can I like and dread one word so much?

"Well," Mother says, "we did say when you're sixteen, you may date college boys, but the rule—"

"I know the rule. You have to meet them first. I think that rule only exists so that Dad will have new people to show his antiques to."

"That's exactly why we created it, yes."

"Maybe that's why he likes Geoff so much. He's still relatively new and hasn't heard all Dad's stories about blood-lettings and cures for female hysteria, which, by the way, I think Kate has."

"Your father and I like Geoff for a number of reasons, not least among them that he makes Kate, who is not a hysteric, happy."

"Well, he makes me unhappy, so what about that?"

"You're not marrying him."

"Since he's marrying into this family, the family should have a vote."

"Well, then my vote cancels your vote, my dear," she says before heading out of the kitchen.

"I'm not done campaigning," I call to her.

"I'm sure you're not," she says, leaving me in the kitchen sensing the faint whiff of toes.

Long after the dishes are done, after I hear Geoff's car pull out of the driveway, Kate knocks on my bedroom door and enters as she asks, "Josie, can I come in?" Inside, she finds me sitting in my desk chair, facing the door, arms and legs crossed in preparation to rebuff her.

"Josie, let me explain," she says, hurrying in, sitting on the bed corner closest to me. "Okay, yes, I told Geoff about your texts, and I probably shouldn't have. Okay, no, I shouldn't have. Not without your permission, but, Josie, I'm just—I was so excited when I got your messages, and I wanted to share this really happy news with Geoff, who's also really excited for you. This is a huge thing. We're happy. That's all, and we want to know everything and share the excitement with you. And—that's—I'm sorry I told him without asking you first if I could. Please don't be mad at me."

"Okay," I say.

"No. You're mad."

"I don't know that I'm mad. I only know I'm stunned that you would do that. I swear you've lost your mind since you got engaged to him. It's as if you've become less of a sister since you met him."

"Don't blame Geoff for this."

"I'm not blaming him. I'm blaming you. Are we to have no more confidences between sisters now?"

"Josie. I'm sorry. I don't know what more I can say than I'm sorry. Really," she says, reaching out to place her hand on my knee and giving a little squeeze. I promptly swivel toward my desk as I say, "I know. I've got work to do."

"What are you doing?"

"Mathematically determining the exact length of eventually."

"What? Is that how long it's going to take for you to forgive me?"

"Yes. And it's a complicated formula, so please close the door on your way out."

When I hear the door latch, I refresh my computer screen and continue with my search terms: + science + "love at first sight."

CHAPTER NINETEEN

Researchers have long studied the possibility of love at first sight. One engrossing article I find online describes how researchers observed the initial introduction of two study participants, Cedric and Adeline, and concluded, given the couple's subsequent courtship, that they had fallen in love with each other in the first three minutes of meeting. Adeline before Cedric. It is only when I reach the end of the article that I discover Cedric and Adeline are orangutans, but the author of the study wrote at length about this phenomenon *possibly* applying to humans too. (Also to peacocks and beavers.)

Apparently, the potential for love at first sight is hardwired into brain circuitry and occurs when we first lay eyes on someone who corresponds with our idea of the Pperfect Person.

I read a few more articles before climbing into bed and falling asleep on the thought that, according to research, it is entirely likely that I fell in love today. I'm fairly certain I fall asleep smiling, since everything I read tonight makes Pperfect Sense.

* * * * *

Text from Stu, 7:33 a.m.
No.

Text from Sophie, 7:33 a.m.
Yes. Y?!

Text from Jen, 7:33 a.m.
OMG yes!!!!!

Text from Emmy, 7:33 a.m.
Not since my mom's third divorce.

They're all responding to this text I just sent them:
Do you believe in love at first sight?

I text them all back:
Just wondering about an article I read last night.

Thursday afternoon, Mrs. Easterday and I have tea and shortbread cookies on her porch, which she calls Mr. Easterday's Room. It was his favorite. She keeps his monogrammed desk set exactly as he left it.

I ask her the same question, and she says, "Oh, heavens, no. I didn't like Mr. Easterday at all when I first met him."

"You didn't?" I can't help grinning when she speaks of him. She reminds me of Jen Auerbach, but in a much more dignified way. Her lips don't produce an actual smile, but her entire face seems to whenever she mentions her husband.

"Oh, not at all. I thought he was a show-off," she says.

"What changed?"

"Nothing changed," she says, sounding surprised at the question. "I just got to know him better." She beams at a nearby black-and-white photo of him in a naval uniform. "And I'm so glad I did. Think of what I'd have missed if I had trusted my first impression."

"What if your first impression had been good?" I ask. "Would you have trusted it then?"

"After teaching children for twenty years, Josie, I have learned to withhold my opinion until I get to know the person better. Sometimes my first impression was right. And sometimes it was wrong. You can never tell."

"Oh," I say, and trace my finger in the capital *E* embossed in black leather on Mr. Easterday's old desk pad.

I text Stu as I walk home across Mrs. Easterday's yard:
Are there days when you find life terribly confusing?

Text from Stu, 5:18 p.m.
Only when I have a girlfriend.

Text to Stu, 5:19 p.m.
That actually makes sense to me now.

Text from Stu, 5:20 p.m.
Who's the guy?

Text to Stu, 5:20 p.m.
There isn't 1. But there could be.

"Eventually," I say quietly, and expel a long, slow, confused breath I'm certain is in the shape of an embossed *E*.

On Friday, Ethan looks at *me* throughout the lecture, which he calls "getting the dry stuff out of the way." I take copious notes on the history of sociolinguistics and its origins in three separate disciplines—sociology, linguistics, and anthropology—and nod periodically so that he knows I find him and this subject fascinating.

He's an excellent lecturer. Doesn't use notes, which means he knows this topic, which means it's important to him, which is one more thing we have in common.

Next week, we're going to start our semester-long Language Variation Project. From then until the end of the semester, we're going to be collecting units of speech—a word or phrase—used by different individuals to mean different things. Take the phrase *cool* or *that's cool,* for example, which Stefan, who won't even look at me in the halls now, says, or said, all the time. Depending on how, when, and where, it has meant:

1. That's really interesting.
2. I approve or like that.
3. I've never heard or seen that before.
4. I guess I don't mind.

After we log thirty examples of our chosen phrase, or at the end of ten weeks—whichever comes first—we'll look for common patterns of usage by sex, age, location, things like this, and write a final paper about it. Some of the other people in the class complained about having to collect thirty examples, but I'm not worried, given the number of different social groups, complete with distinct languages, I interact with. I actually think this is going to be a breeze and wish I could write more than one paper on it.

Kate meets me at the breakfast table every day this week so far, including Monday, which was Labor Day, when I didn't have the excuse of school to get me away from her, so I spent much of the morning with Mrs. Easterday. Here Kate is again on Wednesday, sipping coffee and waiting patiently while I perform my breakfast routine.

For the past two days, she attempted to engage me in conversations about the news, and I answered as politely as possible. *Hmm*. Since she speaks fluent Josie, she knows not to push me just yet for elaboration.

Today, she says, "Josie, you can't still be mad at me. I told you I'm sorry. What more can I say?"

"How can I ever trust you with anything important if you're going to blab everything I tell you to Geoff?"

"I won't. I promise. From now on, when you tell me not to, I won't."

"I don't like that I have to tell you. You should know that. What's happened to you?"

"Nothing's happened, Josie. I just wanted to share your happy news with the person I love most in the world. I won't do it again without your permission."

"Maybe," I say, and leave the house sick with an inchoate misery.

Ethan ends the class with, "Okay, that's enough about speech communities for today," and, as usual, people hang around afterward, talking. Not Stu, who is hungry and says he'll wait for me outside Fair Grounds. I linger, collecting my books slowly, hoping to time my exit from the classroom with Ethan's, when I hear Samantha mention Styx.

"What do they sing that I'd know?" she asks.

"'Lady.' 'Babe.' 'Come Sail Away,'" Ethan says, but she shakes her head to each title.

"'Mr. Roboto,'" I say.

"Oh, right," she says, and Mr. Football adds, "That's so random. I love it."

And I actually hear myself mentally translating this phrase—*"so random" equals good; this is good*—which I've translated a hundred times before, at least. It's particularly popular here on campus but not unique to my mother tongue. I make translations like this all day, every day, but lately, for some reason, I'm more aware of the shift.

The general agreement then is that "Mr. Roboto," I say, quoting Mr. Football, rocks.

I join the group on their way out, and we all talk about music but not necessarily about Styx anymore. Not until I suddenly find myself alone with Ethan, walking away from campus.

"Going my way?" he asks.

"Looks like it," I say.

"So let me ask you something, Josie. How did you end up a senior at fifteen?"

"Well, I'm almost sixteen," I say. "October third. That's a Friday this year. Mark it on your calendar and shop now for best deals."

"Send me a wish-list."

"I'll do that. But I skipped second grade."

"I skipped third," he says. "And Stu?"

"Stu's seventeen. Never skipped anything. Including a meal."

"You two seem really close," he says. "You and he are . . . going out?"

"Stu and I? No." I look ahead in the distance at

nothing, trying to appear and sound casual when I say, "Neither of us is going out with anyone at the moment."

He responds with a cheery nod I cannot interpret.

We have come to the corner, where we wait for the light. Down the block we see Stu standing outside of Fair Grounds, eating a muffin the size of a softball. It's probably his second one.

"So I'm told there's a better coffee shop down here than the one back on campus," Ethan says.

"Fair Grounds," I say, pointing. "That's where Stu is. That's where I'm going."

"Mind if I tag along?"

"I don't mind. We come here every day after class."

"You shouldn't have said that. You'll get sick of seeing me."

"I doubt it."

"That's sweet."

Light turns. We cross, and once again I feel that force—that rush of energy—I felt last Wednesday, and now, walking so close next to him, I want to ask him if he feels it too. But it seems a little early in our burgeoning relationship to discuss the physical phenomena of love or the research behind love at first sight, so I decide to wait.

We will have endless conversations about it and other things eventually. I hope.

"So what's your favorite Styx song?" he asks.

"I fell in love with them over 'The Best of Times.' First song of theirs I ever heard."

"Love at first listen?" he asks playfully.

"Exactly," I say. "And my devotion has never waned. What's your favorite?"

"Oh, I'd have to say 'Lorelei,'" he says, and, oh, I wish my name were Lorelei.

When I think of Lorelei,
my head turns all around.
As gentle as a butterfly,
she moves without a sound.

"So I imagine there aren't a lot of Styx fans at your school," Ethan says.

"Are you suggesting there is no universal appeal of the greatest musical talent of all time?" I ask.

"No. It's just an, um, unusual thing to find a fan of theirs under thirty."

"It's funny you say that because the joke in my family is that I'm going on thirty."

"I can see that. So I imagine all your tastes run in that direction. Different from your friends. Older, maybe?"

"Some. Okay, many. But they stop short of sensible shoes. Although, I do see the value of sensible shoes. I just don't own any. Yet."

"So let me ask you, Josie. Given the choice between the coolest party on Friday night or, say—"

"Making fudge with my eighty-one-year-old neighbor?"

"Yes."

"I'd rather make fudge with Mrs. Easterday," I say. "She and I have a really nice connection. We have great conversations."

"Easterday?"

"It's a great name, isn't it? But I go to the parties too. I just don't feel as comfortable there as I do with Mrs. Easterday."

"What don't you like about the parties?" he asks.

"They're okay for a little while, but then I've had enough. Enough noise, enough shouting, enough drunks, enough being bumped into, enough everything, and I *have* to leave."

"Ah!" he says, appearing happy and excited by the thought. "Let me ask you. If a shirt has a tag or knot—"

"I can't wear it."

"And what about strange noises? Not loud but strange and repetitive?"

"Can't be near them."

"Sensual Overexcitability."

"Exactly," I say.

Sensual Overexcitability is a term coined by a Polish psychologist who performed some of the first large studies with gifted kids. He found that people with very high IQs profoundly overreact to certain sensual input—lights, noises, smells, textures—to the point, at times, of impaired functioning.

"You are the only other person I've ever met who

knows what this is," Ethan says, and I don't tell him that Stu does too. We're quiet for a few more steps before he says, "I think we may be a lot alike, Josie. If you ever want to talk to someone who's been there, my door is always open."

"Really? Thanks."

"Anytime. I'm serious. I know how rare it is to meet people who can understand where you are and what you're going through. Rare and important."

People who speak the same language, I want to say, but say this instead: "It is."

Then he nods contentedly, or so he seems to.

We meet up just then with Stu, who asks Ethan, "So how do you like Cap after a week?"

"Yeah, I like it." He looks right at me and turns my ears hot with: "The people are sweet, easy to talk to, and have excellent taste in music."

"Want some?" Stu asks, holding his muffin toward us both.

"See?" Ethan says. "Everywhere you go, people offer you their muffins."

"We're that kind of place," Stu says, and takes an enormous bite.

"Looks like you've got a head start on Josie and me."

"Ahuhhizer."

"Appetizer," I translate.

On our way inside, Ethan asks, "Are you guys staying here? Getting it to go?"

"We usually stay," I say.

"I'm just going to grab coffee to go today," he says, and they're so efficient at Fair Grounds that it takes thirty-two seconds, darn it. "But maybe next week I'll stay. You're making that muffin look awfully good."

"You shu hie a by."

"You should try a bite," I say.

"Next time. I'll see you guys," he says, and wishes us a good day and waves from the door.

I turn to Stu to ask, "Does Jen Auerbach know that you cannot wear socks with seams in them?"

"Probably not."

"Don't you think she should know this about you?"

"No. It's more important to me to find out if she can walk in misaligned, seamed socks."

"I knew you liked her," I say.

"Actually, I need to know this about everyone, but it's a topic that rarely arises naturally," he says.

"All right. I'll find out for you."

"Yes, it was my plan all along to get you to ask her."

"You like her."

"The way you like the teacher?" he asks, smiling wickedly.

"What?!" I protest.

"I saw you walking with him. Looking kind of cozy."

"We were talking about Styx. How else am I supposed to look?"

"Okay," he says, raising his shoulders high, still smiling that smile.

"Eat your muffin," I order, which is Josie for *Shut up,* which, in this case, is Ohimig*d for *You're right and I have no comeback.*

Later in the afternoon, on our perfectly aligned walk back to the high school, I lose myself in the mental recall of "Lorelei."

When I think of Josephine, my head turns all around
As gentle as a butterfly, she moves without a sound.
I call her on the telephone. She says, "Be there by eight."
Tonight's the night she's moving in, and I can hardly wait.
The way she moves,
I gotta say,
"Josephine, let's live together . . ."

Stu doesn't ask me what I'm thinking. We never ask each other that. It's not that we don't need to. It's that we know how rude it is to interrupt.

CHAPTER TWENTY

Friday morning. I have just set my backpack on the classroom floor when Ethan approaches me and asks through that fabulous look of shared, personal information that only exists between close friends, "Fudge with Mrs. Easterday tonight?"

"Hanging out at his house tonight," I say, pointing at Stu.

"Have fun," Ethan says, walking toward the big desk at the front as Stu asks, "You are?"

"Yeah. Sophie and I have some theories to discuss."

"About what? Don't say Josh."

"Okay. Monkey grooming theories. Is poosking innate or the result of social pressure?" I scrunch my face at him. "Of course Josh."

"Poosking?"

"Yeah. Picking bugs off some—"

"I know what poosking means."

"Your knowledge of primate hygiene is one of the things I like best about you."

"I thought you dug my beard." He pushes his chin toward me and asks, "Want to pet it?"

"How long are you going to keep that thing?"

"I was going to shave tomorrow, but now I have to keep it so that you don't think I shaved it for you."

"I didn't ask you to shave it. I asked how long you were going to keep it."

"Your implication being that I am going to, at some point, get rid of it."

"I don't even know why you have it."

"Because I can," he says. Then he wrinkles his forehead and points across the room to where Ethan is standing, preparing for class. "Hey, how does he know Mrs. Easterday?"

And I just smile, content with the feeling of sharing a little information with Ethan alone. This is like the feeling of an inside joke—a bond, and a private one at that.

This is a good beginning.

Late this afternoon, I walk home with Sophie. She's this year's art director for the yearbook, whose staff meets every day after school, same time as my volleyball practice. If one of us finishes early, we hang out with friends—Note to Geoff: I *still have* them—and wait. Stu would have waited for us after his soccer practice if Sophie weren't in love again. He says he can't stomach listening to her prattle on about Josh, says he prefers her post-break-up complaints to her pre-relationship gushing.

All the way home, Sophie describes the perfection

of Josh Brandstetter's flirting skills. She doesn't want to go out with him just yet. It's only the end of the second week of school and obviously a little too warm and green still for what she considers the best season for love.

"Fall is the perfect time of year to be in love," Sophie says. "When it's getting cold at night, and all the leaves have turned. I love that." She turns quickly to me. "But I'm not stringing him along. He knows I like him. He just doesn't know how much."

"I know that. You're just prolonging the run-up."

"Prolonging the run-up. Yes, perfect."

"I heard him call you hot today."

"Shut up. Who did he say it to?"

I name a couple of his friends.

"Shut up," she says again, which only makes me smile.

Shut up is the unit of language I'm recording for my Language Variation Project. Translated situationally, it means:

1. Stop talking.
2. Thank you.
3. I am not.
4. You're kidding.
5. You're right, and I have no comeback.

I already have four examples since Wednesday, when my dad bought me, especially for this project, a black, hardback journal from an office supply store—the third store we visited that night. Dad bought a small brown leather journal with a red silk ribbon attached as a bookmark. I asked him what he'd be using it for and all he said was, "Wouldn't you love to know."

Kate's car is in the driveway when I get home, and on the counter in the kitchen is a package from Victoria's Secret, addressed to her. Next to it lies a note:

Dear Josie,

I got you this for the wedding but am giving it to you early as a completely frivolous peace offering.

xo,
Kate

Upstairs, I crank up "Lorelei" on my computer, peel off my T-shirt, throw it on the bed, scramble into the new bra—"padded for extreme lift"—and squint old-lady-like at my reflection in the mirror until I finally put my glasses back on.

Hmm.

I look the same but for boobs. I thought I'd look . . . different. Not exactly the swanlike transformation I imagine Kate envisioned.

Josephine, let's live together. Bah-bah-bah. *Brighter than the stars forever.*

I flip through the accompanying catalog to get a sense of what I am doing wrong and contort myself—butt out, knees slightly bent, arms wrapped all the way around me. Oh, wait. I have to take my hair out of its ponytail. *Tousle, tousle.* Then holding the pose just so, I call for Kate.

"Yes?" she asks as she enters my room and tries not to laugh.

"Who stands like this?" I want to know.

We shout over the music.

"Josie."

"Have you ever stood like this in front of Geoff?"

"I'm not telling you that."

"You have!" I giggle and sham more poses. "And like this too, I bet." I shove one arm up in triumph. With the other, I push my hair around. "And this."

"Josie," she laughs, and turns the music off. "Mother!"

"Don't call her!" I shriek and quickly put my T-shirt back on, stretching it out over my brand-new bust.

"She's not home. So how do you like it?"

"I'm not sure." I poke at the bra cups. I think they may be bulletproof. "How does this look?" I thrust my chest out. "Do you think Dennis DeYoung will want me now? Actually, I hope he doesn't. I wouldn't want him to leave his wife for me."

"Isn't he a little old for you?"

"He's entirely too old for me, but I hate thinking of him as having any imperfections, so I choose to think of him as ageless. Like his voice."

"I see. So am I forgiven?"

"Because you bought me this? No. You're forgiven because I love you." She squeezes me into a quick hug as I say, "But this is ridiculous. I can't wear this."

"Of course you can. It's convertible. The straps unhook to make it strapless, so it will work perfectly with your bridesmaid dress."

"It's still ridiculous."

"It'll look great under the dress. Trust me."

"When's the next fitting?"

"October eleventh."

"Will it be the last one?" I ask, hoping it will. We've already had two.

"We'll probably have four altogether."

"Four fittings?"

"Yes. Sit," she says.

I sit on the edge of the bed, and she starts brushing my hair.

"Are all the other bridesmaids going to be there again?" I ask.

"Yes."

"I'm not going."

"Yes, you are."

"They make me crazy."

"I know," she says, robbing me of the chance to list my complaints. "But be nice to them, because they adore you. Especially Madison."

"I think you stay friends with her to torment me," I say of Kate's lifelong best friend, Madison Orr.

"Josie, this may shock you, but my friendships have very little to do with you."

"They should have more to do with me when their behavior affects me."

"Madison loves you."

"Madison talks about me in the third person when I'm right in front of her."

"Yeah, she does," Kate says, wrinkling her nose just a little. "But she means well."

"Plus, doesn't it bug you how she holds her pen? She puts too many fingers on it and presses too hard," I say, awkwardly miming it.

"Are you going to tell me about this guy at Cap or not?"

"I can tell you right now that if he holds his pen wrong, our relationship is going nowhere. Except I already know he doesn't."

"Ooh. So you have a relationship?"

"I don't know. No. Well, technically, yes, but it's just from class." I twist around to face her, and she sits when I do. "But I really think we have a connection."

I go on—at length—telling her every pertinent bit of

info but his last name, every gorgeous detail, especially the ones highlighting our many similarities, and when I am done gushing, which I manage to do with punctuation, Kate asks, "How old is he?" And I feel as if I have just run full speed into a wall I saw ahead but chose to ignore.

Crash! Ow!

Erm.

"Older," I say, and flop back on the bed.

Defeated.

"Josie. Come on. Sit up."

"I can't. This bra is too heavy."

I'm barely able to see over it, so I'm happy when Kate lies next to me, cuddling her shoulder into mine.

"Is he a senior?"

"No, he's not a senior, but he is older, and I'm—" I can't even say it, so I puff the last of that sentence out and close my eyes.

"You're nearly sixteen, and you're going on thirty. Sometimes. Other times twelve."

"This is actually not helping," I say.

"No. I know. But, Josie, you have to know you're not the typical sixteen-year-old. I'm sure Ethan sees that."

"He sees sixteen. And so do I. And so do you, and so does the whole world."

"Josie, you're not always going to be sixteen."

"I know that. Kate, I do know that, and I keep telling myself that maybe, eventually, we'll get to know each other, and he might like me. A lot. But that's a long way off, and in the meantime, I already know I like him. A lot. And I don't know what to do with these feelings. I don't even know what my feelings are. Only that they're real, and they're huge, and they're completely confusing."

"Just be easy with them," she says as she sits up. "Love is a huge thing."

"You think it's love?"

"Maybe. And if it is, it will last long beyond sixteen. And you just have to deal with it. It isn't something you can work out like a math problem."

"I can work everything out like a math problem. Well, almost everything."

"Not this," she says. "What's Ethan's last name."

"He doesn't have one. He's like Sting, Madonna, Bono. Ethan."

"I'm not going to Google him."

"Yes, you are," I say as I prop myself up on my elbows.

"Yes, I probably would," she says, giggling a little.

"Your feelings for Geoff are really this huge?" I ask.

"My feelings for Geoff are very real and very strong," she says, "and I know how you feel about him, so I'm going to go."

She's at the door, ready to leave, when I ask her, "You really *love* him? Him?"

"Josie," she says, and sighs. "We've had a really nice conversation, and I'm happy to talk to you about Ethan, but you're going to spoil it all by bringing Geoff up, just so you can insult him—"

"That's not *why* I bring him up. That's just an organic bonus."

"You're starting. I'm leaving."

She closes the door behind her, and I am left alone in my room and in my confusion and in my bra, which is, no matter what Kate says, ridiculous. I need socks or hamsters or something to fill out the cups.

A couple minutes later, I return my hair to its ponytail and start to slip out of the bra when it occurs to me what it represents. The bra, next contacts and pierced ears—all of them alterations, improvements of me apparently yet to come. I toss the new bra into a dresser drawer, close it and drop, deflated, onto my bed, stewing over a new word.

When?

CHAPTER TWENTY-ONE

This Saturday morning, my dad is at the table when I come downstairs and begin my routine. Something is different. And terribly, terribly wrong. The cereal box is on the wrong shelf in the cupboard. The milk is on the wrong side in the refrigerator, and all the cereal bowls are in the dish rack, drying.

I quickly assess. Bowls. All of them. Milk. Cereal. All of them? All of them?

And then I look over at my father. He's sitting at the table, a maniacal grin on his face, watching me, pen in hand, brand-new leather journal with attached silk bookmark open in front of him.

"Very funny, Dad," I say.

"Don't mind me. Don't mind me. I'm merely observing."

I dry a bowl and set about my routine, first putting everything back *in its proper place*. Then getting it out again.

About twenty minutes later, I shout to my dad from the downstairs powder room, "Very funny again, Dad!"

He has removed the toilet paper from the holder and placed two rolls of competing brands on the back of the toilet. It takes me a long handful of seconds and a thorough touch-test to decide which roll to use, which I report to him upon my return and add, "Slow at work, is it?"

"Merely taking an interest in my girls," he says, writing in his journal. "Noting your response to unpredicted changes in your environment."

"I hate unpredicted changes in my environment. You could have just written that down."

"Self-reporting is usually inaccurate. And experiments are so much more entertaining."

"And what experiments do you have planned for Kate?" I ask.

"This wedding is enough of an experiment. If I could have cooked it up in a lab, I would have."

"If I were conducting the wedding experiment," I begin, "I would record in your journal that it has changed Kate for the worse, and I would end the experiment for her own good. Call off the wedding before someone gets hurt."

"I agree Kate's not herself at the moment, but a lot of that is just stress, Josie. She'll be back to her old self after the wedding."

"I can't agree that it's the wedding, necessarily, that has changed Kate, nor that the change is temporary. I noticed a deterioration of sisterly-ness long before she set the date but *after* she got engaged. Therefore, since Geoff is the only new variable in our relationship *as* sisters, the cause of her decline is Geoffrey Stephen Brill."

"And how has this deterioration of sisterly-ness presented itself?"

"Broken confidences and direct and indirect criticism of my appearance," I say, raising three fingers at my father. "We had this great talk yesterday. She was the old Kate, but then, of course, Geoff came into it, and the mere mention of his name drives a wedge between us. She actually got up and left at the sound of his name." I sigh. "Oh, and she's doing things *he* says just because *he* says to do them." I'm thinking of the weeks-long silent treatment and later traffic cop gesture. "You know, he could be a master manipulator, plotting to use Kate as his patsy in some future criminal enterprise. You and Mother should be very concerned."

Dad closes his notebook, puts the pen down.

"What is it you most dislike about Geoff?" he asks.

"I have a list of eighteen things I dislike about him, including the way he pronounces *Ren-wah*. And can't you get him to stop winking at me? It's completely disturbing."

"What is number one on that list?"

"That he's changed Kate. That he's made her more *his* fiancée than *my* sister. Ross didn't do that to Maggie."

"Kate is no less your sister just because she's getting married."

"Yes, she is," I say, "and apparently I'm the only one who can see this. He is coming between us."

My dad and I share a long, solemn look. His eyes tell me he takes me seriously. Mine tell him, I hope, that I agonize over this—more than I do over his pronunciation of French names.

"Do you want me to speak to Kate?" he offers.

"I want you to cancel the wedding," I say. "I'm not kidding."

"I'm not going to cancel the wedding, but I will employ my skills as . . ." He pauses and puts his hands on his hips. "Super Shrink."

"How?"

"I will observe without bias as much as I am able," he says.

"And if I'm right? And you see that Geoff really is coming between Kate and me, what will you do?"

"I think I'll probably talk to Geoff," he says after some careful thought. "I will talk to him very seriously, Josie. I promise."

"Good. Because if he's a gentleman, *he* will call off the wedding just to restore harmony to this family, which, by the way, we had before he came along. You have to acknowledge that."

"I can acknowledge that," Dad says.

"Thank you," I say, and kiss his cheek and start to leave.

Before I can head upstairs, though, he takes my hand and directs me back to my chair by pointing.

"I will do my part, Josephine, but I expect you to do yours as well," he says.

"My part?"

"Yes, which is equal to mine. I expect you to observe Geoff and Kate without bias as much as you are able, which—"

"I'm—"

"Which," he says a bit louder, "you are capable of doing if you will try."

"I already know he's wrong for her," I say.

"Is he?"

"Yes. I'm just waiting for the rest of you to see it."

"Huh," he says, his head tipped back a moment before he returns his attention to his journal.

I smell toes as I trudge up the stairs to my room because *huh* never, ever means *huh*. Not in the Dr. Sheridan language. It means so much more, which I am left to contemplate on my own, which is part of the meaning of that word.

Jen Auerbach regularly answers her phone by predicting what the call is about. With me, she's been right sixty-six percent of the time. She is wrong this afternoon when she says, "It starts at eight."

"I'm not coming," I say.

She's having the whole volleyball team over to her house tonight for her annual team party. I nodded off at it last year and woke up when the girls were making a tinfoil hat for me. I let them finish. We made hats for everyone then and posed for ridiculous photos. And we hugged and laughed and shouted over loud music and ate cold pizza. It was exhausting.

Emmy passed out that night from all the shots she drank and found herself wrapped like an aluminum mummy when she finally came to. I guess she freaked out and started screaming and refused to speak to Jen for about a week. I was gone by then. Went home about ten thirty. Sober and with my hat.

"Josie, aww," Jen says. "Why not?"

I tell her only that we're having another Family Dinner, and she asks questions about Kate's wedding, which I answer succinctly.

Then she asks, "Is Stu going to be there tonight?"

"No. Why?"

"Curious."

"No, it's just a family and temporary fiancé thing tonight."

"Oh. Cool. Okay. Call me later."

"Okay. Have fun tonight."

Why would she ask if Stu is going to be there? I know she still likes him. Now I wonder if she knows he likes her too.

Tonight, when I enter the kitchen, Geoff is already here. Maggie and Ross too. Geoff is standing next to Kate, smoothing his hand over her back as she carries on about the greatness of this photographer they've hired and his incredible eye for angles. And Geoff does it again. He winks at me.

I turn my back so he won't see my irritated squint, turning seamlessly into an eyeball-roll. It was gorgeous, I'm sure. My parents should have gotten it on film.

"His photos are works of art," Geoff says to my parents. "If you have any aesthetic sensibilities, you immediately appreciate his work. If you're not going to have an artist take your wedding photos, I have to be honest"—he puffs out a laugh—"I actually don't even see the point in having any. People should just save themselves the expense and have an aunt or grandmother take the things."

"Excellent," my father says. "Excellent. I'll call Aunt Toot this minute and tell her to be sure to bring her Polaroid."

"Dad," Kate giggles.

"Have you ever seen Aunt Toot with a camera? She's a genius. No one can ever guess what the actual subject is. Now that's art," Dad says.

"I guess it's all a matter of how you define it," Geoff says, and then fakes a sniff.

Aunt Toot is Dad's seventy-eight-year-old sister—Uncle Vic's wife—who refuses to wear her glasses in public because she thinks they make her look dowdy. The woman has never taken a perfectly centered photo in her life.

"Oh, I've brought a little something for us to try tonight," Geoff says, pulling a bottle of wine out of a bag and showing it, cradled in his hands, first to my father, then to Ross.

Apparently, the womenfolk don't rank in this exchange.

"Hmm," my father says in a perfectly noncommittal tone as he looks at the bottle.

Ross does the same.

Hmm—like *huh*—is one of those fabulous responses that means so many things, and if Geoff spoke Sheridan, he'd know that, tonight, my father means *I am onto you.*

"This wine," Geoff says as he begins pouring, "comes from the Marlborough region in New Zealand." I start to wash lettuce for tonight's salad as everyone else waits for Geoff to distribute the glasses. "Sniff it first," he says, demonstrating the rare and difficult talent of sniffing.

He leaves the bottle on the counter next to me, so I lean over and sniff as if I'm inhaling my last breath.

"Smells like wine," I say, and am ignored except by Mother and The Look.

"Now, a sip," Geoff says. "Do you taste honeydew and peach?"

They nod. I tear lettuce as if it is the very essence of Geoffrey Stephen Brill's lecture.

"Now another sip, and pay attention to the finish this time," he says.

"Lemon?" Kate guesses, and Geoff smiles as he shakes his head.

"No," he says. "Grapefruit. This is a very straightforward and approachable wine. And I particularly like the lingering citrus finish."

"'Enjoy the straightforward and approachable style of this sauvignon blanc with flavors of honeydew melon and peach and a light but lingering grapefruit finish,'" I say to silence and stares. "It's on the bottle."

"Hmm," Geoff says as he turns away from me. "Well. Then I was right."

"Remarkably. Astoundingly and, dare I add, accurately," I say with mock enthusiasm as Mother quietly scolds, "Josephine."

"I'm something of a wine connoisseur," Geoff explains, squinting at the bottle as if seeing it for the first time. "I don't really bother with these labels." And he adds a proud *huh* as he pretends to read. Then he returns the bottle to the counter and leans in close to kill me, except there are witnesses, so he'll have to whisper, instead.

"You know, Josie," he says through a crooked smile, "you catch more flies with honey than you do with vinegar."

"What makes you think I *want* to catch flies?"

And then—he has this coming—I wink.

He's quiet then at dinner. Mostly quiet. It's spaghetti, so he's keeping an eye on me. And during one of those organic lulls in the conversation, I scare the daylights out of everybody by—*SLAM!*—slapping my palm flat on the table.

"Sorry," I say a second before Mother says, "Josephine, explain."

I smile some at Geoff when I say, "I thought it was a fly."

My father's aspect—inky blue eyes fixed emphatically upon me as he holds himself perfectly still for far longer than comfort and propriety dictate—says *That's enough out of you tonight, my dear*.

In the kitchen in the midst of after-dinner conversation and clatter, my dad sternly whispers, "Forcing a subject to respond the way you want him to only confirms your bias, my dear. And it makes your results worthless."

"Sorry," I whisper back, and realize it's my turn to be quiet, especially when my dad adds a solemn "Huh" in conclusion.

CHAPTER TWENTY-TWO

7. Stu Wagemaker

Written in Jen's perfect script.

We crane our necks or lean in close around her and Emmy as they compare their lists. *Top Ten Seniors I Wouldn't Mind Hooking Up With*. Today is Friday, September twenty-sixth. We have a match in thirty-five minutes, but, clearly, first things first.

At the moment, our coach is in the locker room with the JV team lecturing them after some pointless drama that happened yesterday, and reminding them, as she does every year with both teams, that your teammates are your BFFs.

I don't understand why membership on a sports team should confer instant Best Friend status to all other players irrespective of compatibilities. But since it is a tenet of this subculture to which I belong and to which I generally like belonging, I acquiesce.

They like to hug on this team—those weird X Marks the Spot Hugs: pull sleeves down over hands, tilt head, and cross arms behind friend's neck in an X, pointing up. It's almost like beginning a cheer with someone's head between your pompoms. I had to learn it last year when I made varsity and discovered that every girl did it.

Again, it's a cultural thing, like bowing in Japan, I suppose. So I practiced at home and now have the reputation for giving the best hugs on the team. Girls actually say, "I need a Josie hug," so I oblige my thirteen "BFFs" and a couple of JV girls too. No one knows how unnatural I find it—as unnatural as I will find bowing, should I ever go to Japan, which I don't foresee, but if I go, I will certainly practice before the trip, and my new Japanese friends will say, "I need a Josie bow," but in Japanese.

And I will feel, after my trip, the way I often feel after volleyball practice: It's a relief to be home, no offense to my teammates or to the entire country of Japan. But after a time, it's hard living in a foreign place.

So we continue craning our necks and leaning in close until Jen and Emmy have finished comparing their lists. They have eight names in common, if not in identical order, but both have Josh Brandstetter at number one, which makes Emmy say through a huge smile, "That's so ironic."

"Also a coincidence," I say, and she pretends to slap my leg, but she also shoots me a bitch smile—the one with little, slitty eyes—so I know she didn't appreciate the correction and is shamming the playfulness.

In all fairness, these lists aren't To Do Lists. Jen and Emmy are not in the running for Class Slut, a title currently held by Cassie Ryerson, who smells unnaturally of pancakes, but I don't think that has anything to do with her morality.

I'm just a little surprised by how cavalier Jen and Emmy are about hooking up. It's not a list I would ever agree to make—no matter which culture I'm immersed in at the moment. And I can't tell if I'm happy for Stu that he's on Jen's list or offended that he's all the way down at seven.

Now I'm not entirely sure Jen is right for him at all, and I'm even less sure by the time the game, which we win, ends. I plant myself next to her on the gym floor for a few final minutes of stretching.

"Let me ask you something," I say.

"Sure."

"Why is Stu on your list?"

"Don't you think he got completely hot over the summer?"

"I guess," I say, thinking quickly about Stu, how he looks now compared to how he looked in May. I noticed changes but hadn't judged them hot. I hadn't perceived them as anything other than natural physical changes teenage guys experience. *Hmm,* I say to myself before turning my attention back to Jen.

"Well," she says, drawing out the word. "I don't know about his beard, though. I mean, it's kind of cool that he grew one, but I don't know about kissing a guy with a beard."

"Yeah," I say. "Let me ask you something. What exactly does the list mean?"

"It means what it means. If something happened between us, I wouldn't mind."

"See, I still don't understand that."

"Josie, I love you, you're so funny."

"I'm serious. I don't know if it means you like those particular guys or not. As more than some one-time, casual thing. I need to know if it's strictly about hooking up, or do you want a real relationship with them?"

"Why? Did Stu say something about me?" she asks, and an open-mouth smile starts to grow.

"No. I'm just curious," I say as I stand.

Jen stands too.

"Come on, Josie."

"No. He's never said anything. I'm just asking about your list. He is one of my best friends, you know."

"After us," Jen practically sings and promptly embraces me in an X Marks the Spot hug.

"You do remember that I told you that he's the love-'em-and-leave-'em type, right?" I ask.

"That's only because he hasn't met the right person yet. Or not met but, you know, gone out with." She grabs my hands. "Ohmig-d, Josie, what if *I* am the right person for Stu? What if *I* am the one who turns him into a completely committed guy? 'Cause you know what they say. When the right one comes along."

"When the right one comes along, what?"

"When the right one comes along, no one else matters."

She talks all the way into the locker room, and I want to interrupt but can't find just the right moment to ask, *But aren't they all the wrong one until you find the one you marry?*

And even then how do you know?

CHAPTER TWENTY-THREE

Monday, September twenty-ninth, begins my private and thrilling countdown to Friday, my sixteenth birthday, the official end to the insignificance of fifteen. It's also the official beginning of Sophie and Josh Brandstetter's great romance—such as it is in these early days. Sufficient rain and chilly nights have turned every leaf in town every color of the autumnal rainbow, inspiring Sophie to inspire Josh to confess "I love you."

He said it at her house last Friday night, and Sophie replied as only she could.

"I know."

She's working on a collage in jewel tones she's going to give him this Friday morning before school. Instead of her signature, she's going to write *I love you* at the bottom. She signs every birthday card to me the same way.

It's amazing to me how different the same words can feel, even when they're written.

* * * * *

I have just joined Stu at our regular table at Fair Grounds. At least twice a week since the beginning of this month, Ethan has joined me on walks here. Sometimes he sits for a few minutes with Stu and me. Sometimes he gets coffee to go. Always, we have wonderful conversations. He knows just the right questions to ask about just the right subjects: What did you think of the "Mr. Roboto" video the first time you saw it? Can you study with music on? How's my teaching style?

That's what he asked me this morning, just a little bit ago on our after-class walk.

"Josie, tell me something honestly," he began.

"As opposed to something dishonestly?" I teased. Well, I partially teased. Okay, I wasn't teasing but tried to sound like I was.

"Yeah," he said, grinning quickly at me. "Yeah, I guess that goes without saying. But I do want to know how you think the class is going."

"Oh, it's great. I love it."

"And what about—do you think my teaching style is okay? Am I lecturing too much? Am I holding people's interest? Am I getting through?"

"I think," *you're perfect*, I wanted to say but said this instead: "you're doing really well, and you don't need to change a thing."

He nodded. Satisfied. Relieved. And I felt pleased that I was the one who made him so obviously contented.

Text to Kate, 11:52 a.m.
If Ethan asks me to assess him, his style, what does that mean?

Text from Kate, 11:53 a.m.
that your opinion is important to him!!!!!

I click my phone off and look up in time to catch Ethan's eye as he leaves with his coffee in a big blue travel mug. He waves. I do the same and return my attention to Stu, who is grinning clumsily at me as he chews an enormous bite of his bagel sandwich.

"What?" I ask.

He mimics my wave, tweaked with his version of shammed girlishness.

"He waved. So I waved back. It was polite," I say.

He swallows, says nothing but "Mm-hmm," and finishes the sandwich in self-satisfaction, to which I say, "Just sit there and chew, please."

"Ha ahl I'h hooing."

That's all I'm doing.

"I can't believe Jen Auerbach finds you hot."

His grin just grows, and I try to ignore him as I sip my tea, but now I'm thinking about his beard and ponytail and now that entirely too amused smile on his face, and I blurt out, "She doesn't like your beard."

"Maybe I'll shave it for her."

"Good," I grump, and grow slightly more irked when I notice the scent of toes wafting my direction.

"Josie!" Kate calls out happily the instant I walk in the back door this afternoon.

"Kate!" I respond in kind.

She and Mother are sitting at the kitchen table with a number of papers spread out in front of them—guest lists, seating charts, responses to invitations that went out two weeks ago, plans for the violent overthrow of Columbus Country Club, where the reception will take place.

"I know exactly what I'm getting you for your birthday," Kate says.

"Good, because it's Friday."

"Contacts. Contact lenses." She turns to Mother. "That solves it. She can wear them at the wedding."

"Solves what?" I ask as I drop my backpack and start to pour myself an enormous glass of water at my dad's wet bar.

"No one's wearing glasses in the photos," Kate says. "There'll be a glare. It'll be awful."

"I'll take my glasses off for photos," I say.

"Josie. *Eh*. You can't pause halfway down the aisle, take your glasses off, have your picture taken, and put them back on," Kate says.

"Actually"—I sip some water—"I'm sure I can."

"You'll be carrying flowers," she nearly whines.

"With both hands?"

"Josie, just let me buy you contacts for your birthday," she says as I take a seat on one of the stools in front of Dad's bar and start spinning slowly.

"I'd rather have a goat," I say.

"A what?"

"A goat. I ask for one every year, and technically," I say, stopping to face Mother, "that means I never get what I want."

"Yet you manage the deprivation with such composure," she says, and I happily return to spinning.

"You actually want a goat?" Kate asks.

"Yes, and everyone else who knows me well knows that. How come you don't?"

"Why do you want a goat?"

"I want to learn how to make goat's milk cheese."

"Why?"

"Because I don't know how."

"Why not just buy goat's milk?"

"If I have a goat, it will be free," I say.

"If you had a cow, so would cow's milk."

"Our yard is hardly big enough for a cow, Kate. Now you're just being ridiculous."

"Josie, I'm not—just—what? Never mind. And stop spinning. You're making me dizzy."

"Then you should be tested for vertigo."

"You're not getting a goat, obviously, so it's going to have to be contacts," she says.

"That's a little bit of a false dichotomy, don't you think," I say as I stop spinning. "It's not contacts *or* a goat. There are tons of other things you could get me, and why don't you have your shopping done yet? My birthday *is* in four days."

She tries the traffic cop stop gesture. I copy the move in a slightly more exaggerated manner.

"Now what?" I challenge, so she lowers her hand.

"I've been busy with wedding plans," she sneers at me as if the answer were so obvious, I was stupid to ask it.

"Well, I don't want contacts. I just won't wear my glasses at the wedding."

"You'll—" She drops both hands with a loud slap onto the table and puffs out a bit of air. "You'll ruin the photos."

"Kate," Mother tries to soothe her.

"She'll squint and ruin the photos," she says. "Tell her she has to get contacts."

"Tell *her* this is just a stupid wedding, not a coronation," I say.

"Girls."

"Josie. Oh! You do not understand these things. They have to be perfect, and you're making my life really difficult."

"Oh, well, in that case, I apologize for my myopia."

"*Err,* Josie!" And with a dramatic shove away from the table, she rises and marches out of the kitchen up to her bedroom.

"She started it," I say to Mother as I make one complete revolution on the stool. "And she's becoming unhinged. You and Dad should be very concerned about her."

"Your father and I *are* concerned about Kate. She has a very low tolerance for personal stress. However, we did not anticipate your contribution to her stress level."

"Can't Dad drug her?"

"Josephine. Are you saying no to the contacts simply to aggravate your sister?"

"I haven't even decided if I'm going to the wedding. *If* it even happens."

"It's happening, and you're going," my mother says in her most imperative voice.

"Well, I don't want contacts. And I don't like Kate's telling me I have to have them or I'll wreck her photos."

"That was a bit much. I'll talk to her later."

"Well, talk to Dad too, because he missed an important exchange here that proves what I told him a little bit ago about Kate."

"Fine. But I would like you to try the contacts," Mother says.

"Are you serious?" I protest, and Mother merely sighs at me. "I could get a corneal ulcer."

"You won't."

"I could go blind from it."

"You won't."

She waits.

I pick at a fingernail.

"Josephine, I would appreciate it if you would try the contacts for the sake of a little peace in my life at this moment. You might even find you like them."

"And if I don't?"

"I would appreciate it if you would try the contacts with the mindset that you might enjoy them."

Erm.

"I'll try them," I say, and spin once on the stool. "For you. Not for Kate, because I don't like how she went about the whole thing."

"Thank you."

"But if I lose my vision as a result, Kate has to donate her corneas to me."

"I'm pleased to see you're being reasonable about this," she says as she picks up papers and tucks them neatly into one of four (4) color-coded folders.

I'm not in my room thirty-two seconds before Kate rushes in *without knocking* and throws her arms around me in a real hug—one thousand times better than an X Marks the Spot Hug, making it very difficult for me to remain mad at her. Yet I manage.

"Josie, thank you," she says, and drops herself onto my bed.

I sit at my desk, pretending to start homework I finished earlier. I rarely have any.

"You're going to be really happy with contacts," she says. "I promise. They're so comfortable. And you know what? You won't have to wear those ridiculous safety glasses when you play volleyball."

"Why wouldn't I keep wearing safety glasses?"

"And," she says, getting excited by the thought, "you won't clink frames when you and Ethan get—uh—close."

I stare. Our relationship is entirely class and conversation on the way to Fair Grounds and she's got me entwined in some awkward, bespectacled make-out session? Even *my* fantasies don't extend that far. I don't know if I should be offended or flattered.

"Oh, now, Josie, I'm not making fun of you. It's just that I have the funniest image of you and him, sitting side by side in the library, working on a dissertation or something, with your glasses on."

Offended.

"Why is this funny?" I ask.

"Because it is. It's classic," she says as she stands and walks toward the door. "Two brainy kids in glasses. I love it." In the doorway she stops to say, "But he's going to see your huge, blue eyes in a couple of weeks and be blown away."

Really?

"And my pictures will be perfect," she says. "All that's left are your ears. We have to get them pierced. And then your hair."

"You're going to pierce my hair?"

"You're so cute. No, I'm going to fix it."

"Fix?"

"Oh, but we're all getting our hair done the day of the wedding, so I didn't mean that in a bad way," she quickly adds.

"Okay," I say, squinting at her in disbelief as she leaves.

Silently, I repeat her list of complaints against my appearance and tick them off on my fingers: un-pierced ears, hair, glasses, boobs (such as they are)—and I think she just told me I'm funny-looking.

Maybe I am. I never pretended I was a great beauty, but I understand now what Kate is saying—brains don't flatter anyone in photos. Maybe I'll just hang out with Geoff at the wedding.

Wait.

What?

CHAPTER TWENTY-FOUR

Mother, Dad, and a groggy Kate sing Happy Birthday to me the minute I enter the kitchen, and then they sing it again after Dad shouts out, "Once more, *goioiso*!"

Goioiso: joyfully.

It's a musical term—a mood marking, connected to tempo.

My dad has a beautiful baritone voice that translated into a beautiful alto voice in Kate, of which I am completely jealous since all I can do is merely sing on key.

Hugs and kisses follow the second chorus of Happy Birthday, which Kate promptly blights by saying, "And you know what else today is? Five weeks and a day to my wedding."

"Oh," I say, and cheer myself with thoughts of seeing Ethan later this morning and being sixteen and older in his presence.

Since it's my birthday—at least, that's the excuse I'm using—I allow myself the diversion of imagining eventualities. I envision the intertwining of Ethan's and my glasses, so to speak, as Kate so kindly fantasized yesterday on my behalf. My hands shake at the idea of it—my daring to script how, when, and where it will happen. I picture his office—warmly lit by a couple of small lamps, an old wooden desk, two small leather chairs of the kind usually found beside fireplaces, and books crowding shelves on three walls. I am a junior. A senior. I no longer take his classes but drop by his office to talk. Just talk. He is always happy, he says, to see me.

We have the marathon conversations I have dreamed of for years about everything that's important to us. And we never exhaust a topic, never find ourselves at a conversational dead end, relying on *hmm, yeah,* and *so* to lead us out of any awkwardness. But tonight, this night, we allow our conversation—about us, how we met, how it was love at first sight, which neither of us believed in to begin with—to trail off. This night is about silence—about smiles and looks full of meaning. About knowing. We will just know that now, right now, all we want to do is kiss each other. For its delicious duration, no one else in the world even exists.

It's going to be Pperfect.

My Facebook page and phone are full of brief birthday wishes with countless smiley faces, *X*'s and *O*'s, which I still want to rub in Geoff's face, but mostly I wish his remark about not having many friends didn't still bother me. Smiley faces, *X*'s and *O*'s. Look at all the friends I have, Geoffrey Stephen Brill. I dare you!

Stu's in his car in his driveway, waiting for Sophie and me. I can see as I cross the street that he has shaved, which I acknowledge—only because I can't help it—with a smile. He rubs his chin and says through his open window, "Tell me what Jen thinks."

"Don't you want to know what I think?"

"I already know what you think—usually before you think it."

"You only *think* you do."

"You like me better without it," he says.

"I *like* you no more or less than I ever have," I say, happy that I get to correct him. "I prefer looking at you without the beard."

"Why?" he asks.

"It's just not part of your identity to me," I say.

"I guess," he says, looking critically for a moment at my face. He points up at me as he says, "My beardless-ness is to me as your glasses are to you."

"Exactly," I say.

"See how well I know what you think," he gloats.

Sophie comes outside then and greets me with a hug and climbs into the backseat of Stu's car, saying, "You're the birthday girl. You get to ride up front today."

"At Cap, I'll be the birthday woman," I tell her.

Stu nods in quiet agreement while Sophie says, "That's kind of bizarre."

"I like it," I say.

"You would," she says.

"How's Josh?" I ask, twisting around to face her.

"Perfect," she says, raising her eyes heavenward for a moment.

"Don't start," Stu says.

"You're just jealous," she says.

"Yes, I'm jealous that you're going out with Josh. Don't tell him," Stu says.

"No, you're jealous that I have a boyfriend and you don't have a girlfriend."

"That's woman-friend to me," he says, smiling quickly at me.

"That's true. I could have a man-friend at Cap," I say.

"Don't you already?" Stu asks under his breath, and I pretend I don't hear him.

"Guys, these words are just gross," Sophie says. "Stop using them."

Later, after depositing a slightly disgusted Sophie at the high school, Stu parks nearby, and under a pale blue sky streaked with cirrus clouds, portending rain, we enjoy a long walk to campus.

"Do you ever find this a little culturally schizophrenic?"

I ask. "You know, man, woman here." I point toward Cap. "Guy, girl there." I point behind us toward the high school.

"I never thought about it," he says.

"I think about it a lot."

"You think too much."

"You think as much as I do," I say.

"Yeah, but not about the same things," he says through something like a laugh.

"That's because you are a guy-man."

"Probably," he says.

"I'm just noticing it more lately. I don't know why."

"Probably because you're aging, and as you hurtle toward decrepitude, your perspective changes."

"Yes," I deadpan in Stu fashion. "That must be it."

"Happy birthday, by the way."

"Thank you."

Across the street from Cap, while we're waiting for the light to change at Drexel, Stu pulls a card out of his backpack and hands it to me. I open it to find that he has traced his hand on a folded piece of white paper and colored it to look like a turkey wearing a party hat. Inside: *Happy birthday from Enoch, the wily birthday turkey.*

This he has written in crayon. Brown.

He's nodding and smiling at me when I finally look up.

"Did it all by myself," he says. "Sophie didn't help me at all."

"Very impressive. No matter what anyone says. In any language."

As we cross the street, I try to work the conversation around to Jen Auerbach, but I can't manage it naturally, so I give up for now.

We arrive at our classroom before Ethan. Stu checks his watch.

"I'm going to run to get coffee," he says. "You want anything?"

"World peace, a goat, and a chocolate chip scone."

"I'll see what I can do."

I set to work pulling notebooks, one folder, and the correct pen from my backpack, when someone taps my desk. It is Ethan, who smiles down at me as he says, "Happy birthday, Josie."

"You remembered."

"Of course."

"Thank you."

He walks to his desk, and I promptly fold myself over at the waist, shoulders on knees, and pretend to dig for something in my backpack, allowing the red that I know colors my face just now to abate. Judging by the heat, it doesn't. I keep digging. I must have seven pens in here. I should have more, though. I usually have more, which means someone is taking my pens, and I'm sure it's Kate.

I have no idea how long he has been standing there—

nor how long I have been contemplating Kate the Pen Thief—but when I finally look up, I see Stu, staring down at me, bemused, as he asks, "Can I help you?"

I promptly produce a pen.

"Found it," I say, and he just nods at me as he places a tissue-paper-wrapped scone on my desk.

"They were out of goats," he says.

"What about world peace?"

"The woman ahead of me got the last box."

"Was she wearing a sash?"

"She *was* wearing a sash. Was that significant?"

"It was Miss America. Did you get her autograph?"

"No. I was afraid she'd hold the pen funny, and it would just bug me all day," he says, adding a quick side-long glance for emphasis.

When class ends, I linger. I tell Stu I'm going to hang around for a few minutes and will catch up with him at Fair Grounds. I don't even make a pretense of stalling anymore, just collect my things, catch Ethan's eye, and wait until he too is packed up and ready to leave.

"Going to Fair Grounds?" I ask.

"I am, and thank you for waiting."

"Anytime."

We start out.

"So tell me about school, Josie. What's going on?" he asks.

"Which school?" I ask.

"Yeah, I guess I have to be more specific with you. Uh—both. Well, which do you prefer?"

"Both and neither, lately, but ultimately here."

"Really?"

"Usually, it's just a relief being home and decompressing in peace and quiet."

"Decompressing is always good. So tell me about home. What are your parents like? Are you close to them?"

"I'm close to my entire family," I say. "My parents and both older sisters."

"You're lucky," he says in a tone sounding slightly sad.

"You know, I know I am. Aren't you close to your family?"

"No, not really."

"I think I would shrivel up and slowly die without my family. Or I'd hope to."

"I'm in no danger of shriveling up and dying, but we're just not close. I think I can sum it up by saying we don't have much in common, and opposites don't attract. So," he says more cheerily, "back to your family. You have two older sisters?"

"I do," I say, and we talk about them and their names and ages and miscellaneous stats, of which Geoff is last, the rest of the way to Fair Grounds.

Opposites don't attract echoes in my head over tea and my second scone of the day, which Ethan buys me, though I tell him he does not need to. He says to consider it a birthday present. I opt not to tell him why I'd prefer a goat.

We join Stu and his pile of food and talk—through Ethan's one cup of coffee and then a little longer—about Columbus, music, Chicago, popcorn, movies. It's one of those lovely organic conversational chains, a word or phrase in one topic inspiring a whole new topic and so on. No long pauses interrupted only by *hmm, so, erm*.

And the whole time my attention is divided between the present exchange and *opposites don't attract*. Ethan and I are definitely not opposites, and I am growing a bit more comfortable with the idea that he and I just may be something more to each other . . . eventually.

CHAPTER TWENTY-FIVE

My birthday dinner is a misery, which is partially my fault. I insist on having it where we always have it—our club, Columbus Country Club, which is where Kate and Geoff's reception will be if I cannot find some way to prevent this wedding.

Kate spends the entire evening verbally visualizing, down to the last shrimp, exactly how the club will look on the evening of November eighth, when three hundred guests, gorgeously attired in tuxedos and evening gowns will mingle, dance, and toast the happy couple.

Three hundred guests. That's my whole class and one-fourth of Sophie's.

By the end of the evening, Mother has thrice admonished Kate to stop the wedding blather and at last resorts to a stern, "Katriane, that is enough. It is your sister's birthday."

Yes, I say thrice but only to inveterate speakers of Josie. If I said it at school, I definitely would have been stuffed in a locker before now. I would have deserved it and wouldn't have put up much resistance.

Mother gave us all French names in honor of her heritage. She only uses them when we've overstepped our boundaries. Naturally, I hear Josephine frequently, but it is rare to hear Katriane and rarer still to hear Maggie called Magdeleine.

I enjoy the sound of Katriane and further enjoy the chagrinned blush it produces in my sister's cheeks. I must see if I can make Mother use that name more frequently.

Kate has it coming. When I climbed into Ross and Maggie's car this evening, Ross said, "I'm glad you're riding with us. It'll give us a chance to hear more about this guy you like at Cap. I hear he bought you breakfast this morning. What's his name? Kate wouldn't tell us."

"No, it's nothing," I lie. "He's just a guy in one of my classes."

Judging by the quick glance Ross and Maggie shared, my lie failed to convince them, but they had the sensitivity to change the subject.

Ross turned on his radio, queued up to play "The Best of Times," and I hear,

Tonight's the night we'll make history,
Honey, you and I . . .

It was in Ross' car and to these very opening lines that I fell in love with Dennis DeYoung. I was eleven. He and Maggie were newly married, and, like tonight, I was riding with them to the club for dinner. Seconds after he turned the car on, Dennis DeYoung's glorious voice flowed through the speakers, and I fell in love. No doubt. No confusion. I just knew.

After that particular dinner, I found that Ross had slipped the CD *Paradise Theater* into my purse, and before I fell asleep that night, I wrote him a long, gushing thank-you note in which I used the words *mellifluous* and *ineffable*.

Mellifluous—Dennis DeYoung's voice.

Ineffable—my gratitude for *Paradise Theater*.

I was already nursing an eleven-year-old's crush on Ross. The gift of the CD only secured his place in my heart.

But even this song earlier tonight could not sufficiently extinguish my smoldering anger at Kate, who I then knew was telling my entire family every single thing I've been sharing with her in confidence. Everything except Ethan's name, as if that somehow counts as keeping my secret.

The night improves with dessert, but what night doesn't? We congregate at home in the living room, where everyone sings Happy Birthday as Mother carries in a tray of iced brownies Mrs. Easterday and I made earlier. Mrs. Easterday gave me a card too, and wrote in her perfect, teacher handwriting, *You're becoming a lovely young woman, Josie, one whom I am pleased to know.* She wished me a happy birthday and sealed the benediction with a kiss on my cheek.

Each of the brownies has a candle in it. I prefer brownies to cake, which makes Geoff say at the end of the song, "Brownies are cake-like. In fact, lots of cakes are as dense as brownies, so can you *really* say you prefer one to the other?"

"Yes," I say. "The same way I can *really* say I prefer Sophie Wagemaker to Emmy Newall. They're both girls, but they're different."

"Excellent," my dad says with a chuckle.

Later tonight, after everyone has gone home, and Kate has gone upstairs to work, I help my parents with the dishes and use a knife to scrape excess chocolate icing from the pan of brownies, which I wipe off with my finger and eat.

"On a scale of one to ten, Josie," my father begins, "one being poor and ten being excellent, how would you rate your sixteenth birthday?"

"Nine. A goat would have made it a perfect ten."

"It's important to always want something," Mother says.

"And on a scale of one to ten," he says, "one being poor and ten being excellent, how would you rate your mother's skill at parenting you?"

"Dad," I say, and smile at them as he wraps his arms around Mother's waist while she rinses the last dish at the sink.

"Come now, Josephine. Your mother requires feed-back."

"I'm giving myself a ten for putting up with you both," she says, and I quickly kiss both their cheeks, thank for them for a nice birthday, and say good night.

I have been in bed for about twenty minutes, trying to read but distracted by my mental replay of the day's events. Verbatim. My dad knocks on the door, waits for me to say *come in,* and sits on the edge of my bed, where he presents me with a small, wrapped package.

"It's something special," he says as I slip the heavy cream paper off to find a red leather journal with lined pages—extremely small lines, just as I like them.

"Dad."

"Now, Josie, I want you to listen to me. There is some work involved in this gift. I want you to use this journal daily and with intention." He touches the book as he speaks. "It is for you and you alone to record your thoughts and your experiences and your views on everything having to do with all the things going on in your life right now, the real things about you and your friends and school and Kate and your heart."

"I know she told you about"—I shrug—"certain things I've told her lately. And that should show you how she's changed as a sister."

"It doesn't matter what she told me. I want you to

write for you and about you, from the depth of you. We can talk about it if you want. Or not, if you don't. But I want you to write in it daily so that you have at least one safe place to record your most searching thoughts. This is important."

"Thank you," I say, and corroborate my gratitude with a kiss.

"You're a good girl, Josie. Most of the time."

After he shuts the door, I flip through the notebook a couple of times, fanning the pages to un-stick their gilt edges—I love that crisp, cracking sound—and I take a pen from the top drawer of my nightstand. And I pause, fully prepared to write. Legs crossed. Notebook open. Pen perfectly poised over the first gorgeous new page. And for what feels like ages, I stare at the paper until my eyes lose focus and the thing blurs into white fluff.

I blink a few times and finally write this:

> I find this very uncomfortable and wish my dad had just given me a sweater.

CHAPTER TWENTY-SIX

Saturday morning I receive my driver's license bearing a frighteningly accurate picture of me, and later drive home from Sutton Court. My dad and I ride home in occupied silence, a complicated session on his mind, my driver's license photo on mine.

Sunday night finds me at the kitchen table before dinner. I'm working on my Language Variation Project and need the uncluttered space of our long breakfast table for shuffling through papers and books. This project turns out, as I had predicted, to be extraordinarily easy, but begins, tonight, to bother me in a strange manner. It feels a little prickly, like a stiff thread on a seam I cannot quite locate.

At dinner, Geoff makes some remark about my being quiet, intended, I think, to draw me into a conversation or at least into the role of audience for one of his monologues. I don't even know if he's speaking when I say to my mother, "I'm done," and promptly carry my plate to the sink.

We understand silence in this house. My parents support it and never intrude, so Kate has no basis for complaint when later, after Geoff leaves, she barges into my room and calls me rude.

I walk past her to my bathroom, where I shut and lock both doors and sit on the closed lid of the toilet. I'll stay in here all night if I have to.

Soon I forget about her and soak in a steaming hot bath while trying to locate, without success, that stiff, prickly thread that bothers me so.

I continue my thread-searching efforts before, during, and after Sociolinguistics, when Ethan calls to me, stopping me at the door.

"You seem lost in thought today," he says. "Everything okay?"

sigh—good sigh—imperceptible good sigh

"It is, thanks."

"Headed to Fair Grounds?"

"Of course."

"Mind if I join you?"

"I never mind," I say, and walk with him outside into the first sunny, cool day of the season.

" . . . like this in Chicago . . . . lake effect . . . . but the winters . . . around here? Josie?"

We've come to the corner.

"Sorry," I say. "What was that?"

"I was asking what winters are like around here."

"Gray and slushy," I say.

We start to cross.

"You sure everything's okay?" he asks. "You seem distracted."

"Just thinking."

"About what?" Then he grins almost playfully as he asks me the single worst possible thing he could ask me, short of my age, which he already knows. "Penny for your thoughts."

sigh—disappointed sigh—imperceptible disappointed sigh

"Just, uh—actually I'm thinking about the Language Variation Project."

"Anything I can help with?"

"No, thanks. I'm just kind of writing it mentally."

"I do a lot of that when I run," he says. "But that's why I like to have a jogging partner. Good to bounce ideas off of."

"Huh," I say, and later write in my new journal:

Monday, October 6

I don't really need a jogging partner. Anyway, I've always thought couples who jog together are one boring step away from becoming couples who dress alike.

By Friday I realize I have not embraced the spirit

of this journal as my father intended. He asked me to write about real things, but here's what I've written so far:

Tuesday, October 7

Stu farted on the walk to Cap this morning, but I did not. He was not embarrassed, but I was for him. We both have boundary issues.

Wednesday, October 8

Walked with Stu and Ethan to Fair Grounds. They talked about soccer. No one farted.

Thursday, October 9

Had my eye exam today. Contacts will be in next week. Two sets—thank you, Kate—and I cannot wait for just the right occasion to show her how much I appreciate such a thoughtful gift.

Friday, October 10

[blank]

Then I say to my journal, out loud, "I'm out of things to write today." It holds me accountable, so I thought I should explain.

But, no, I'm not out of things to write, and it and I know this. And I swear this thing plagues me. I know its purpose in my life and that I have failed it—and my dad.

Great. I get an F in Journaling 101.

Later this evening, I position myself with some solemnity at my desk, open my journal, and write *Dear Ethan*. Here I pause, allowing my thoughts to stream through every encounter, every smile, every walk, and every word we've shared since the moment our eyes met across a crowded room.

> Dear Ethan,
>
> Do you believe in love at first sight? I didn't until I met you, but since then I've read some articles about the science behind it, and it appears to be a valid phenomenon—or valid experience if not phenomenon. I don't know the statistics of its frequency, but I can tell you that, to my knowledge, I am the only person I know it has ever happened to. I think—I believe—I'm nearly certain enough to say I know that it happened to me when I first saw you. Something happened. Something strange and exciting and wonderful happened, and, as I get to

know you, this something grows stranger and more exciting and more wonderful, because we are so alike, so connected in our similarities. You yourself even spoke of the connection we have the first time we walked to Fair Grounds—how we understand each other, how we speak the same language—well, I said that, or meant to. I thought it, anyway. You said you understand where I'm coming from and how rare that is. You're right—opposites don't attract.

"Whatcha writing?"

I jump half a foot and spin around in my chair to see Kate.

"Don't you ever knock?"

"What is it? A looooove note?"

"Shut up, by which I mean shut up."

"Oh, it is. Let me see."

"Get away," I say, slapping her hand as she reaches for my journal, which I quickly stash in my desk.

"Sorry," she says. "I'm sorry, Josie. I was only teasing."

"Well, it's not funny. And it's not a love note. I was just—writing about the day."

"Okay. Okay," she says, dropping with a bounce onto a corner of my bed.

"Do you want something?"

"Wow, are you in a bad mood."

"Well, what do you want, Kate? I'm kind of busy."

"How come you're not at the game tonight?" she asks about a football game at the high school.

"Cramps," I lie.

"Ah. That explains your mood."

"*You* explain my mood."

"Geez. All right. I'm going. I just found out from Mom that you were home, and I thought you might like to watch a movie with Geoff and me."

"Something about ticks, maybe? *The Tick of Oz? Tick-tanic*."

Kate starts to leave.

"*Ticks and Sensibility*."

She's out of my room, nearing the stairs.

"I know. I know," I call. "*Harry Potter and the Half-Blood Tick*."

I close the door, return to my desk, and finish my note.

> Someday, I will be brave enough to say these things to you in person. For now, I remain in happy, quiet contemplation over you and can say tonight that I just might love you. Or could someday.
>
> Love—eventually,
> Josie

Later I fall asleep content with my new journal used as my father intended it. I wish I had a red pen handy. I'd give tonight's entry an A.

CHAPTER TWENTY-SEVEN

We congregate this morning at Millicente's, a small bridal salon that takes customers by appointment only, and are offered croissants, orange juice, tea, and coffee in the cream-colored living room before being taken into the cream-colored fitting room where the alterations take place.

Millicente is Mrs. Millicente DeGraf, a French émigré with a round accent, sun-damaged skin, and hair the color of straw, expertly brushed off her face and flipped up at the shoulders. Married for the third time, she liked telling us this morning that her first husband was a boy; her second a mistake; and her third the great love of her life.

"*Pourquoi?*" I ask.

"*Mon coeur,*" she says. "*Il est à mon couer. San lui, une partie de moi est allée.*"

Why?

My heart. He is in my heart. Without him, a part of me is gone.

"Josie," Madison Orr says as warmly as she'd speak a puppy's name. She turns to my mother and Maggie, right there next to me, and says, "Listen to her. She's speaking *French*."

"You should hear me cipher," I say.

"Isn't she great? Don't you just love her?" Madison asks Mother and Maggie.

"I do," Mother says as Maggie shoots me a quick smile.

Madison looks more like Kate than I do, and always has. This resemblance, no doubt, is what has led her to the erroneous conclusion that I am as much her little sister as Kate's. And it is what persuades her to hug me now and kiss my cheek and turn back to Mother and Maggie to practically sing, "Love her."

We bridesmaids stand, in our elegant if ill-fitting gowns, stealing glances at our reflections but not daring yet to pose on the carpeted stage rising in front of the three-way mirror in the center of the room. We agree Kate should be the first. She, the progenitress of the Grand Entrance, has chosen to slip into her wedding dress in the living room and join us only after we've changed.

"Okay, ready?" she calls.

Madison quickly surveys us and catches me tugging at the bust of my dress to keep it up.

"Josie, are you—?" she begins, but turns to Mother. "Is Josie ready?"

"She is," Mother and I say in unison, which earns me a semi-reproachful glance, ameliorated by a hint of my mother's everlastingly patient smile.

"Ready!" Madison calls, and then we wait. One . . . two . . . three . . . four . . . sigh . . . five.

The door opens, and in walks Kate, slowly, as if the

invisible and ill-balanced crown on her head weighs eight pounds. Then, as if on cue, her ladies-in-waiting gasp before their cacophony of compliments ensues, and the words *beautiful* and *stunning* and *gorgeous* reverberate through the room. Even though we've seen Kate in her dress at previous fittings, she elicits this reaction from all of us each time, and I privately seethe that her visage should be wasted on Geoff, who I feel certain has no appreciation whatsoever for invisible crowns.

While the other bridesmaids surround Kate, who basks in their praise and returns it in near equal measure, Millicente DeGraf says to Mother, Maggie, and me, "*Elle fait une belle mariée.*"

"*Pas encore,*" I say to Mother's wholly disapproving glance and to Millicente's surprisingly polite response.

She merely bows her head toward me as if to say *Very well, then*. Then she claps her hands to get the attention of the room, calls for two seamstresses, orders us where to stand, and runs the rest of the morning in like fashion.

Millicente: *She makes a beautiful bride*.

Moi: *Not yet*.

I am the last bridesmaid to be fitted and receive a quick and concerned *hmm* from the rounder and grayer of the two seamstresses, who directs her eyes at the puckered bodice I still hold to keep from slipping. Even "padded for extreme lift," I am not sufficiently filling out the top of the dress. The seamstress produces two foam falsies from a shoebox and promptly—"Excuse me?!"—shoves them into my bra.

"Josephine," Mother cautions me, and before I can protest any more, the things are in place, and the seamstress begins pinching and pinning fabric.

"Oh, geez, how funny," Madison says to Kate. The two, still in their dresses, stand just behind me a few feet, leaning close together to talk and conspire, or so it seems by their reflections, which I assiduously watch.

"Yeah, she can be funny about stuff like that," Kate says.

"She was always funny about stuff like that," Madison confirms, and I feel my ears burn and corroborate their beet-red color with a quick glace at my own reflection.

Maggie and the other bridesmaids carefully slip their dresses off, with Mother's expert help, and begin changing back into their jeans and such. Meanwhile, Kate and Madison continue their confab, critically squinting my way every now and then.

"What about her hair?" Madison asks. "Ponytail? Up-do?"

"I haven't decided," Kate says.

I have, I want to say, but don't.

"What about cutting it?" Madison asks. "Have you thought about that? She'd look so cute with bangs."

I almost protest when Kate says, "No, she'll never do it." Thank you, Kate. "Plus I just couldn't handle the scene after the one she made about contacts."

You're the one who threw the fit. Again—wanted to say. Didn't.

"Contacts?" Madison asks, thrilling wide-eyed to the

idea. "Oh, good. I always thought you should do something about her glasses."

I'm getting really sick of the phrase *do something*.

"Done," Kate says. "I mean, her glasses are cute for every day."

"Oh, sure, but not a wedding."

"Well, not my wedding. They'll look ridiculous," Kate says. "I'm working on getting her ears pierced now. And the padded bra"—she points at my reflected bust—"was the best I could do for her figure."

"Are you aware that I am three feet away from you and not deaf?" I ask them both as I twist around, furious, and interrupt my seamstress's work.

"Josie, we're just talking," Kate says.

"About all of my *ridiculous* flaws. I know. I heard."

"No," Kate corrects me a bit more harshly than I think I deserved. "About *my* wedding and how *my* bridesmaids, including *my* sister, are going to look so that *no one* looks ridiculous."

"Everything okay here?" Mother asks, stepping closer.

"Fine," Madison says.

"No, it isn't," I protest. "You're both standing there picking me apart."

"No, we aren't," Kate says as Mother walks closer. "We're simply discussing how I want my bridesmaids to look on my wedding day."

"You didn't criticize any of them," I say, pointing. And as I talk, my throat starts to throb, and I grow even more irritated that Kate's about to make me cry. Here. In front of everyone. *And* my own reflection. "You didn't say you have to *do something* about their glasses and their hair and their figures."

"That's because I don't," Kate snaps at me.

"Enough," Mother says, looking deliberately at each one of us.

I turn back around so the seamstress can finish pinning the dress. Kate turns sideways to Madison and says, "I'd like to *do* something about her mouth as well."

"How about my hearing too?" I snap at her over my shoulder, and Kate whips around to face me and to say, "No, Josie, just your appearance and your mouth."

And when Mother scolds her with a stern, "Katriane," I am not remotely soothed. Especially since the only comeback I have is *shut up* in any of a number of useless languages.

But at least as Mother continues to address Kate, neither one of them notices when the seamstress hands me a crumpled tissue from her pocket, which I quickly use to dry my eyes and stash down the front of my dress—naturally, there's still room—before anyone sees.

I spend the remainder of my fitting pretending to find great interest in the tips of my shoes and trying unsuccessfully to ignore the lingering pain in my throat.

CHAPTER TWENTY-EIGHT

Sunday night I have trouble falling asleep. Kate has refused to apologize for what I call insults and she calls
wedding planning. She hasn't even acknowledged that
her remarks *were* insulting, making me feel doubly miserable as I stand in front of my dresser tonight, leaning
close to the mirror and attempting to evaluate the aesthetic difference between glasses on, glasses off.

Until yesterday, I thought no more of my glasses than
I did of my shoes. They are something I need and use
every day. But tonight, each time I put them on, I hear
one word in Kate's voice. *Ridiculous.*

My mood lightens considerably Monday morning, when
I spend all of Sociolinguistics practically channeling Sophie as I privately gush over the perfection of Ethan
Glaser. Right down to his gorgeous wire-frame glasses.
No one, not even Kate, would presume to tell him he
needed to change a single thing about his appearance, no
matter the occasion.

By the end of class I am determined to fight for my right to choose my own form of vision correction, but I change my mind during dinner, after Mother informs me my contacts arrived in the mail that day.

"I put them upstairs on your desk," she says to me.

"Oh, good," Kate says, sounding both relieved and excited.

It's just the four of us for dinner tonight. Geoff's hanging upside down in some dark old belfry near the river. Or working late. I think Kate said working late.

"Josie, go put them on," she says. "I am dying to see how you look in them."

I remove my glasses.

I set them on the table.

I look at Kate.

"I look like this in them," I say.

She giggles when Dad says, "Excellent." Then she adds, "Well, after dinner then."

"Tomorrow," I say.

"Tomorrow morning," Kate says.

"Tomorrow night."

"Tomorrow before dinner," she says.

"After dinner."

"Josie," she nearly whines.

"Okay, after the salad but before dessert," I say.

"Josie," Kate says, sighing and quitting a game I was enjoying. "Just put them in before dinner tomorrow," and I concede with, "Fine," and Kate hijacks the rest of our dinner conversation with topics such as monogrammed stationery, personalized church programs, and the global televising of her vows on NBC. Something like that. I stopped listening when she mentioned inviting the Queen. No, *being* the Queen. I think that's what she said. Or what I *thought* she said.

Monday, October 13

Kate was more fun before she started planning this wedding. (I pause to consider the events that brought her to such a fate.) For which I blame Geoff.

Tuesday evening she bursts through the back door, practically shouting the rest of the week's schedule to a colleague over the phone. "Sorry," she mouths to Mother and me before starting up the back stairs.

I am chopping tomatoes for a salad when Kate rushes back down the stairs, saying, "Hang on, hang on, hang on," into the phone.

"Josie," she says to me in much the same tone she's been using to her colleague. "Contacts. Dinner. Go."

I arch my eyebrows in exaggerated displeasure at my mother, who returns, without comment, to whisking oil and vinegar in a large measuring cup.

I take my time. I finish chopping the tomato. Then I set the table. Kate returns to the kitchen, dressed comfortably in jeans and a white top, and before she turns apoplectic at the sight of me in my glasses still, I tell her, "I'm going," and hurry up the stairs to my bedroom.

There, I combine my two sets of lenses—a clear one in my left eye, and a dark gold-colored one in my right. Technically, the color I ordered at the optometrist's last week is called *warm honey brown,* but it is the color of whole-grain mustard, which I think matches rather well with tonight's dinner of turkey burgers and battle.

Downstairs, I take my place at the kitchen table and promptly lower my eyes for Dad's grace.

Amen.

Then I stare bug-eyed at Kate as she begins the riveting details of the manifold ways to secure one's veil on one's head for one's Big Incomprehensible Wedding.

"Maggie seems to think the best way is to put a little bit of hair in a ponytail here," she says, touching the top of her head.

"Uh-huh," I say too enthusiastically.

"But I don't know. I mean, if it slips, then I look completely stupid, but Maggie says—"

As she continues, Mother passes me the salad, notices immediately, and sighs disapprovingly at me.

"Josephine," she says quietly.

And not wanting to leave Dad out of the loop, I glance over at him as I pass the bowl, but he sets the thing down, folds his hands in his lap, and simply waits for the inevitable.

" . . . and I know there's a clip on the veil already, but I was thinking," Kate says, "that if we ask one of the seamstresses at Millicente's to add a comb, a small comb, I'd be—"

Boom . . . goes the shot across Kate's bow.

"A small comb. Go on," I say.

"Jos— Mother! Josie! Take those out!"

"You wanted to see what I look like in contacts. Here I am."

"Josie, *er*! Take those out!"

"But then I'll have to wear my glasses," I say, "and we all know how *ridiculous* you think I look in those."

"I didn't— You're not—you're not wearing those at my wedding," she says, pointing across the table at me.

"First you say I have to wear them. Now you say I can't. I really wish you'd make up your mind."

"You little monster!"

"Josephine, Katriane," my parents caution almost simultaneously.

"You're the one who wanted me to be *pretty* for your wedding," I say, startling even myself as I hurl the word *pretty* at her.

"That's not— You can't—you can't wear those!"

"Oh, I think you know very well that I can and that I will."

"Josie! Oh!"

"Just wait until I get my ears pierced and you see the earrings I've picked out." I look over at my mother. "They're pigs in bondage."

"Josie!" Kate slaps the table.

"Kate, settle yourself," Dad says.

"Settle myself?! She's going to ruin my wedding just like she ruined Maggie's!" she practically screams as she storms up to her bedroom, and I take a bite of turkey burger and privately triumph as Mother calls out, "Ka-triane."

Mother puts ketchup, soy sauce, Worcestershire, breadcrumbs, hot sauce, and lemon juice in these. They don't need whole-grain mustard, but the mustard was a nice flourish, nonetheless.

"She ha i cuh-ing," I say.

"She had it coming?" my father asks. "Why is that?"

I finish chewing and swallow before I say, "She's been picking at how I look for weeks now." I turn to Mother. "You heard it."

"She has been . . . unusually critical," Mother says. "Kate has very definite ideas about how she wants you to look for her wedding."

"She's been insulting. And I don't like it. And I don't like it that she hasn't even noticed how hurtful she's been."

"So," Dad says, pointing at my eyes, "you did this."

"I knew the colored pair would come in handy one day."

"Well, that day is over now. You've had your turn,"

he says without the slightest trace of condemnation. "I want you to go apologize to your sister for your part in tonight's contest. Your mother and I will talk to Kate later."

"Yes, sir," I say, and on my way past his chair, he stops me by taking my hand and saying, "And when you return to this table, I would like your eyes to be the same color."

"Okay," I say, and as I start up the stairs, my mother calls out, "Blue."

Darn.

For the record, I did not ruin Maggie's wedding. She had taken to calling me darling around that time, and I asked her to stop because *darling* is a word grandparents and great-aunts who give you two dollars and mints for your birthday use. Not sisters. Not equals. *Darling* in the language of Family means *cute enough to be observed but not to be taken seriously*.

She ignored my request, even when I wrote a list of eight objections to the word, which she called darling and displayed on her refrigerator. This, coupled with my role as *junior* bridesmaid, vexed me to the point of torment. My job entailed herding a flock of small, sticky flower girls here and there and managing all their hundreds of grubby little hands reaching for every single food and utensil at the rather long buffet. Maggie understood my aversion to all things—and children—gooey, but declined my petition for a different role in the ceremony.

So at her wedding reception, I told all of her new in-laws that I was her daughter from a previous marriage and that, "you understand, we really don't like to talk about my real father, considering all the pending lawsuits."

I might have mentioned an outstanding warrant.

Or two.

Apparently, some of the in-laws bought it and spread it through the in-law grapevine, ending with Ross' parents, who hazarded a few worried questions the next time their new daughter-in-law came for dinner.

Ross and Maggie laugh about it now, but Maggie sufficiently scolded me at the time, and my penance was writing letters of apology to a handful of those in-laws, who, Maggie later told me, found my notes and the whole situation just darling.

Kate is not in her bedroom or her bathroom. Or mine.

I grow increasingly irritated as I walk through the upstairs looking for her, but she's not anywhere, which is probably good since I've lost the spirit of repentance.

In my bathroom, I re-organize my lenses. The yellow ones really are bizarre, and I'll save them for Halloween, or for distracting opponents at volleyball games.

As I leave the bathroom, I adjust the newly inserted clear lens a bit with just the tip of my finger, blink twice, inhale, stop breathing and prepare to die—right there—from the sight of my desk drawer, slightly open, which is not how I left it.

Text to Stu and Sophie, 6:42 p.m.
Kate has stolen a deeply personal page from my journal!!!

But before I hit SEND, I delete the text with a shaking hand. They would ask about its content, something I would not want to share with anyone but . . . Kate. The Kate I used to know, Kate before there was anything in the world better than her brushing my hair and making up stories about birds and angels, Kate, who I could communicate with by mere looks while she carries on a phone conversation about work. Kate before she became bride-to-be-Kate. Kate before Geoff.

I could almost cry.

Except that there's no time for that—now that the war has begun.

CHAPTER TWENTY-NINE

Dinner is nightmarish.

When I return to the table, I find Kate happily gloating by pretending she is no longer angry with me and forgiving me with, "Oh, Josie, that's okay," when I say, "Kate, I'm sorry I upset you."

As I slip into my seat, I add, "I'll pay you back for the colored lenses."

"That's very considerate," Mother says.

"She doesn't have to," Kate says. "You don't have to, Josie. Have fun with them. I really just don't want to see them at the wedding."

"You won't," I say.

What else can I do but concede?

"Josie, how's everything at Cap lately? You haven't said much about it," she says.

"It's fine."

"Now, I know you're taking history and religion. But I can't remember the name of that third class. What is it again?"

"It's a soc class."

"Which one?"

"Introduction to Sociolinguistics." I turn to my dad in an effort to ignore the giant crow that is Kate. "My Language Variation Project is coming along. I have forty-one examples of how 'shut up' is used to express different meanings. I only needed thirty, but its prevalence made it easy to collect more, so now I'm starting to analyze the differences, the intended meanings, the real meanings. Actually, I'm almost done."

"That does sound interesting. Tell me about that," Dad says, and for the next few minutes, he and I talk about the evolution of words and how definitions change from group to group and also within distinct groups.

At a natural pause in our conversation, Kate chimes in with, "Stu's in that class too, right?"

"That's right," I say.

"You know, I don't think I have him or Sophie on my Facebook page. I should add them."

"Sure. I'll give you their e-mail addresses," I say, because there's nothing else I can do.

Later, as we're clearing the dishes, she whispers to me, "Your room, soon as we're done."

I think we wash the dishes in record time.

* * * * *

Upstairs, she follows me so closely I'm sure she can feel the heat of anger emanating from my body. She closes the door, and I shove my finger in her face.

"I can't believe how cruel you're being. You never used to be like this."

"Oh, please," she says, pushing past my finger and lowering herself onto the edge of my bed. "What were the contacts if not cruel?"

"There's a world of difference between antagonism and cruelty, Kate."

"So you admit you're being antagonistic?"

"Are you admitting you're being cruel?"

"Josie." Kate sighs. She softens a little when she says, "I don't want to show this Ethan your letter."

"Good," I say, and plant myself in my desk chair, arms tightly folded across my so-called chest. "I'll wait here while you get it."

"I'm not giving it back."

"What?"

"Josie, look, I have no idea how else to keep you from saying and doing the things you've said and done lately that are driving me crazy. Geoff said I need a little—"

"What?!"

"—leverage in our current relationship, so that's why I took the letter."

"I knew he was behind this. You never would have done this on your own."

"I'll give it back to you at the wedding."

"Don't take it there."

"I'll give it back to you in private unless you pull one more stunt like tonight's contacts. Then I will find out from Stu who Ethan is, and I will give him this letter."

"I'll just tell Stu not to tell you."

"Then I'll find a different source. I'll call the professor, make up some story. I'll find out, Josie, and you know it."

"I cannot believe you've become this kind of person. You never used to be like this."

"Neither did you."

"I am merely reacting to you. You're the one changing to suit some guy. Some guy who's not even right for you."

"Geoff and I are getting married, and it's time you accept that," she says with the edge returning to her voice. "This is my wedding. It's not a game. It's not some party. It's my wedding, and it's important to me and to Geoff, and I want it to be perfect. And I *am* going to marry him, and he *is* going to be part of this family, and we're both sick of all your remarks and stunts that you think are so cute and clever." I narrow my eyes into my best, angriest stare as Kate continues. "So from now on, at showers, at fittings, when Geoff's over, I want you to be pleasant and supportive and happy. In *every* language you speak. And if you can't be these things, then be quiet, or I make a few phone calls and mail the letter."

She stands, starts to leave.

At the door, she says, "It's just insurance. That's all. Like I said, you can have it back at the wedding. Understand?"

"*Je comprends,*" I say, and she leaves.

Tuesday, October 14, 8:02 p.m.

I hate Kate.

Tuesday, October 14, 11:17 p.m.

I never thought I'd say that—that I hate one of my sisters. I've never said it to anyone even semi-playfully, the way friends tell Sophie they hate her. "You're so beautiful, I hate you." I always assumed the second half of this alleged compliment was merely an expression of jealousy, not the actual expression of hatred. But now I wonder if I've gotten the translation wrong. I wonder now if there is some measure of truth in these words.

I

Hate

You

Maybe, deep within their hearts, some girls—
friends of Sophie's, for example—are so consumed
with jealousy over her beauty that they cannot, at
times, contain it, and it spills out as hatred, which
they disguise with humor and whitewash with praise.

Or maybe it doesn't spill out. Maybe they say it
because they choose to, because if they don't, they
will hurt so much that they believe the only way to
ease their pain is to cause a little of it in Sophie.
But does that give them the right to say it?

I hate this journal.

Wednesday, October 15, 1:42 a.m.

I don't hate Kate. I am angry. I feel trapped
by her. I am hurt to discover that my own sister
would threaten to humiliate me in this way simply
for what she's calling leverage. And I'm completely
irked with her for keeping me up this late, sitting
here dissecting my feelings in this demanding
journal and stewing over the control she has in our
relationship now. But, no, I don't hate Kate. Did it
feel like hatred when I wrote that? Yes. Initially.
Was it? No. Just a strong and temporarily convincing

emotion—a burst of anger, masking—I don't know—
frustration, sadness, misery. It's easier to hate
than to hurt.

I'm relieved I did not say the words to her. I
understand now why my parents dissuade us from
using that word. I think it would be very difficult to
take back.

I think "I love you" would be too.

But Emmy Newall is wrong. Love and hate aren't
remotely close in the spectrum of emotions. She's
either gotten the meanings wrong—or she's wrong
about how she actually feels about Nick.

I put my pen down.

I am done with, i.e., exhausted by, my journal tonight,
but I am not done stewing, and stare for some time at
the fuzzy, white nothingness of my ceiling, until some-
time between 2:15 a.m. and falling asleep, my stewing
turns fruitful—even producing a wicked grin that rivals
Kate's of late, and I set my alarm for 5:55 a.m.

CHAPTER THIRTY

I stand in the empty, dry shower for ages. Hours. Feels like hours. If necessary, I will miss Sociolinguistics. If necessary, I will stand here all day.

Seconds tick by. Then minutes. Then more. Then . . . I hear the door close.

I think I will pass out from lack of oxygen, but I know if I breathe, I'll laugh, and that will ruin everything, and I refuse to waste this moment. Three more seconds. Two. One, then, slowly I pull the shower curtain back, and *click-flash!*

Kate screams.

I run!

In my bedroom, I shut and lock the door and download the photo onto my computer before Kate has a chance to pull up her underwear and flush. And before she can pound on my bedroom door—because neither of us at this point wants to involve Mother or Dad—I open it and proudly show her the photo I have entitled: *Queen Kate on the Throne.*

I click my computer off just as she lunges for it.

"You little monster," she hisses.

"Give me my letter back, and I'll delete it."

"Delete it, and I'll give it back."

"Uh, no," I say lightly.

She folds her arms tight across her chest.

"So now what?"

"Stalemate," I say. "Have Geoff define it for you."

"I know what it means."

"And you say you're not gifted."

"Josie," she snaps through clenched teeth.

"You show one person that letter—one person—and that photo goes viral. It goes on your cocktail napkins at the reception. Coasters. Matchbooks. It goes on postcards." Four fingers up. "I'll even print posters of it and give them as Christmas presents to Aunt Toot and Mrs. Easterday."

"Eh," she practically grunts. "I wasn't—I wasn't really going to show anyone that letter. Unless I had to. I was just keeping it for insurance."

"Well, consider this your new policy."

"Josie—erh!" she huffs, and storms out of my room.

Once she's gone, I bring the photo back up on my computer and lose all my breath laughing into the pillow I have pressed against my face so that I don't wake my parents. I had not noticed it at first, but Kate—God bless you, Kate—is not only on the toilet, but she is picking her nose. One small part of me actually hopes she gives my letter to Ethan. It would be such a shame not to share this photo with the world.

Oh, geez. If it's possible to pull muscles from laughing, I may need a neck brace.

By breakfast, fatigue sets in. I am too tired to care that the cereal box is on the counter instead of in the cupboard, where it belongs. I just grab it and dump a pile in a bowl, which causes my mother to ask, "Are you feeling all right?"

"Just tired," I say. "I didn't sleep well. Lots of things on my mind."

"Anything you want to talk about?"

"Dad's already making me write about it."

"Is it helping?"

"It's hard," I admit.

"Ah," Mother says as she cleans up the crumbs I've made. "Then it's helping."

It doesn't feel like it's helping. Earlier—a couple times, anyway—it felt good, relieving, to write, almost as if the mere act of putting pen to paper legitimized me. Now, for the same reasons, it feels as if the problem worsens or becomes harder or more unbearably burdensome than I imagined. And aside from the letter, I haven't written a thing about Ethan. Because it will be worse or harder or more unbearably burdensome if I do.

I drop myself into the backseat of Stu's car and grumble good morning.

"Late night?" Stu asks.

"Didn't sleep well," I say.

"It shows, even through your glasses," Sophie says.

"Sophie," Stu says with quiet caution.

"What? It does," she says, and then produces, from her backpack, a tube of under-eye concealer and gives me explicit instructions on how to apply the stuff.

After she exits the car, I squish a bit of the sticky stuff between two fingers, shudder some at its thick gooeyness and determine to go to bed early for the rest of my life if this is the only way to conceal dark circles.

I dread walking into class this morning. I don't even want to see Ethan and merely glance politely in his direction when I do. I feel that somehow he knows about my journal page. He can tell by looking at me that it's out, that I have feelings for him, and that, by writing that letter, which is now in Kate's custody, I've somehow stripped myself of the protection of secrecy.

He knows.

Everybody knows.

"Are you all right today, Josie?" he asks as I take my seat in class.

"Just tired," I say, and make myself busy with books

and folders and pens, and that is the last time I even look at him this morning.

After class, I practically run out of the room, leaving Stu, for the first time ever, hurrying to catch up with me about a block from Fair Grounds, where he grabs my elbow to slow us down and says, "Okay. What's wrong?"

"I had a fight with Kate last night. I've got a lot on my mind."

"That's it?"

"It was a big fight."

"The wedding?"

"A bunch of stuff."

"You want to talk about it?"

"Talking about it only makes it worse," I nearly snap. Then I sigh. "Sorry."

"Josie, what's going on?" he asks, putting his hand on my arm and worriedly searching my eyes with his.

We are stopped outside of Fair Grounds. I look around nervously.

"I'm tired of this place. Can we go to Juliana's?" I name a less popular coffee shop, across the street and east by a block.

"Sure. On the condition that you yell at me every time I ask if you're okay."

"I'm sorry," I say, half smiling, and we start walking. "I really didn't sleep well last night. Almost not at all."

"Why?"

"Kate and I got in a huge fight. Huge, and she's just—I don't understand her anymore."

"Why do you say that?"

"I'll tell you exactly why. Because Geoffrey Stephen Brill is changing her. She does whatever he says. I can't stand it. The stop sign." I mime it. "Spaghetti. Insurance policies, and Kate goes along with all of it."

"In the words of more than one songwriter, Josie, 'Love changes everything.'"

"That's your explanation?"

"I don't really know what we're talking about."

"Kate."

"Not Geoff and insurance?"

"Kate."

"Well, what do stop signs and spaghetti have to do with her?"

"What do song lyrics have to do with any of it?"

"Josie," Stu says, holding his shoulders in a huge shrug. "I need subtitles here. Or footnotes."

I expel a breath I didn't know I was holding and I ask, "Signal flags?"

"That might help. I need the one that says 'Get me out of this conversation with Josie. Send big men with large hats.'"

"Large hats?"

"I think that would be a cool message to send with flags."

"So back to Kate."

"And clarity," he says as we start walking.

"I don't know what to do about her," I say. "About Geoff. About the wedding. About anything—except, apparently, these enormous blue circles I have under my eyes today."

"You can hardly notice them."

"You did."

"Yeah, actually they're huge," he says, smiling some and shooting me a quick sideways glance. He bumps my elbow with his. "You just look a little tired today, Josie. Not bad. Maybe sleep some this afternoon. Things will probably be clearer then. For all of us."

"Thanks," I say, and we walk the rest of the way to Juliana's in silence.

Along the way, too tired to talk, I consider Sophie's many love affairs and their inevitable tragic outcomes. I consider Stu's many love affairs and their inevitable fizzling out. I consider Ross and Maggie's perfect harmony. I consider my dad with his arms wrapped around my mother's waist in the kitchen. I consider Ethan standing in front of the class, expertly teaching. And I consider Kate and Geoff cooking spaghetti, and before long I consider the very meaning of the word *love,* which suddenly feels massive, unwieldy, intimidating.

I wish I had my journal with me—that rotten, demanding, affirming, awful journal. I'd write: *Kate changes everything.* No, I mean love. *Love changes every-*

thing. Geez, that was Freudian. I'm glad I didn't write that down.

Later, I fall asleep last period in my government class for a second or two, waking when my head bobs forward. Lots of people fall asleep in my government class, some shamelessly, with their heads resting on their folded arms on top of their desks. Old Mr. Bloom appears not to care, appears to struggle against his own somnolence, exacerbated, no doubt, by his monotone voice explaining the relationship between land, labor, and capital for the four thousandth time.

"What is with you today?" Emmy practically snaps at me at my locker. And because I am too tired to translate both her words and her tone, I respond in irritation.

"I'm tired. Aren't I allowed to be?"

"All right. Sorry."

We don't speak on the way to the locker room.

Volleyball practice does not revive me, but further wears me out. I get hit twice in the face—not bad—by balls I just plain miss. At the end of practice, Jen bounces up to me and laces her fingers through mine.

"So I've been thinking about something you said," she says, smiling her big round smile at me.

"About what?"

"About Stu."

"What about Stu?"

"You know," she says, "if I like him or not."

"Uh-huh," I say.

"And what would you say if I said I do?"

"Uh . . . I don't know."

"Josie, come on. I thought you'd be happy."

"Oh, yeah. Sure. Jen, I'm so tired."

"I know. You really look it." She squeezes my hands before saying, "Okay, so don't say anything to him, but find out if he likes me, okay? I mean, since he's your cousin and all, I thought you could ask him so that it doesn't seem like I like him."

"Sure."

"You're so fabulous, I love you," she says, and hugs me, and I really do not have any energy left for anything else today.

Stu drives me home, and I say nothing on the way other than an apology for my continued fatigue. I collapse on top of my bed and sleep until almost six o'clock, waking with slightly puffy eyes and a faint imprint of my watch on my left cheek.

A quick splash of cold water and a readjustment of my ponytail does little to improve my appearance, but at least the circles are gone, and I feel better than I have all day, so I give no thought to puffiness or sleep scars as I walk downstairs or as I open the front door when someone rings the bell.

And as if by magic—black magic—I promptly turn into a statue the moment I see him, standing at my front door, smiling at me, holding, of all things, a purse. My purse. I think he says something.

I.

Cannot.

Move.

I don't know how long I've been standing here, frozen. Long enough for Kate to enter the foyer and ask, "Josie, who's at the door? Josie?"

She squints a little at me—irked, but what's new—before she opens the door more fully, and he introduces himself to her.

"Hi, I'm Ethan Glaser," he says. "I'm Josie's sociology instructor at Cap."

CHAPTER THIRTY-ONE

Peripherally, I see a smile grow gorgeously across Kate's face—the kind of smile that usually precedes a bit of wicked laughter, but Kate exercises impressive control and just basks in satisfaction.

"Instructor? Ethan Glaser?" she asks, then directs her eyes at me for a second, just long enough to tacitly harass me.

"Ethan," he says, and they shake hands as Kate invites him in.

I still haven't moved. Can't seem to move anything but my head, enough to watch Ethan step inside and extend my purse to me.

"Josie, you left this in class this morning. I'm sorry. I haven't had a chance to get it here sooner."

"Uh-huh," comes out of my mouth, and I manage to raise one arm to take my purse from him.

"'Thank you,' Josie would say if she hadn't just woken up," Kate says.

"Long day?" Ethan asks me. "You did seem a little tired in class this morning."

"Uh-huh." I clear my throat. "Uh—yes."

"I don't want to keep you," Ethan says. "I've probably interrupted dinner."

"Ladies, what's going on out here?" my dad asks, entering the hall from the kitchen. "Oh, excuse me. I didn't know you were expecting company. Hugh Sheridan," he says, reaching to shake Ethan's hand.

"Ethan Glaser."

"Ethan is Josie's sociology instructor at Cap," Kate says.

"Ah. Josie talks about your class all the time," Dad says. "I know she enjoys it."

"Thank you. I enjoy her insights."

"What brings you here, Ethan?"

He explains. Then Dad asks, "Ethan, have you ever seen an authentic eighteenth-century barber bowl?"

"No, I haven't," Ethan says, and that's when Kate leans close to him—she puts her hand right on his arm—and she whispers, "It's a blood-letting bowl."

"Is it? I'd love to see one," Ethan says, and my dad brightens.

"Well, then you have returned a purse to the right house," Dad says, leading Ethan—one hand on his back—to his study for the medical antiques tour.

Kate follows, intentionally bumping me with her elbow as she passes, and whispers, "We'll talk later."

In perfect synchrony, we narrow our eyes at each other, but Kate wins the contest by adding that fiendish grin to her gaze.

Then I bolt—BOLT—up the stairs.

In record time, I wash my face, apply what little makeup I own—eyeliner and mascara, concealer, and note to self: Thank Sophie for showing me how to use this—re-comb my hair and secure it with a black band that matches the black T-shirt I scramble into. And just before rushing downstairs again, I grab my new padded bra and pause long enough to consider donning it. Hold it up. Stand sideways.

Maybe.

Oh, forget it.

I toss the thing back into my underwear drawer and stroll down the front staircase as if Ethan's arrival were both routine and insignificant. But he is gone. I lean into Dad's study and smell the light remnants of Ethan's cologne lingering in the air, but apparently I have missed him. The house is quiet, and I find myself relaxing neck and jaw muscles I had unintentionally flexed.

In the kitchen, I find Mother chopping an onion, which promptly obliterates the memory of Ethan's sweet scent from my mind.

"Need help?" I ask

"You could keep me company," she says, and I hop up on one of the bar stools at the far end of the room.

I start spinning slowly, soothed by the repetitive, near-hypnotic motion.

"You were awfully tired today," Mother says. "Do you feel okay?"

"I was up late. Too late."

"Doing what?"

"Contemplating," I say.

"Anything you'd like to share with me?"

"The complexities of all relationships on Earth."

I start pushing myself a little faster.

"That *would* keep one up late," Mother says, and I catch a glimpse of her smiling at me as I zip round and round on the stool. "Which particular relationships do you find most vexing?"

"Ethan Glaser," Kate says as she enters the kitchen by the back stairs, with Ethan and Dad following. "This is my mother . . ."

Er . . . *crash!*

That would be me, falling off the barstool as the introductions are made.

"You know my daughter, of course," Mother says, one hand gesturing to the twisted mess of me on the floor.

Dad leans close to Ethan and adds a somber, "We normally don't mention it in public, but she *is* gifted, you know." To me he calls, "How's the floor routine coming?"

"The dismount's not exactly where I want it yet," I say, rising, brushing myself off, ignoring the raging embarrassment that I'm certain has turned my face scarlet. I can't even tell if I've hurt anything.

"Well, the dismount is the hardest part," Dad says as Ethan asks if I'm okay.

"Yes, thank you. Clumsy and mortified, but fine," and as I gather my limbs and thoughts, I miss some important exchange, because when I turn my attention back to the other end of the kitchen, Mother, Dad, and Kate are drinking wine with Ethan. Drinking wine and talking. Drinking wine, talking, and laughing. And, wait, when did Geoff get here, and how can anyone be that entertained in his presence when all the man can talk about is ticks?

I wander to the sink and busy myself pouring a glass of water. As I sip, I try to find a contextual handle in their conversation, something I can grasp and process that will allow me entry. But nothing makes sense. Geoff and Ethan speak quickly, their voices rising, rising, then laughter. Dad says something about Chicago, adds a sweeping gesture, then more loud, happy chatter. Kate says, "And there I am . . ." And Geoff joins her to say, in two-part harmony, something that sounds like, "no kings mettle in thespian tea." And over the roar of laughter, I nervously sip water, stunned and perplexed that the five of them are speaking a language I do not know. Stunned, perplexed, and irritated. I do not like this one little bit.

My shock turns to abject panic when I hear Kate ask Ethan, "Are you seeing anyone? I have a friend you would love."

And suddenly Madison Orr is on the phone and a foursome date is arranged for the upcoming weekend, and I'm at the door, shaking Ethan's hand as he leaves and offers me this benediction:

"See you Friday in class, Josie."

＊ ＊ ＊ ＊ ＊

After the blur that is dinner, I walk almost robotically to my room, lower myself onto my bed, and direct my eyes to the abstraction of the floor. There, I replay, with wretched accuracy, the alien conversation from earlier—the one involving Mother, Dad, Geoff, Kate, and Ethan. The adults. I swallow hard. Everyone but me.

The words were familiar, but the rhythm felt foreign. And the gestures. And the laughing. In that way. It seemed as if it were the language of a private club I was not asked to join.

"Oh, for G-d's sake, Josie," Kate says as she walks in, scaring me into jumping up quickly and snapping at her, "Don't you ever knock?"

She shuts the door behind her.

"He is twenty-six years old," she says.

"So?"

"He's too old for you."

"Now, yeah. In a few years he won't be."

"Josie, come on."

"No, you come on. You know how I feel about him, but there in front of me you set him up with Madison."

"Madison is his age. My age. Our age."

"It was cruel, no matter how old you are."

"Josie, enough."

"Four weeks ago you completely understood how I feel. We talked about it right here in this room."

"Four weeks ago I thought you were talking about a college kid."

"Four weeks ago the only thing that was different was that you didn't know Ethan's age. Nothing else has changed." Kate puffs out a laugh, and my face flushes hot. "How can you stand there laughing at me?"

"Because it's funny, Josie."

"I can't believe you're saying that."

Again, that puff—that dismissive, airy kind of smirk.

"You have a crush on your teacher," she says.

"It's more than that."

"It's a crush." *Puff.* "Ross, Dennis DeYoung, Ethan Glaser." She ticks them off on her fingers. "Crushes all."

"Yeah, maybe Ross and Dennis. But how do you know I'm not in love with Ethan? Why is this one a crush? Why isn't this one different?"

"Okay. Then tell me what love is."

"It's—*uh*." Now it's my turn to puff.

"It's a crush. Frame his picture and put it there," she says, pointing to Dennis DeYoung on my desk. "And I love it. Because it makes you just like everyone else. And trust me," she says as she walks to the door. "It makes that letter you wrote even more valuable for the *darlingness* factor. Think global embarrassment."

"Uh!" I say after she closes the door, and it's a full-body *uh*! Jaw and fists clenched, shoulders shuddering. Then I act. Within seconds I take my seat at my desk, bring up her wedding photographer's site, hack into her account on the third attempt at her half-witted password—kate&geoffbrill—and upload *Queen Kate on the Throne* in the file that reads *Reception Slide Show*.

Emotionally paralyzed somewhere between rage and satisfaction, sadness and determination, embarrassment and confidence, I look across the room at my journal. But I make no movement toward it.

Its very existence irritates me more than sounds and smells and seams and bugs, and if it actually started speaking to me—*"Jooosieee. Jooosieee. Here I aaa-aam. Come and tell me every scrumptious detail about your disconnected little life"*—I would not be surprised.

I think my mother finds me distracted lately and wants to ask but doesn't, which I appreciate. I'll tell her everything—almost everything—once I'm ready, once I've worked out what I want to say and how to say it. Couple years from now. Or maybe never.

Did I just say disconnected? Oh. No, my journal did. My word was distracted.

Finally, I open it up and write:

Wednesday October 15, 8:17 p.m.

What is the nature of love?

I don't answer. I want my journal to do it for me.

CHAPTER THIRTY-TWO

When I enter class Friday morning, Ethan greets me with a smile, emphasized by raised eyebrows that seem pleased to say *I've been to your house now and know where you live.* Two days ago I would have thrilled—maybe even swooned—over this confirmation of intimacy. It is intimate, after all, when two people share knowledge or history or even jokes that few if any others are in on. Or speak a language all their own. But today I do not thrill or swoon. Today, I shrink—collapsing inward on myself, or wanting to, anyway.

I smile back briefly, politely.

"You okay?" Stu asks, leaning over a little.

"Yes. Why?"

"You look like you're about to dissect a fetal pig."

"Don't you think if I were about to dissect a fetal pig, I'd be vomiting about now?"

"How do you know I wasn't suggesting you look like you're about to vomit?"

"*Are* you suggesting I look like I'm about to vomit?"

"No. Bad but entertaining metaphor. Let's start again. You okay?"

"Yes," I say, trying not to smile, which always amuses Stu. "Why?"

"You look like you just realized you're not wearing pants."

"You honestly think I could get this far from home before realizing I'm not wearing pants?"

"No, I don't. That's the irony. That's why I had to ask if you're okay."

I concede my thanks with a smile he shares as I say, "I'm fine, thanks."

Class begins. For the first few minutes, I take unnecessary notes just for someplace to put my eyes other than on—I gulp—my teacher. When I finally hazard a glance, I see him as I've always seen him—handsome, bright, perfect. And today, handsome, bright, and perfect turn me small, pink, and miserable.

"Think about it," Ethan says to the class. "If I stood here not speaking but merely handed you copies of my lecture and demanded that all questions and answers be submitted in writing, every one of you would drop this class. It would be weird. A weird relationship. Awkward."

I nod.

"Language transcends awkwardness," he says. "Now

think about the number of times I've seen you guys outside of class. We've talked. Right?"

To my left and right, lots of heads are nodding. Lots. Wait—lots?

"I didn't just walk up to you guys and stand there without saying anything. Or walk with you without saying anything," he says, and a couple people in the class laugh. "Yeah. Too weird," he says. "No, we talk. Mostly about neutral subjects. Safe subjects as we get to know each other. That's one of the functions of language. It contributes to civility and to a sense of polite comfort between strangers. It fills awkward silence."

I leave. Get up and leave. It happens in class. No drama. Nature calls in most cases but not in mine. Not today. My face is hot; my heart is pounding; my stomach is trying to turn itself inside out. I mentally tick off the possible causes:

massive coronary
delayed anaphylaxis
slowly bursting cerebral aneurysm
hot flashes
This is serious.

In the ladies' bathroom, I pull my phone out of my pocket.

Text to Mother, 9:17 a.m.
I think I'm having a cerebral aneurysm.

Text from Mother, 9:18 a.m.
No you're not.

Text to Mother, 9:18 a.m.
I can feel it swelling.

Text from Mother, 9:19 a.m.
No you can't.

I click my phone off, return it to my pocket, and avoid my reflection while I wash my hands and splash a little water on my face. If not an aneurysm, heart attack, allergic reaction, or early onset menopause, I can be in the midst of only one life-threatening condition: global embarrassment.

Back in class, Ethan's presence—his handsome, bright, perfect presence upon which all eyes and ears are directed—forces me to confront three painful questions that lead in only one mortifying direction.

What if Kate is right?

What if this is a crush?

How could I have mistranslated my feelings so profoundly?

What is the nature of love?

There must be a way to figure this out.

I contemplate the possible formulae lying on Stu's bed, staring at the ceiling but seeing only x's and y's and parentheses and question marks. Stu lies next to me and joins me in my ceiling-ward gaze.

"It's a good question," he says. "I have absolutely no idea how to answer it."

"You have a ton of experience," I say.

"That's what you keep telling me."

"Hey—" Sophie enters the room. "What are you guys doing now?"

"Interpretive dance," Stu says, and raises his left leg and right arm toward the ceiling for a couple seconds.

"We're contemplating the nature of love," I say as Sophie lies on the bed next to me.

"*You're* contemplating. I'm practicing my routine," Stu says.

"Who wants to know about love?" she asks.

"I do," I say.

"Really?" she asks. "You're not thinking about Stefan again, are you?"

"No," I say.

"Is there someone else?"

"No." *Not anymore,* I want to say. Maybe. I don't know. "No. I thought I was ready to be in love, but now I'm not even sure what it is. Plus, I figure that if I understand precisely how it feels, how it looks, how it sounds, how it acts, and why it's different from liking, from liking a lot, even from hooking up, then I'll be able to understand Kate better." And by *Kate,* I mean myself.

It's been over a week since Ethan showed up at my house with my purse and spoke Ethan with my family. Since then I've walked with him three times to Fair Grounds. Along the way we talked, or so I thought. I talked. This time I also listened. He asked questions— about me, about class, about music, about volleyball, about high school, about Cap, about my family. Music. School. Pastimes. All these weeks I have failed to notice that while I was speaking fluent Josie to Ethan, he was merely transcending the awkwardness of silence with me. Geoff tried that with me the night we met but with much less success.

After school this afternoon, I wrote this in my journal:

Friday, October 17

Ethan has a good rapport with adolescents.

"I've been telling you for months that Kate *is* in love," Sophie says to me there on Stu's bed.

"How do you know?" I ask.

"She's getting married."

"But you can't point to marriage as proof of love, since so many marriages end in divorce."

"You can fall out of love," she says. "I've done it like nine times."

"Well, then why do some people fall out of love while others stay in love for life?"

"I have no idea, Josie. You're making my head swim."

"But it's in the shallow end, so you won't drown," Stu says, and Sophie reaches across me to slap her brother's arm.

"I thought the two of you would be more helpful," I say.

"Nope," Stu says, getting up and settling in at his keyboard. "I am no help at all, having no experience of it myself."

"He's so in denial," Sophie says to me. "You know he's going to homecoming with Jen Auerbach."

I prop myself up on my elbows to ask, "You are?"

"Yeah," he says, and plays a few, quiet chords.

"Composing a song for her too?" I ask.

"A looooove song," Sophie teases.

"I would, but I no longer know what the nature of love is thanks to Josie's questions and *your* answers," he says.

"So you admit you did understand its nature until this moment," I say, and he merely shakes his head at me as he plays the first four chords of the Hallelujah chorus.

"No, he admits you're both over-thinking it," Sophie says. "You can't over-think love, Josie."

"Well, how are you defining over-thinking?"

"Oh, you're impossible," she says, and marches out of the room.

This is impossible, I tell myself, and lie back for a better view of Stu's ceiling.

"So Jen? And homecoming?" I ask.

"Yep."

"You realize she's all wrong for you," I say.

"I thought I was wrong for her by your account."

"You are."

"So don't two negatives make a positive?" he asks.

"I'm not entirely sure there *is* a formula for this," I say. But I wish there were. I would have followed it, plugging in all my data for x and all of Ethan's for y. And I would have worked out the results before involving my emotions, and I wouldn't feel as I feel now—like I've been dumped for real by an imaginary guy.

CHAPTER THIRTY-THREE

All this week, the cultural shift from Cap to BHS jars me. It's homecoming, both places. Cap's is Saturday. Bexley's is Friday. Cap gives the event a weekend. My high school gives it the whole week. On campus, I hear of events I have nothing to do with—fraternities, sororities, alumni reunions. At the high school, I experience only the remnants of each day's activities, which are really only fun in homeroom, anyway. I haven't had a homeroom for two years. I can't decide at the moment if I miss it.

My two school IDs provide me with little sense of community lately. Maybe they never really did.

Tonight, October 25, is Bexley's homecoming, also Kate's first shower and my excuse for not attending the game or dance when, in truth, I have no energy for them. Also no date. Lately, I have little energy for anything and am relieved we ended our volleyball season with a record that precluded playoffs.

Stu pops into the Wagemakers' kitchen just long enough to say good night. He's headed out to pick up Jen for dinner and the homecoming dance afterward. Sophie left with Josh fifteen minutes ago. Stefan, I heard, is taking Sarah Selman, and I privately wish them both a good time. He's still not speaking to me, and it still hurts.

I am alone in the kitchen, attempting to lure Moses closer to me with a shrimp intended for tonight's party, but he's been reluctant to approach me since I last dropped him.

"Next time rub it on your face," Stu suggests as he pops a cube of cheddar cheese into his mouth.

"Yeah, I'll do that," I say as I stand, and Stu jerks his head back slightly.

"Yes?" I ask.

He finishes chewing before answering, "No, you just look great. All dressed up."

"You've seen me dressed up before."

"Yeah, but tonight you look really nice."

"As opposed to all the other times when I didn't?"

"Yes. As opposed to all those times," he says, trying unsuccessfully not to smile.

"Well, it is a party," I say of my black dress and absurd heels. "I figured overalls were out of the question. Also bathrobes and wet suits."

"I have flippers you could borrow."

"Oh," I say, momentarily thrilling to the idea. "Three weeks ago I would have taken you up on that."

"And now—what—change of heart?"

"Maybe. I don't know."

"Yeah. I know how it goes."

"Oh, nice."

"What?"

"You're already thinking about breaking up with Jen," I say. "You haven't even been out with her yet."

"I'm not thinking of breaking up with her, because we're not a couple."

"Yet," I say, and he shrugs.

"At least I warned her about you," I say.

"And were wrong again."

"Not wrong."

"Good night, Josie," he says.

"Good night, Stu."

He starts out, stopping at the back door, looking as if he wants to say something—something good; he's smil-ing—but he just waves and leaves.

Earlier tonight, I flipped through a few dozen response cards while Kate styled my hair into a low ponytail with a piece of hair concealing the band. Mrs. Easterday wrote on the bottom of her card, *I wouldn't miss it for the world.* Lots of people wrote similar sentiments.

When Kate finished my hair, she called me "the best" for missing homecoming for this, her first shower. And I said in the language of Kate's Wedding, "I wouldn't miss it for the world." We said very little otherwise.

Now we Sheridans and Wagemakers and one, soon-to-be two I suppose, Brills stand in Auntie Pat and Uncle Ken's kitchen, waiting for the guests to arrive to celebrate what I fear I cannot prevent and what I understand even less than I did back in March, when this whole convoluted affair began.

"What are you doing?" Kate asks Geoff, who has hooked the side of his collar with one talon-like finger.

"There's a tag here that's poking me."

"Just yank it out."

"You can't yank it," Geoff and I say practically in unison, which surprises neither of us.

"Here," I say, removing a small pair of scissors from the drawer where Auntie Pat keeps them.

Kate takes them and snips the tag, muttering, "Geez, the two of you." Geoff gives me one of his standard winks, but nothing shakes this heavy sadness I continue to feel.

Ethan and Madison are the first to arrive. She fills the foyer with her hugs and voice. I share a nice-to-see-you nod and smile with Ethan—who produces a tangle of feelings within me I cannot begin to describe—and promptly make myself useful to Auntie Pat, passing platters of finger foods she spent the day making.

I don't feel like talking tonight, even though I speak many of the languages represented. Not all but many. Still, I have never felt so utterly disconnected from everyone—including Kate, with whom I do not speak at all. Not out of anger or in a fit of pique. I find that tonight I just don't have much to say to her in Josie that I think she would want to hear. She and I, tonight, stand in two different worlds.

All night I strategically position myself in the crowd to observe her, stunning in a merlot satin cocktail dress with spaghetti straps and light beading on the bodice, her beauty enhanced by her unawareness of it. Her smile is the natural, bright-eyed smile of a woman enjoying herself and looking forward to whatever thrills the evening brings. Behind her stands Geoff, one hand placed gently in the small of her back. Periodically, they share a warm, quick look.

This is Kate as she is at work—confident, welcoming, cheerful, and dancing that invisible dance I've seen Ross and Maggie, and Mother and Dad perform so often as couples. But Kate's dance card is full of different partners. Lots of them. In fact, she dances with every person here tonight as if this is her own private ball, her coming out party. Every person but me. And each of her dance partners will return home tonight feeling as if he or she received the special gift of attention from the dazzling guest of honor.

I cannot help thinking it was made all the more possible not only by the looks she shares with Geoff—the looks that convey a private, happy, unspoken connection. But by the looks he shares with no one else. I have not noticed before tonight that Geoff is the only guy I've ever known who did not take his eyes off Kate to ogle Maggie.

He has eyes only for Kate, and they say to her: "You are uniquely special to me and to me alone." No wonder she loves him.

And I accept the previously unfathomable—that Kate and Geoff do, in fact, speak the same language, and it is one that does not include me.

Geoff catches me watching him—watching them—twice. And each time, he winks. The second time he does it, I find it hard to swallow for the developing lump in my throat. So I distract myself by finding Moses in the kitchen and continuing my efforts to lure him close with shrimp.

A much more useful distraction presents itself toward the end of the party when Sophie bursts into the kitchen, startling Moses into running away.

"Josie," she cries, and drapes herself into a hug around me and sobs. "Josh and I broke up."

* * * * *

Saturday evening, Jen pulls into my driveway and honks. When I climb into her car, she says, "Right there in the middle of the dance. Well, not the middle like the center, but, you know, the middle of the thing."

"Chronologically," I say, not yet knowing what she's talking about.

"Right. Time-wise. Like halfway, it happens. And it's not really a scene, but I was standing right next to Sophie, and I could see she was getting upset," she says, and tells me her bystander version of Sophie's break-up with Josh.

"—wait, Josie, are you listening to me?"

"Yes," I say. "Yeah. Go on."

Jen continues, but I'm not listening. I'm trying, but I'm finding it difficult. Jen's conversation blends with my constant replay of last night's conversations—the ones I heard rather than joined—and they quickly become intermingled in my memory. I see Madison standing with Jen at the homecoming dance and Sophie breaking up with Josh in front of Kate in Auntie Pat's living room.

We pick up Emmy from her house. She climbs into the back and immediately says, "Don't be mad at me for being happy Sophie and Josh broke up."

"I'm not mad," I say, but wanted to say I don't even feel like I'm fully here. I don't want to go out tonight. To Easton of all places, Central Ohio's Grand Bazaar, where thousands of us Saturday night pilgrims can buy anything from flip-flops to diamond chokers, dine on anything from popcorn to sushi, walking and talking the night away.

Tonight my ears are overly tuned, a carryover from last night when I recognized so many different languages distinct from my own. And my translating skills overload before Jen parks the car. I manage a smile. I manage weak pleasantries. I manage to pretend I'm not three seconds away from running, screaming, from this place to one of total quiet. But I cannot manage any other language but Josie when Jen asks me if I'm all right.

"I actually don't enjoy being here and really just want to go home," which Jen promptly translates into Jen and asks, "Why? Are you mad at me? You are, aren't you? Because I was talking about Sophie and Josh?"

"She's mad at *me,*" Emmy says dismissively. "Because I'm glad for Josh."

"I'm not mad at anyone," I say.

"Yes, she is," Emmy says to Jen.

"Well, I'm not happy when you talk about me in the third person like I'm not here," I say, causing Emmy to turn to Jen to say, "See? She's mad."

"I'm not mad," I say.

"Josie, don't be mad," Jen says, hooking her arm through mine and squeezing us close. "Maybe you're just hungry. Come on. Let's go eat first."

So we bump and thread ourselves through the crowd

of foreigners, and I do find some visceral relief downing a soft pretzel and a soda, but it comes more from the distraction of chewing and swallowing—the respite from having to talk—than from anything else.

We spend a few hours there, during which time I come to feel like I'm viewing the world through the concave end of binoculars. Instead of magnifying the world, mine appears smaller, farther away and distorted and fraying at the edges. Or maybe it's not the world but me in it.

I end the evening by reassuring Jen I am not mad at her. I have just stepped out of her car into my driveway when she leans across the seat and asks, "So it's Emmy? You're mad at her?"

"Yes," I say, and Jen smiles.

"Okay, cool. As long as it's not me."

"It's not you," I say.

It's me. It really is me.

Upstairs, I drop my purse on my dresser and flop backward on my bed, luxuriating, as if in a hot bath, in cushy pillows and perfect silence. I am exhausted living life in foreign places among so many hospitable tribes. Even Kate's wedding brings yet more languages and more societies into which I must contort myself, however much, to fit. All this contorting, constantly shifting from one language to the next, one culture or subculture to the next, physically and mentally, girl and woman, hugging and bowing, proms and weddings, not only fatigues me but seems, at times, to consume me. High school, Cap, home, Easton, Sophie, Stu, homecoming, prom, my parents, the track team, the volleyball team, Kate, Geoff, juniors, seniors, bridesmaids, Ethan.

What made my Language Variation Project the breeze I predicted it would be illustrated a point I have long denied. This, at last, is that invisible prickly thread that has irritated me lately.

I can speak the languages of lots of groups and learn others with some ease, but no matter how fluent I am, when I'm not speaking Josie, I am merely acting. We all are when we interact outside of our natural cultures. It is inevitable, because it is impossible to be fully yourself in a foreign language.

In someone else's language, you become a visitor, a guest—sometimes a very welcome guest received with shrieks and hugs—but still always a guest. Because as soon as you stop speaking the native language of the group, you stop being one of the group. And then you're just alone, no matter who you're with.

October 26, 11:22 p.m.

I don't think I have as many friends as I thought
I did.

I close my journal and finish the entry mentally. It's not something I want to write down.

I don't think I have as many friends as I thought I did, not close ones, not many who I connect with on that deep level of language that doesn't just allow us to be ourselves with each other but allows us to be understood, even when we're not saying anything.

Silence—awkward or comfortable—is a language too. Awkward silence screams, "We have nothing in common." Comfortable silence proves just how much we do.

I swallow hard at the thought that Ethan and I were never comfortably quiet with each other. I swallow harder at the thought that I am not comfortably quiet most places.

As Stu often reminds me, I really do talk too much.

CHAPTER THIRTY-FOUR

It's Sunday evening. I am lying on Stu's bed. Auntie Pat and Uncle Ken are across the street at my house, having a formal review of Friday's shower over dinner and card games, which my mother usually wins. Sophie has cloistered herself in her room to paint a tree-lined river, frozen and flowing nowhere. She breaks her concentration only to phone or text friends, berating herself for ever telling Josh Brandstetter "that I love him. I hate him!"

They broke up over Sarah Selman, whom Josh had the temerity to call hot, the same adjective he had once used for Sophie, which she understood as both a threat and a betrayal. Refusing to believe his assertions that she was and is, in fact, hotter than Sarah, they argued. She cried. And the rest is unfolding on canvas and Facebook.

"How can Sophie hate Josh tonight when Friday morning she loved him?" I ask. What I mean is *How can I have had such strong feelings for Ethan when now I don't know what I feel aside from overwhelming mortification?*

Stu spins around on his music bench to face me.

"You're making this overly complicated," he says.

"It *is* complicated," I say. "You should know."

"Why should I know?" he asks, stretching out on his bed next to me.

"Because of the many and varied girls to whom you have professed your love who now either hate you as Sophie hates Josh or, in at least two cases I know of—count 'em, one, two—lie pining for you at this very moment."

"Who's pining for me?"

"You know very well."

"Josie," he nearly laughs, "it amazes me how little you know me."

"I know you."

"No, you don't," he says in a way that makes me turn my head quickly toward him. "You don't."

"You realize we're going to go back and forth now— you don't; I do—until you tell me what it is I allegedly don't know about you."

"You don't know," he says, propping himself up on one elbow, "that the reason all these girls break up with me is because I don't love them."

"I know that."

"You don't know that they have said it to me, but I have never said it back."

"What?"

"I have never said 'I love you' to anyone. So they get upset or mad—usually both—and break up with me."

"You never said 'I love you' to a single girlfriend?"

"Never."

"Why not?"

"Because I intend to say it to only one person. When I'm sure. When the time is right." He leans closer and smiles just a little. "And when I can predict with certainty what your response will be."

And he kisses me—gently and lingering. I feel his hand against my cheek, his warm skin against my own, his tongue twisting around mine, the pressure of our mouths intensifying, the very weight of my own body lightening, until, at length, he slowly pulls away.

And in my heart-thumping anxiety, I shoot out from underneath him, manage something like, "I have to go," and stumble a little at the door to avoid Moses. "I'm fine. Cat's fine." And I race across the street to my house, to my bedroom, in record time.

Text from Stu, 7:27 p.m.
U OK?

Text to Stu, 7:28 p.m.
Fine, thanks. U?

Text from Stu, 7:29 p.m.
I'm great, but I'm not the one who set a new land-speed record leaving here.

Text to Stu, 7:30 p.m.
Was surprised. And now double-checking. Are

you honestly telling me you love me? Or might?
Or do? What just happened?

Text from Stu, 7:32 p.m.
Do you honestly think I'd tell you in a text?

Text to Stu, 7:33 p.m.
No.

Text from Stu, 7:34 p.m.
Good night, Josie.

Text to Stu, 7:34 p.m.
Good night, Stu.

I click my phone off, drop back against my pillow, and perceive so many thoughts racing through my mind at dizzying speed that I find it impossible to grasp a single one, let alone a single emotion, and instead I find great interest in my own, soothingly plain white bedroom ceiling.

CHAPTER THIRTY-FIVE

I can't sleep tonight. So I open my journal to this eleven-days-old entry:

Wednesday October 15, 8:17 p.m.

What is the nature of love?

And I see there is no answer yet. So I flip back through the thing, hoping to entice it to start speaking to me, but all I see are loosely connected thoughts, fragments of thoughts appearing like flashcards—a sweater, jogging partner, Stu, eye exam, Kate, hate Kate, don't hate Kate.

I close my journal, flop back on my bed, and mean to think of Stu, mean to answer my own question about the nature of love, but I only see Kate when I close my eyes. Kate brushing my hair. Kate introducing Geoff. Kate laughing with me over a padded bra. Kate yelling at me over spilled spaghetti. Kate excited for me. Kate irritated with me. Kate and Geoff in our kitchen.

I can think of nothing but Kate. *Kate, Kate, Kate, Kate*. And then this—*I love Kate so much I hurt,* and very easily I begin to cry, warm tears falling out of the corners of both eyes, washing out the familiar definition of all objects in my room. Even me.

I cry until I no longer feel like crying. In my bathroom, I wash my face, wipe my glasses dry, and then sit down at my desk to finish my Language Variation Project, which, weeks ago, I changed from *Shut Up/Thank You* to this:

Cool, Sweet, Hot, Love, and Other Impossible Words
by Josephine Sheridan

Over the course of the first nine pages, I tackle the easiest words—*cool, sweet,* and *hot. Love* comes last. And I write:

Finally, *love.* There is an old adage about poets and playwrights forever struggling to define the term, and I believe the reason is threefold:

It is an ambiguous term.

It is often misused.

There is more than one kind of love.

It is an ambiguous term. In the past several months, I have used the word *love* or heard it said in reference to: sisters, family, Styx, studying languages, quilting, running, chocolate peanut butter cookies, Shopping Commando Style, love itself, weddings, "Mr. Roboto," "The Best of Times," two brainy kids in glasses, Dennis DeYoung, the crisp, cracking sound a new journal makes, wedding dresses, Josh Brandstetter, Geoffrey Stephen Brill, and a few other people.

How can one word with one definition apply equally to cameras, weddings, sounds, cookies, and people? It can't. Therefore, it has to have more than one meaning, to be determined contextually, and words with more than one meaning are ambiguous.

It is often misused. The word *love* is used in reference to people when *like* would do. *Like very much. Attracted to. Infatuated with.* Attraction and infatuation produce strong, exciting emotions that could easily be taken for love. But attraction wanes, and infatuation passes. Love doesn't end.

Sometimes, people think they're in love when they choose to see in someone else only the good qualities, none of the bad ones—only the qualities they most admire, none of the flaws or obstacles. Good becomes perfect, but perfect is an illusion. And illusions are like all spells—temporary and soon broken. And when that happens, feelings change.

Often, when feelings change, people who once loved now claim they hate. But maybe the word *hate* is misused the same way *love* is. Maybe it isn't hate but hurt that comes from embarrassment or regret or sadness or frustration or all of it. I misused the word *hate* once against my sister and can honestly say that no one who truly loves another person could ever treat that person with any of hate's real qualities. If the hate is real, then the love was not.

So what is love—the kind that applies not to cookies but to people? It is a connection, almost like a private language between two people, or an invisible dance. It is an invincible force that binds us to one another and can never be broken. Stretched and tested, even worried over, but never temporary, never fleeting, never broken, which I know from recent experience and which brings me to my third and final point.

There is more than one type of love. Since March, I have watched, studied, scrutinized and analyzed my sister Kate's relationship with her fiancé, Geoffrey Stephen Brill. Their wedding is thirteen days from the date of this paper, and I can conclude the following:

I know my sister and Geoff love each other.

I know I don't understand that.

I don't know if I have ever experienced that kind of love.

I know I experience one kind of love because of my sister Kate, whom I can confidently say I will always love, and who I know loves me, even when I am, at times, unlovable. (Though many of those times are her fault.)

I can't explain why my sister and I love each other, and I cannot prove it mathematically. I know it because of those times when it is tested and worried over. Because it is in those times when I want nothing more in life than love's very restoration, which puts everything else in my life in proper order. And somehow, Kate's love makes all other unhappiness a little easier to bear.

And then there is romantic love, of which I have little experience, though, perhaps, my experience is developing. But based on my observations, it shares the enduring strength of family love plus whatever element accounts for romance, a word that comes from medieval French and means *narrative*—usually a heroic, inexplicable, or otherworldly story. And I think there is something heroic, inexplicable, and otherworldly in every love story.

There is in Kate's and mine.

Both types of love remain a great mystery to me, and I wish, with all my heart, that love were as easily defined and understood as the word *teepee*. But then what would poets and playwrights do with all their time?

I hit SAVE, too tired even to reread what I've written, and I reach for my phone.

Text to Kate, 10:47 p.m.
I love U, and I will try my hardest to love Geoff 2.

Text from Kate, 10:47 p.m.
Where R U?

Text to Kate, 10:48 p.m.
My bedroom.

Seconds later, Kate bursts into my room without knocking, and I don't care and hope she always does so, though I'm certain to get mad at her next time. She wraps her arms around me, and I do the same in equal measure, equal pressure, equal sisterly-ness, making this the single most perfect hug in the history of hugs.

"Okay, tell me," she says, grabbing both of my hands into hers and sitting with me on the bed. "Honestly, Josie. What is it about Geoff?"

"He's a little odd-looking. He talks about ticks. He thinks he knows everything. He thinks there's—" It hits. My throat starts to hurt and my voice thickens. "He thinks there's only one way to do things. His way. And he always wants to be the . . . the smartest guy in the room." Tears. Tears pour out of my eyes, and my bottom lip quivers as I sob, "He's me, and you already have me. And I don't have that many people who are just mine. So now, when you marry him, I have one fewer."

"Oh, Josie," Kate says, pulling me into another hug. "I will always have room for you in my life and in my heart."

"Nobody wants two of me. I certainly don't."

"No, Josie, one of you is more than enough," she teases, which makes me laugh, which comes out of me as a wet, disgusting snort.

She grabs a handful of tissues for me, and I dry my face.

"First of all, neither one of you is funny-looking," she says.

"I know what I look like, Kate."

"No, I don't think you do. And I don't think you're looking at Geoff accurately either." I shrug a maybe at her. She continues, "And yes he found an article about ticks interesting, but he finds lots of things interesting.

The way you do. Correct me if I'm wrong, but aren't you interested in learning if you've eaten an entire rat in your lifetime?"

"I think that's important information to have."

"I think Geoff would agree with you." She tucks a loose strand of hair behind my ear for me. "He is a lot like you, Josie. Why do you think I love him so much?"

I concede with a nod and a considered grin.

"And I'm not replacing you. As if anyone could," she says. "I have, of course, wanted to throttle you at times."

"You will again, and, by the way, you haven't been the easiest person to deal with lately either."

"I know," she says through a conciliatory smile. "Josie, I'm sorry. I just got caught up in all the plans and the pressure of throwing a wedding. I kind of lost my head."

"You were a fruit loop."

"I'm sorry," she says again before squeezing my hand. "You know I would shrivel up and die if I didn't have you in my life."

"Please don't ever stop speaking to me again," I say, and describe how that particular silence felt—the pain, the loneliness—to her repeated apologies, and we talk like this all night, falling asleep on my bed, heads and shoulders touching.

CHAPTER THIRTY-SIX

First thing this morning, my phone beeps.

Text from Stu, 7:01 a.m.
U riding 2 class with me this morning?

Text to Stu, 7:01 a.m.
Yes. Of course. Probably. Y? U want me 2 or not?

Text from Stu, 7:02 a.m.
Just making sure U R OK. Should I even bother
asking you to stop over-thinking?

Text to Stu, 7:03 a.m.
Do you really need to ask that?

My phone rings.
"Yes?" I answer.
"Come out here," Stu says, and when I look out my
bedroom window, I see him waving to me as he jogs across
the street, his breath visible on this chilly, pale morning.

When I meet him at my front steps, he says cheerfully, "We do have to talk about last night, you know."

"Stu, I don't know what to say," I admit. I also don't know what to say about the smell of him, which is spicy like dried fruit and cloves, which is from the cologne he wears every single day. I just don't remember it feeling this warm to me. And since when do fragrances have temperatures? I shake my head just a little. "But I know I need a lot more time to think about it than one night, especially last night, which turned out to be a good night but long, between Kate and the paper, which I finished by the way, and I probably have huge under-eye circles again, which Sophie will point out . . . Where was I?"

"Needing a lot of time," Stu says, smiling at me.

"Well, some time."

"Are you sorry I kissed you?"

"No," I say quickly, so quickly it startles me. "No." I clear my throat and try not to smile overly and try, unsuccessfully, not to turn red as I recall warm skin, soft tongues, and the very color of the inside of his lower lip. I wish it came in a lipstick. It would be more perfect for me than Candy Bliss. "It was nice. Surprising. But nice." I consider that a moment. "Really nice," I qualify. Then I reconsider my qualification and try to improve it with, "Definitely nice. Are you sorry?"

"No."

"But it changes things."

"I knew it would."

"I hate change."

"I know that too," he says.

"Then why did you do it?"

"Because I couldn't stand not to one second longer."

"Oh. Well, that's . . . kind of . . ." Oh, geez, the only word coming to mind is the one I say. ". . . cool."

I roll my eyes at myself, which thoroughly entertains Stu.

"You have to give me time to think about this," I say.

"By which you mean over-think it."

"Probably."

"Don't over-think this, Josie," he says, and nudges my elbow with his before walking back to his house.

I, perfectly contented and nearly giddy, watch him all the way. Just after he reaches his front door, he turns and flashes me a very confident smile.

My dad walks out of his study, several papers in hand, as I enter the house, and he greets me with, "Out all night again, my dear?"

"You caught me."

"Partying?"

"Over-thinking."

"That'll get you in more trouble than partying," he says, glancing at his papers.

"It probably will," I say, heading toward the stairs. But I think I may be addicted. I'm not sure. I'll have to give it some thought.

* * * * *

A short time later, in Stu's car, we shoot each other ridiculous smiles—of the bottom-lip-biting kind—via his rearview mirror, but we remain quiet.

"What?" Sophie finally demands.

"What?"

"What?"

"What is with you two?" she asks.

"Nothing."

"Nothing."

"Are you doing this to bug me? Is it to try to get me to say something? Or do something? What?"

"Yes," Stu says.

"No," I say.

"Then what?"

"Nothing."

"Nothing."

We bite our lips some more, and when Sophie finally gets out of the car at school, she leaves us with, "You two are getting weirder by the day."

Stu tips his head toward the passenger seat, and I step across the console into it.

"Music?" Stu offers, and I shake my head no.

No, I'm happy sitting here in silence full of possibilities, which we'll address once I've sorted through them all.

Or will I? Will we?

Stu parks, and we walk as we rode—in goofy, grinning silence from which a new thought starts to percolate. I try to ignore it all the way to my seat in Sociolinguistics, through settling in and pulling out my notebook and finding just the right pen and taking notes and sharing quick sidelong glances with Stu.

I try to ignore it later when I walk to Fair Grounds with him and Ethan, who asks us how our weekend was and who won the homecoming game. And I try to ignore it through a quiet lunch with Stu, who contentedly downs two bagel sandwiches and finishes my plain bagel when I cannot.

For the first time in my life, I want him to ask *Penny for your thoughts*. I want him to rudely interrupt the silence with a question about what is on my mind because what is on my mind is this: *I don't know what to say to you now. And I want you to tell me, "Everything's going to be okay."*

Stu would say it. I know he would if I asked him to. But I recall my dad's admonition from some weeks back. *Forcing a subject to respond the way you want him to only confirms your bias, my dear. And it makes your results worthless.*

Suddenly I am not convinced that everything between Stu and me will be okay, and I do not want that confirmed by his honest answer. Surely he senses what transpires between us. This isn't self-possessed silence anymore. It's awkward, and I have no idea how to fill it.

Stu was right. So was Stefan. Love—the possibility

that it exists between two people and the possibility that it doesn't and never will—changes everything. I already lost one friend to this. I look across the table at Stu, who finishes my bagel and asks, "You weren't going to eat that, were you?"

I shake my head.

I cannot lose another.

On the quiet walk back to the car, I apologize for my silence, which I've never done before, and add, "Thinking." Then, like an idiot, I point to my head—for what? Emphasis?

"You realize your head's going to explode someday."

You'll clean it up, I say, and whew, talking as usual. Except we're not, because I meant to say that but didn't. I couldn't get the words out for all the thoughts overburdening me. And now that I want to say it, the moment is gone, and I only know that I want it back.

Stu's soccer practice runs late today, so I walk home with Sophie, who berates Josh Brandstetter, without repeating herself, for nearly a whole mile. Closer to home, she tells me, "But Danny Shiever is kind of cute, don't you think? Not real chatty, but so what? Find out if he likes me, okay?"

I nod, relieved to have the distraction of Sophie's life, and doubly relieved she never notices how lost in my head I am.

Text to Stu, 6:44 p.m.
I like us how we are.

Text from Stu, 6:45 p.m.
I like us how we are too.

That's not what I mean. And he knows it.

Geoff comes for dinner tonight. He comes almost every night now that the wedding is only two weeks away. After dinner, he and Kate spend a few minutes opening the presents that arrive and writing thank-you notes together at the desk in Dad's study. Tonight, they laugh quietly about their ability to gush so effusively over their sixth set of candlesticks.

"It is impressive," I say, popping into the room for a handful of M&M'S from the leeches jar, which, I see from Geoff's expression, is a hidden treasure to him.

"Want some?" I offer.

"Thanks," he says, indulging in a handful just as Kate's phone rings.

"Work," she says to us, by way of apology, and takes the call out of the room.

I return the jar to its proper spot on the shelf, next to a Civil War field surgeon's kit complete with amputation saw and tourniquet. Dad keeps the worn leather lid closed. He really needs a new hobby.

I pretend to straighten the leech jar a couple times, twice shooting a sideways peek at Geoff, who contentedly munches on M&M'S and reviews his and Kate's note. Finally, I turn toward him to say—I don't know—something about the wedding, maybe, when he winks at me, and I say, "You know that really freaks me out when you do that."

"Why do you think I do it?" he asks, smiling almost victoriously, and I concede his win with a self-directed eyeball roll before taking a seat in the nearest armchair.

"You know last summer when you said you knew how hard it was to lose a friend because I didn't have that many?" I ask.

"Yes, and I'm sorry about that. I didn't mean it—"

"I know what you meant," I say quickly. Too quickly. I exhale and say earnestly, "I know what you meant."

"Everything okay, Josie?"

"I don't think so. I think I'm about to lose another one, and the list is shrinking."

"Who?"

I shake my head, which he translates correctly. *I don't want to say.*

"Okay," he says. "Can I help?"

"I don't think so," I say, and stand. "But I like that you understand."

"Sure," he says, and I start to leave, but stop in the doorway to say, "Oh, and the spaghetti *was* an accident."

And then—and I have this coming—he winks at me.

* * * * *

I am not two steps up the stairs when I get a text from Stu:

I'm at your front door. Come out here.

"Come in," I say when I open the door.

"No," he says, holding his phone up for me to see my previous text. "Tell me." I step outside and close the door behind me. "You've made a decision about us. Already?"

"Stu, you're my best friend in the world. I don't want to lose that."

"You're the person I see myself with forever. I don't want to lose that."

"We risk losing everything if we end up on a path that doesn't lead where you think it's going to."

"You're worth that risk, Josie. Aren't I?"

"I am not"—my voice thickens with impending tears—"willing to risk losing you as one of my only friends."

"You're not going to lose me," he says.

"How can you be so certain?"

"How can you not be?" he asks, and this time, instead of holding his mouth halfway between a smile and a laugh as he so often does, he holds it halfway between nothing at all. Nothing I can read.

It startles me into a silence full of rotten possibilities. Finally I remember to breathe and confess, "I don't know. I am sure of very few things right now, but one of them is . . . that we are already changed."

"Yeah," he agrees. "Yeah, we are. I thought it was for the better."

"I think it isn't," I say.

He turns and jogs across the street to his house. I step inside and jump half a foot when I hear his front door slam shut and echo down our quiet street.

CHAPTER THIRTY-SEVEN

Text to Sophie, 7:00 a.m.
Tell Stu I'm getting a ride with my dad to Cap this morning. Have to be there early.

Text from Sophie 7:22 a.m.
OK! XOXO

The language of Sophie does not involve too many probing questions, especially when she is consumed with the grief of yet one more break-up. It is exactly the language I need to hear today.

Stu arrives late to class by only a few minutes. He takes his seat next to mine, leaving me wondering if he's as wholly wrenched as I am. I feel and suffer my connection to him. Our unique bond of friendship and lifelong history has become all the more palpable because of its injury. It's similar to that acute, sudden awareness of how often you swallow each day only after you develop a sore throat. And all you want—all *I* want—is restoration. But to what now?

Neither of us can even look at the other.

After class, he leaves with, "See you later."

I barely even remember Ethan at the front of the class and am startled when he calls out to me afterward, "Fair Grounds, Josie?"

"Library today," I say.

"Studying for a class?"

"Yes," I say. Just yes.

Ethan catches up with Samantha and Mr. Football then and asks Mr. Football, "Who are you playing Saturday, and are you ready?"

I see them—Stu and Jen—hanging out in the senior lobby after school this week. By Wednesday, Jen leans in close to him, speaking pleasant things in a low voice. On Thursday, they pass by me at my locker, Jen smiling her hello at me, Stu staring abstractedly ahead, searching, it appears, for the former comfort of our relationship, which is nowhere to be seen. On Friday, Jen kisses him, there in the senior lobby, but he pulls away quickly, sharply, stung. After, our eyes connect for the briefest moment before he grabs his backpack and walks out, leaving Jen hurrying to catch up.

"What's with him?" Sophie asks.

"Oh, you know. Love-'em-and-leave-'em," I say.

"He's never going to change," she says, walking past me to join a group of her friends and to flirt with Danny Shiever, who is standing next to Stefan Kott, who looks my way and nods. No smile. No grimace. Just a nod.

I nod back and produce that warm smile I had so long ago practiced because that is my natural response in Josie. And I don't feel like speaking anything else at this moment.

Later, I consider texting Stu, calling him, sending him an e-mail, throwing pebbles at his bedroom window. Something. Anything. And nothing. There's no time this weekend, this last weekend before Kate and Geoff's wedding.

On Saturday we have our fourth and final dress-fitting, which takes remarkably little time. Afterward, we congregate at the hair salon for a rehearsal of hair and makeup. Kate stands with her stylist the whole time she does my hair, instructing her how, precisely, to do it so that I won't bolt screaming from the chair.

I have not gotten my ears pierced. Kate apologized this morning for pressing that issue and said, "Geoff got a little irked with me for suggesting it. He said I was going over the top in small details."

"You should listen to him more often," I said. "It's amazing how insightful he's become in the last few days."

We enjoyed ourselves—we bridesmaids and Kate—once I manually shifted into the culture, which I found rather pleasant. I had little but questions to contribute when they spoke of work and boyfriends, but we found common ground over the wedding itself, and then weddings in general.

But behind the hair and the makeup and the infectious happiness of Kate's fast-approaching Big Day, I continue to feel the ache of missing Stu, of missing what really was a Pperfect friendship and knowing now we can't go back to it and find it as it was.

Sunday night. Geoff comes for dinner. Afterward, long after I thought he had gone home, he knocks on my bedroom door, asks if he can come in. I open my door to find him standing with both hands behind his back.

"Close your eyes," he says.

"Wh—"

"And don't ask why," he adds quickly, making me grin just a little as I comply. "Okay, open them," he says, and I find him holding a stuffed, plush white goat with yellow horns and pink ears.

"I saw this today and thought of you," he says. "Next best thing to a real one."

"How did you know?" I ask, delighted and taking it from him and happy to find it has no prickly parts.

"Kate," he says. "She tells me everything, you know."

"I know."

"I also thought it might cheer you up." He shrugs slightly when I look questioningly at him. "You haven't mentioned Stu at all lately. From the other day, I figured it out. It wasn't tough to deduce. I'm . . ." he says. "Well, I've been there too, Josie. And I just want you to know that, if you ever want, you can always talk to me. Anytime."

"Thanks," I say, and following the permission of mutual smiles and polite head-bobs, I close my door.

Seconds later, I open it and lean over the railing and call to him at the bottom of the steps, "Hey, Geoff."

"Yes?"

I am on the verge of asking "If you give up your seat on the bus every day to a pregnant woman," but instead I say, more sincerely than before, I hope, "Thanks."

He shoots a crooked smile up at me. I'll ask my thirty-seven questions later. I'll also define *irony* for him and tell him that oregano is Greek, not Italian. And someday I will convert him to a true Dennis DeYoung fan. If he's going to be a member of the Sheridan family, he's going to have learn.

I walk alone to Cap each morning this week. Sophie asks me why one afternoon at school.

"It's just better. Right now."

"Okay," she says, and produces a sad if knowing smile,

which reminds me that, when she wants to, she speaks Josie very well—and probably Stu and Stu Chewing too.

In Sociolinguistics, Stu sits a few rows behind me with Mr. Football and laughs with him before and after class and then seems to disappear. Stu more than Ethan, more than this class, more than anything, occupies me entirely. I look for him at Fair Grounds, at the library, and later back at the high school, but I never catch more than the back of him, walking away. And I refuse to run to catch up.

I still don't know what to say to him, anyway.

At the rehearsal dinner, which Stu skips, we finally meet Geoff's parents, Alan and Dee, in from Wisconsin. Apart from an unnatural interest in the flora and fauna of state parks—and that Dee Brill sounds like something you do to a duck before you pluck it—they seem perfectly normal. Moreover, they respond to Kate exactly as their son does—gently and attentively, content in the background while Kate shines.

Auntie Pat explains, regrettably, that Stu worked himself into exhaustion this week, and he just couldn't rouse himself in time for the rehearsal dinner.

"But believe me," she says, "he will be making his apologies to his hosts and reimbursing them for the cost of his dinner."

"He'll be at the wedding tomorrow, won't he?" I ask.

"I hope so," Auntie Pat says. "If he isn't, his car will be mine until he has made amends to your parents and to Kate and Geoff."

"Huh," I say, which, as usual, means a whole lot more than *huh*.

"But you'll insist he goes."

"I'll do my best," she says.

Seventy-two are in attendance tonight. Earlier tonight, Aunt Toot gave me a mint and a package of tissue. "Just in case you need them tomorrow," she whispered.

Uncle Vic addresses me as "you young people."

"You young people listen to music too loud."

"You young people drive too fast."

Youyoungpeople Sheridan. That's me, tonight. If Stu were here, that's what he'd call me.

I am seated next to a bridesmaid called Stephanie, at the far right end of the head table. We are arranged in ceremonial order—Happy Couple in the middle, honor attendants next—so that's Maggie—and then the rest of us according to height, shortest to me. My seat allows me to survey the room, round tables of eight decorated with flickering white votives and strategically placed vases of ivory roses and red berries that Dee Brill earlier told me are hypericum berries and warned me not to eat since they are poisonous.

"Oh, thank you, because I do like to nibble on centerpieces," I said to her bewildered face and to Mother's directed *ahem*.

Through the steady buzz of conversations, sporadic laughter, clinking glasses, and heartfelt toasts, my attention is drawn, as an arrow to magnetic north, to the one empty chair in the room. One table away, between Sophie and Ethan, who is here as Madison's date, I can even read his place card, thanks to my nifty new contacts. Stu Wagemaker. At last, when I can no longer endure its pull, I excuse myself for the ladies' room and tip the card facedown on my way.

The morning of the wedding passes in a delirium of bridesmaids and brunch foods and caravans and makeup artists. Fortunately, my mother has scheduled two hours of quiet in the Sheridan house, from four o'clock until we must depart for the church. She stands sentry downstairs while Kate flits about the house, and I retreat to the dark solitude of my bedroom.

There, I sit on my bed, propped up against three pillows, and tell myself I have two or three hours before I see Stu, two or three hours to figure this out. Because he and I *need* to talk.

But by the time my mother gently taps on my bedroom door to let me know the limousines have arrived to ferry us to the church, I have come to absolutely no conclusions about what to say when I see him. In the limo, I begin to wonder if I'll see him at all. By the time we reach the church, I worry I won't, but I am happily distracted, then, by the sheer collective fun of us brides-maids changing into our gowns in the undercroft, where coffee hour is usually held on Sundays. And we all prac-tically swoon—no, we do swoon—when Kate enters the room in her gown and veil. I really wouldn't have missed this for the world and am overjoyed to be included as a member of this particular group. I wish we had ID cards, though. But I suppose the dresses serve that pur-pose well enough.

I don't see Stu during the ceremony. Once I see Kate on my father's arm, I forget to look for him. I forget about fights over contacts, tick lectures, and Aunt Toot's tissues stuffed in my bra since I left my foam falsies at home. My mind is wholly occupied first by the sight of Kate, and then by the sight of Geoff, waiting patiently for her to join him at the altar.

The service proceeds with the tradition and speed of all Episcopal wedding services complete with homily, exchange of vows, and seemingly endless hymns that force *G-d* and *blood* to rhyme. There follow prayers and blessings and of course, just before the recessional, the wholly secular kiss.

The wedding party and both sets of parents exhale laughter in the undercroft while the guests depart the sanctuary. Kate fairly pushes through the crowd straight to me for a reassuring hug that brings tears to both our eyes.

I pull two of Aunt Toot's tissues out of my bra for us and we hug again, giggling through sniffles.

Columbus Country Club buzzes with the joyful chatter of two hundred forty-eight friends and relatives—give or take a Wagemaker—who break into applause when Geoff and Kate finally enter. I make my way through the club's crowded living room, stopping repeatedly to say hello to my parents' friends, who, in the language of wedding guests, repeatedly compliment me on a "job well done," and say, "Isn't that a gorgeous dress."

At last I find Sophie, talking with some girls I don't know, and pull her aside to ask, "Is Stu here?"

"He didn't come. Can you believe he'd miss this? He's such a guy."

"Yeah," I say, not even attempting to mask my disappointment.

I continue mingling, or moving about, anyway, while the band plays and people dance and excuse themselves in and out of small crowds around the buffet stations. I move from group to group, receiving more jobs-well-done, letting people admire the dress, and agreeing with Millicente DeGraf among others that, *oui,* Kate makes a beautiful bride.

At last, I find myself face-to-face with Ethan, who promptly tells me "job well done."

"Thank you, but Kate's job was harder, even though

she made it look effortless, like she's doing now," I say, pointing across the room to the star of the show with her husband proudly supporting her nearby.

"So how's your Language Variation paper coming?" he asks.

"I'm done," I say, adding "Excuse me," as I indicate by pointing that I need to keep circulating, but, in truth, I don't want to speak Student-Teacher with him. I'd much rather be alone in my thoughts tonight than have to translate one more language.

Soon I find myself standing between the gray marble foyer and the raspberry-carpeted living room, looking toward the smattering of guests congregating in the front hall, taking a breather from the crowds and the music. A few guests I recognize. One in particular smiles at me—a hesitant smile, unsure as he is of my response. It's Stu.

I march straight to him, or straight-ish, anyway, twisting my ankle once but remaining, inelegantly, upright. I grab him by the wrist and lead him through a corner of the living room, out the French doors, and onto a side patio, crowded with guests in the spring and summer but now empty and quiet and cold.

"Josie," Stu says, promptly taking off his tuxedo coat and wrapping it around my shoulders.

"Just listen," I order him. "I've been working this out, and this is as far as I've gotten. I miss you." I blink a few times, clear my throat. Stu grins at me. "I miss everything about you. Okay. Okay. The kiss changed everything. It did. You know that. And, yes, I admit, in the most scientific terms, it wigged me out, but only because I was not expecting it, so I wasn't prepared, and you should have known that I wouldn't be. And you know how I dislike surprises. But I'm not sorry you did it. You are my best friend in the world, the one person outside my family who understands me, and the one person in the world who makes the most sense to me without either one of us having to translate a thing. I have deep, strong feelings for you that just got deeper and stronger when you weren't there, and I don't know if that's love, but I know I am willing to risk what we have to find out, to be able to say to you, one day, eventually, that I love you, because it's worth the risk, you're worth it, and I want you in my life forever."

"Josie."

"Yes?"

"You talk too much," he says, and he kisses me, and it feels new and familiar at the same time, his lips pressing gently, then firmly, then gently again against mine, our breathing becoming one breath, his hands touching my face as if this is the first time he's ever touched me. And all so natural, so seamless, so graceful—even for me— that it feels like we've done this a thousand times before, even though we've both waited a very long time for this. I don't know how long we kiss. I only know I don't want it to end, but when it does, I know there will be more times like this.

I lean back while he puts his arms around me, and I ask, "So what do we do until we reach eventually?"

"We work it out," he says.

"I can work just about anything out."

"That's what I hear," he says, and we kiss a little longer, while eventually seems nearer than ever before.

"Come dance with me," he says, taking my hand, and someday I'll explain to him that I already am.

Stu leads me onto the dance floor, where I step effortlessly—Pperfectly—into his arms, and after just a few seconds, we turn so that I now see the large screen above the fireplace onto which are projected shots of Kate. Kate in a highchair. Kate on a swing. Kate in pigtails. Kate in braces. Kate graduating high school. Kate graduating college.

I gasp.

The room freezes as *Queen Kate on the Throne* appears on the screen, and above the music, she screams, "Josie, you little monster!"

And I say to Stu, "What do you know? Kate was right. Senior year is turning out to be the best."

ACKNOWLEDGMENTS

My heartfelt thanks, with hugs and smiles, to my agent, Faye Bender, for her support of and belief in both this book and me, and also for phone calls, e-mails—and especially sticky notes—that made me laugh out loud. And also for introducing me to my editor, Jess Garrison, whose guidance and insights made this book so much better. Thank you, Jess!

Thanks also to my dear friend Libby Marx for acting as my pop culture consultant, to Kristin Boes for her valuable critique, and to Jeff Salon for taking the time to explain the work-life of drug reps to me.

To my OHYA friends: Rae Carson, Julia DeVillers, Lisa Gerber, Margaret Peterson Haddix, Lisa Klein, Edith Pattou, and Natalie Richards. There were difficult times during the writing of this book when I would have been lost without you. Thank you so much for being so wonderful! You are the best!

Great big thanks to Denny Fultz, Alex Li, Lori Moomaw, Lisa Martinuzzi, Jack Johnson, Leslie and Matt Marx, Dennis Adams, M. Theadelphi, and my mother, Bunny Hardy, for letting me share book news with you and for celebrating with me.

And very special and continued thanks to my husband, Tim, who gave me invaluable insight into general guyness for this book, and who also wrote a few of Stu's lines and even a couple of Josie's. And who keeps me laughing through all the ups and downs of this writing life we share.

AUTHOR Q&A — ERIN McCAHAN

What languages do you speak?

English comes to mind first. I'm pretty good at English. Also, I've studied, in order, Latin, Spanish, French, Hebrew, Greek, Japanese, and I'm currently learning German. Once upon a time I was proficient in Spanish and Hebrew, but it was ancient Hebrew, which is no longer spoken, so not terribly useful if I ever need to rent a car in Israel. Currently, my level of proficiency in Spanish is limited to asking where Juan is, and if he's not at school or in the library, I won't be able to find him.

What is your favorite foreign word in any language?

Monkey! In any language: *Affe, singe, mico*. Those are the only ones I know—German, French, Spanish. Because everything's funnier with a monkey in it! Drop a monkey into *Romeo & Juliet*—instant comedy!

What was your inspiration for this book?

One extraordinarily boring bridal shower (in desperate need of a monkey) and a radio interview of a cultural anthropologist who kept referring to modern social groups as tribes. They both had to do with speech communities—discrete groups that just organically develop their own languages. Not foreign languages.

But all cohesive groups, like school jocks, new moms, siblings, nurses, law students, postal employees, pilots—the list is nearly endless—develop a way of speaking that doesn't easily translate outside the group. And it's always hard for an outsider to enter an established speech community, which I acutely felt at that bridal shower where I was openly pitied—"Oh, you poor thing"—for not owning hand-painted drinking glasses, and sat in bored silence listening to some of these women describe their individual collections of said drinking glasses while the rest of the group hung on the words as if they formed the climax of the world's greatest art heist. It didn't take long for me to realize that, to paraphrase that cultural anthropologist, I was just not tribal with these women. That's no one's fault, but it made for a long afternoon!

Ever since then, I've thought about the role language plays socially—in terms of inclusion and exclusion. And when I found myself wishing I had understood this in high school, I started fooling around with the question, "Well, what if I had?" How would high school have been different? And from there, Josie was born.

Are any of the characters based on real people?
Yes. I worked with a Geoff.

Were you surprised about the way the characters or the book grew or changed as you wrote?
No, but only because I know now, after years of prac-

tice, to expect that. I think that's part of every writer's evolution. You learn that you must give your characters room to grow, and very often they will say and do things you didn't necessarily predict but which fit their personalities. And then they start telling their own stories.

What experiences did you bring to the book? Were you anything like Josie—or any of the other characters, for that matter—at that age?

Without exaggerating, I cannot get through a single day without tripping over or bumping into something. I do it so often, I can't even explain new bumps and bruises to my husband because I just don't pay attention to how I got them anymore. Also, my IQ is unusually high, higher than Josie's actually. But like she says, I mean this as a statement, not a boast. Again, just like Josie says, I came this way. I have blue eyes, blah-colored hair, a high IQ, scoliosis, attached earlobes, freckles, and lots of other organic features I had absolutely nothing to do with. But IQ and clumsiness are about all I have in common with Josie. I think the biggest difference between her and me is that I was pathologically shy in high school. And shy or not, I just never would have said some of things Josie says.

What is your writing process like? What are your favorite and least favorite parts?

I never start to write until I have the framework of

beginning and end. So I'll chew on an idea for months if I have to, but once I know where I want the characters to start and where I want them to end up, I start writing. And I love that moment in the process when the story starts to tell itself, and all I have to do is get out of its way. My least favorite part, though, is knowing that the story is going in the wrong direction and can only be corrected by cutting thousands of words. Hitting that delete button is always right, but it's so painful—and more than a little deflating—to see that word-count shrink as days or weeks of work disappear!

To which character do you most relate?

I relate to Josie as I am now—thinking like she does, but knowing better, I hope, than to express certain thoughts in public. But because I was so shy in high school, there's no character teenage-me would have related to. I can't imagine there ever will be either. Who wants to read about a high school senior who spends the entire novel trying to get herself written out of the story?

Do you have a Geoff in your life? How did you learn to understand him or her?

I had a Geoff in my life, who knew everything about everything even when he was wrong, which he never was, even when he was. But he could be sweet and funny, too, if you got him alone and unguarded. Fortunately, I saw the sweet and funny sides of him early in knowing him, so that made the public obnoxious side of him easier to endure. Most of the time. Okay, sometimes.

Which is more Pperfect: the word *teepee* **or Dennis DeYoung?**

Dennis DeYoung, because I'm sure he appreciates the universal clarity of the word *teepee* and how much fun monkeys are. Have you heard that man sing? Wait, I need to take a moment here to swoon.

Which is more insufferable: lectures on tick-borne diseases or myna birds? Or is there something even worse than both?

Yes—lectures on tick-borne diseases complete with slides, accompanied by music on a church organ. Written and performed by a guy named Geoff. Who collects hand-painted drinking glasses. And has slides of those, too.

What's your favorite thing to do at Easton on a Saturday night?

Avoid it. It's always crowded, and I feel claustrophobic and panicked in crowds. Favorite thing to do there on a weekday afternoon, though, is meet friends for coffee or lunch, then browse through The Container Store afterwards. I can always find some reason to buy something in that store.

Have you ever used the wrong language when speaking with someone? Was it disastrous or insightful?

Literally, yes! Years ago, during orientation for one of those wilderness-experience courses in Colorado, I was paired with a very nice guy from Japan, who introduced himself, told me where in Japan he was from, and said, "Nice to meet you." So I just started talking. Then, after several minutes of my yammering—and I mean several minutes—I asked him some question about Japan, and he said to me, "I speak little English." I said, "Okay. Well, just tell me what you can." And he said, "Nice to meet you." After our fourteen-day course, I and the eight other Americans on the thing managed to teach this guy a whopping three new American phrases: *granola*, *George Bush*, and *shit*.

What are some unexpected types of love that you have in your life?

I never expected to fall in love with certain authors' words so much that I'd feel something like love—certainly respectful affection—for the author him- or herself. It began with F. Scott Fitzgerald and now includes Nathaniel Hawthorne, Annie Dillard, Henry Wadsworth Longfellow, and Francisco X. Stork.

JOSIE'S 37 QUESTIONS FOR GEOFF

1: If you give up your seat every day on a bus for a pregnant woman but then discover she's not pregnant but faking it to trick her boyfriend into marrying her, will you still give up your seat to her? And will you tell the boyfriend?

2: You come into possession of a magic potion that will cure all cancer in all people for all time if it is ingested by one person you love, but it will claim the life of that one person. Will you give it to someone you love, or will you leave it untouched?

3: If you could hypnotize anyone in the world, who would it be, and what would you make that person do?

4: If you could live inside any movie for one year—as yourself, not as one of the characters—which movie would it be, and what's the first thing you would do?

5: Who would be the worst person in the world to get stuck next to on a twelve-hour plane ride?

6: Secretly, what superpower do you wish you had?

7: What song are you singing when you have your rock-star, singing-to-a-packed-stadium fantasy?

8: What's your happiest memory, and which of your five senses reacts to it most profoundly?

9: What's the most embarrassing thing my sister would learn about you if she spent an afternoon talking with every teacher you've ever had?

10: What was the last apology you had to make, and to whom did you make it?

11: Do you find the Victoria's Secret catalog innocuous, insulting, or titillating?

12: What does your best friend think is the weirdest thing about you, and is he right?

13: If my sister's job takes her to France for three months, what are the three things about her you will miss most?

14: Without mentioning her appearance, what are the three most beautiful things about Kate?

15: If you wanted to make a romantic evening for Kate but weren't allowed to spend any money, what would you do?

16: What is the one thing you wish more people understood about you?

17: One Direction just wrote a song about your life. What is the title?

18: If you could live one day over, would you relive a good day or would you try to change a bad one?

19: *Time* magazine chooses a Person of the Year every December. Who would you choose this year for the honor?

20: If Kate were applying for a new job and you found yourself talking to her potential future boss at a party, what two reasons would you give the boss for hiring her?

21: What is the perfect gift for you?

22: What is the perfect gift for Kate?

23: If you could ask the President of the United States one question that he had to answer truthfully, what would you ask him?

24: Which three adjectives describe the worst moment you've had yet with Kate? And which three adjectives would she use to describe the same moment?

25: If Kate read all the text messages between you and your last girlfriend, what's the first thing she would say to you when she finished?

26: Imagine you just got on an elevator with your single least favorite person in the world. Who is it, and what's the first thing you say?

27: What's the best compliment you've ever received? Who gave it to you? And did you deserve it?

28: What should the 34th Amendment to the United States Constitution be?

29: If you were the judge at the trial of a guy who punched several old ladies and stole their purses and jewelry, and you could sentence him to anything but prison, what would the sentence be?

30: If your life during high school were a reality show, what would the title have been?

31: If you had the power of invisibility (which is my answer for #6) for twenty-four hours, what would you do with it?

32: What are the three most important things you own that are not electronic?

33: What will the front page headline in tomorrow's *New York Times* be if it's about the stupidest thing you've ever done?

34: Imagine writing a letter to the one person in your life who hurt you the worst. What's the first line of the letter, and what's the last?

35: If you could pass a law requiring every eighteen-year-old in the country to do one thing, what would it be?

36: One hundred years from now, if people remember just one thing about you, what do you want it to be?

37: Imagine that my sister has just asked you to tell her the three things you like least about her. If you tell her the truth, what do you say? Or do you lie?